WINTER'S CURSE

WINTER BLACK SERIES: BOOK TWO

MARY STONE

To my husband.
Thank you for taking care of our home and its many inhabitants
while I follow this silly dream of mine.

DESCRIPTION

A blessing? A curse? It's not easy to possess the gift of knowing too much.

What at first seems like a standalone bank robbery becomes something much darker as a pair of masterminds hack their bloody way onto the list of the most notorious US heists. It's not a job exclusive to the FBI, but Winter's office nemesis, Sun Ming, is convinced that she holds the key to taking down the murderous criminals hungry for fame.

Forced into the spotlight, Winter wants only one thing...to solve this case so she can focus on tracking down The Preacher. But the "gift" he left her with might destroy her first.

Welcome to book two of Mary Stone's debut crime fiction series. If you love a page-turning, cat and mouse thriller, Winter's Curse will keep you guessing until the end.

Download your copy of Winter's Curse to discover if Winter's team will outsmart a killer's intricately designed plot for infamy. And if Winter will survive the curse that is growing more and more out of her control.

1

Ashlyn Freitas was running late for work, but she stopped and bought her usual Starbucks nonfat decaf latte anyway. What was the good of working your way up to branch manager if you couldn't come in a few minutes late once in a while?

Vanilla-scented steam wafted up from her cup, and she sipped at the hot coffee on her way out the door. Her blue, sensible-height heels clacked out a staccato tattoo on the concrete sidewalk as she made her way next door to the American Bank and Trust.

Lenny, the aging security guard, beat her there as usual. His buttons strained against his dark blue shirt as he sat up in his chair in a rush, brushing Pop-Tarts crumbs from his belly with a sheepish smile. He got up from his usual post, where he lounged in a chair beside the door. He was nothing if not consistent.

Ashlyn gave him a cheerful hello as he unlocked the front door and waved her through. He grinned wide enough to show a missing back molar. "Good morning, boss lady."

"Good morning, security man."

More consistency. The greeting had been their routine for the last twelve years.

The "boss lady" part, though, had only been added eight months ago, when the promotion she had worked her ass off for finally came through.

She passed the empty teller cubbies and hurried through a hallway on the other side that led to the business offices. Her own was the largest. She still got a little thrill walking into the nice-sized, windowed room, with its big cherry desk and sleek computer. She'd worked hard for this office and adored every part of it, from the potted majesty palm to the printer/scanner combo she didn't have to share with any of her co-workers.

Ashlyn set her coffee next to her keyboard and shrugged off her navy linen blazer, hanging it on the back of her office chair. Then, she booted up her computer for what would be the last time.

In two hours and twelve minutes, she'd be dead.

At 9:56, the first gunshot echoed through the building. At first, Ashlyn thought a car had backfired. She shot an automatic glance out her window, toward El Camino Real, where traffic sat motionless at a red light. Before she could even scan the street, she heard Louise, their newest teller, scream. The high, shrill noise was cut off almost as soon as it had begun.

Ashlyn stood up swiftly, her chair rolling backward to thump against a filing cabinet. Her heart fluttered in her chest, and her palms went damp in an instant. Another shot rang out, and there was a grunt and a heavy thud just outside her office door. She tried to push it open with one shaking hand, but the door bumped against something heavy. She shoved harder, but the door wouldn't open more than about a foot.

In the open space, a spreading pool of red marred the once freshly vacuumed carpet.

Ashlyn backed up, bile rising in the back of her throat. Black dots swirled in her vision, and for one horrible moment, she thought she might pass out.

"Come on, Ashlyn." Her words sounded pathetic and weak to her own ears, especially in the confines of her office. She'd trained for this, she reminded herself. She swallowed hard. Security seminars. Online training classes provided by corporate, where she'd had to watch low budget, poorly acted videos about what to do in case of a robbery.

Needless to say, the tacky training videos hadn't prepared her for the sight of Lenny on the hallway floor, staring up at the ceiling with a surprised expression in his lifeless eyes.

She looked out of the window for a half-second, longing to break out and lose herself in the blessed normalcy of the downtown Monday morning bustle. The urge to climb out and run as fast as she could, leave this situation behind, almost overwhelmed her.

But, she couldn't. In a burst of movement that left her short, frosted blonde bob swinging, Ashlyn grabbed the phone on her desk and dialed 911 as a precaution. The three tellers had call buttons below their countertops. But as the emergency response operator buzzed in her ear, she heard one of them call her name. It was Greg, she realized, his voice high and frightened.

For a moment, she froze. An image of her husband, Robert, popped into her mind. The way he'd smiled at her over his granola and yogurt that morning, still as handsome and charming at fifty-eight as he had been at twenty-four. He'd sold his business for enough to keep them comfortable the rest of their lives and retired. He'd been bothering her to do the same—he could afford to take care of them both—and had started making noises about buying an RV and doing some traveling.

She set the phone gently on her desk as the tinny-sounding voice of the 911 operator repeated a question. She wished she'd done as Robert had asked, but she'd been so proud of her new job.

She struggled to hold back tears and squared her shoulders.

There were others in the office. Someone else would have called 911 by now. The police were already on their way. She had to believe that.

But she was the Branch Manager. She couldn't wait for them.

"I'm coming out," she yelled, trying to sound calm. "Greg, my door is stuck, if you could help me, please."

"Go ahead," she heard a woman's muffled voice order. "And hurry up."

Too soon, the door swung open a bit wider as Lenny's body was rolled away from the other side. When she heard the sound of miserable retching, her own stomach tightened in a sympathy cramp. She stepped out through the widened gap, trying not to think about the way her shoes squelched in the wet carpeting.

"I'm sorry, Mrs. Freitas," Greg moaned, looking younger than his twenty-six years. His dark brown eyes were huge in his pale face. His thin arms trembled as he pulled Lenny's limp body farther away from the door. "They told me to get the manager on duty."

"It's okay." She gave him a weak smile, and jerked her head to the right, motioning for Greg to go farther in the back of the bank. He did, scuttling low and hunched over, like he was afraid he'd get a bullet between his shoulder blades.

She hoped he'd warn the other employees. Find some place to hide.

Stiffening her spine, Ashlyn stepped through the doorway, pasting on her most professional smile without consciously meaning to. "I'm Ashlyn Freitas. Can I help you?"

Before her, on the other side of the counter in the empty lobby, stood two Nixons.

A male and a female, both intruders were tall, around six feet. They were dressed in business casual clothes that wouldn't seem out of place if she passed them on the street outside. But their faces were covered by leering Richard Nixon rubber masks. Her older brother had worn a similar one for trick or treating one year when they were kids, just to annoy their dad, a die-hard Republican.

Through the eyeholes in the masks, two pairs of eyes glittered at her. The man's were bright blue, the expression in them unreadable. The woman's were brown, lit with glee.

"I need you to help these young ladies fill a bag for us. Fast." The man gestured with a large pistol toward a big, black canvas tote.

"No dye packs or I hunt down your fucking family," the woman added with a snarl. "And don't tell me you don't have the cash available, because I checked your system before I got here. I know how much you've got, down to the penny."

"Of course."

Who was this woman that she could have gotten into their system? Or was she bluffing? Ashlyn's mind whirled with the questions.

Ashlyn's hands shook as she punched in the code to unlock the cash-dispensing machines at each teller station. Her hands moved in awkward, jerky motions. The whole situation felt surreal.

"Empty these," she told Louise and Chantel. Both women looked near collapse. Chantel was wracked with silent sobs, tears rolling down her rounded cheeks. She was six months pregnant.

Ashlyn hushed her, keeping her voice gentle with effort, worried that the girl's crying would irritate the thieves enough to shoot her. Chantel stifled a shudder.

Ashlyn looked up at the female Nixon. "The rest is in another room."

Female Nixon nodded toward her partner. "Take him with you. And don't try anything or I'll have to kill a couple more of your employees, Ms. Branch Manager."

"I'll accompany you." The man's voice was smooth and polite, almost kind, with a hint of an Irish accent.

His eyes, though, were so icy, a bright, cold blue that held no emotion. She didn't for a moment doubt he was any less dangerous than his cohort. He, too, carried a gun, and he grabbed the canvas tote. He gestured in a parody of politeness for her to lead the way.

She opened the locked room where their cash was kept and fumbled to drop handfuls of paper-banded twenties, fifties, and hundreds into the tote he held out.

"Hurry up, sweetheart," the man murmured. "I'm afraid my associate is running out of patience."

Task finished, they headed back to the lobby. Male Nixon loaded the money from the cash machines into the bag and then swung the heavy tote over his shoulder. "Ready to go, love?" he asked the Female Nixon.

Thank you, God. They'll leave now.

Ashlyn Freitas almost sagged in relief. She didn't care if they got away. She wanted them to get away. When the police showed up, who knew what would happen. They'd be taken hostage. Maybe killed.

Like poor Lenny.

Her legs felt near collapse, too rubbery to hold her upright anymore. She blocked Lenny's fate from her mind with deliberate effort.

"We'll leave," the woman replied. "There's just one more thing."

She leveled the pistol at Ashlyn, who stood only a few feet away.

"Wait—" The man took a half-step forward, but he was too slow.

Almost at the same moment, there was a deafening roar, a bright flash. Instant darkness followed. Blindly, Ashlyn felt herself being propelled backward, slamming against something hard. A woman's shriek echoed through her head before it faded into silence. It was strange…she didn't feel any pain. Didn't feel anything at all.

Ashlyn Freitas, Branch Manager of the American Bank and Trust in San Clemente, California, was dead before she hit the floor.

2

Winter ignored the argument between Special Agents Sun Ming and Miguel Vasquez that raged outside of her cubicle. She didn't look up from her computer screen.

As an FBI agent, she now had access to a boatload of resources for tracking down criminals. She planned to make use of every one of them to find one of the deadliest serial killers in modern history. Right now, she was knee-deep in murderers.

"Black," a gruff voice barked out.

That voice, she registered. It reminded her of a muffler dragging on gravel.

She rolled her chair back fast, shuffling the files on her desk, and stood. "Sir?"

Special Agent in Charge of the Richmond Violent Crimes Task Force Max Osbourne stalked toward her cubicle, irritation vibrating in his stocky, muscular frame. Even Sun and Miguel backed apart a step and broke off, mid-argument.

His stare nearly pinned Winter to the floor. "Your arm healed up all right?"

Behind Max, Noah Dalton raised his head over his own

wall and shook his head in the negative, giving her a warning look. She read the look clearly. It said she was in trouble.

Winter and Noah had gone through Quantico together, and after the last case they'd worked, knew she could trust him with her life. She'd done it once. Noah disappeared again, and Winter opened her mouth to tell Max she had one more check-up before she was cleared for regular duty.

Unfortunately, Max didn't wait for Winter to answer.

"Vasquez, back to your desk," he ordered the man still inching away from Winter's cubicle. "I don't care if your doctor says you're fighting fit. You still look like hell."

It was true. Miguel's face was an uncommon shade of pale except for two bright red patches of angry color high on his cheekbones. He was fresh off the disabled list and still not one-hundred-percent. He shot one last killing look at Sun, who just smiled back in triumph, baring even white teeth. Shoulders stiff, Miguel muttered something uncomplimentary in Spanish and headed back to his seat, still moving slowly after his appendectomy.

Sun's grin widened at what she clearly saw as a win. She turned to walk back to her own desk, but Max stopped her.

"Black, you're working with Ming now."

The smug-to-horrified transformation of Sun's face would have been comical if Winter hadn't been just as appalled. Osbourne just chuckled, a raspy sound that sounded rusty from disuse.

"Come on now, girls. Be team players. Ming, you're the case agent on this one. Bring Black up to speed."

He headed back to his office, careless of the dynamic he'd just set into play.

Sun hated Winter's guts, and the feeling was reciprocated.

When Winter had first been assigned to the Violent Crimes Unit, the other members of the team had taken good-natured advantage of her lack of experience. They had put her in charge of the virtual reams of paperwork their jobs generated.

She'd graduated Quantico in the same class as Noah, and they'd been hired in at the same time, but he at least had law enforcement experience. Between that and his easygoing attitude, he'd been an easy fit within the unit. Winter, not so much. He'd tried to let her work it out on her own. Eventually, though, he had let her in on the prank.

Winter had used Sun as an example to let everyone know she was done being their administrative assistant. Sun had been the biggest dog in the yard, or at least the one with the loudest bark, and Winter had taken her down in front of the rest of the team.

Judging by the expression in Sun's dark eyes, Winter hadn't been forgiven for that, and wouldn't be any time soon.

Sun broke the tense silence first. Her words sounded as enthusiastic as if they'd been dragged out of her at knifepoint. "It's too late to brief you now. Be here at seven, and I'll catch you up then. Have a go-bag packed. We'll be traveling."

She didn't wait for a reply.

"Awesome," Winter muttered to her retreating form, sinking back into her seat. "Can't wait."

She pulled out the small sketchpad she'd tucked under a manila file folder when she'd heard Max Osbourne's voice. The face of a killer stared up at her from the thick, white paper.

Rounded face, soft and unassuming, the man drawn there looked like someone's benevolent grandpa. Or, maybe a mall Santa, with his close-trimmed beard and rosy cheeks. But his eyes were an inky shade of black. The evil in them roiled. It was visible, almost tangible, even with her less-than-expert art skills.

The Preacher.

He'd taken her family from her in the most brutal way

possible when she was just thirteen years old and left her for dead. After over a decade, she was going to do what the rest of the FBI agents assigned to the case hadn't been able to do. She was going to find the sick fucker and bring him down.

"Who's that?" Noah's voice was casual as he leaned over, but his green eyes were sharp when they met hers.

She glanced up at him. He knew her story. He also knew better than to pry.

"You heading out?" she asked instead, snapping the sketchbook closed and tucking it into her bag.

"Yep. Want to walk me to my car? Gets dark out there early this time of year." He grinned, a dimple creasing one cheek. "You know I'm afraid of the dark."

Winter rolled her eyes, for the most part immune to his easy charm by now. "Sure." She gathered up her things and shrugged on her light wool peacoat. Noah tugged her braid free from her collar in a casual move she barely noticed.

"You know," he started in as soon as the elevator doors began to slide shut. "You should give Sun a chance."

"To do what? Slide a knife in my back? If you saw her face like I did today, you'd know she's actively considering it."

Noah shook his head and huffed out a breath. "You two are a lot alike, you know."

Winter scowled at that. Jumping to the defensive was a no-brainer after such an idiotic statement, but she couldn't let that slide. "I—"

He held up his hands in a placating gesture. "I'm just saying. Both of you are strong, brilliant, capable women. Neither of you are what I'd call flexible. But she's good. With those porcupine quills of hers, Max would have fired her years ago if she wasn't."

The ding of the elevator arriving on the main floor cut off her pithy response.

"You're too much of a nice guy, Dalton. Always trying to be the peacemaker."

Noah shrugged his broad shoulders and stepped ahead of her to hold open the door. "When everybody gets along, darlin'," he drawled, laying on the Texas twang like barbecue sauce, extra thick, "things get done a lot easier."

The sky was dark, and lightning licked along the horizon. It had been cold in Richmond the past week, even for early December, but a warm front was trying to push in. Severe storms were in the forecast.

The weather matched her mood. Unsettled and pissed.

Thunder rumbled with distant menace, and a breeze whipped up as they walked toward their cars. "So, how would you recommend I deal with Sun, Dr. Phil?"

He smiled at her, his teeth gleaming in the darkness. "Just do whatever she says and bite your tongue."

Winter snorted, digging in her purse for her keys. "Right. That's *so* how I operate. What was all the yelling between her and Miguel about?"

"Apparently, he didn't buy into her take on the case she just picked up. Told her she was crazy."

Winter snorted. "He's just out of the hospital for an exploded appendix, and he already has a death wish?"

"He's got a point, though. Most banks don't keep enough cash on hand to make it worthwhile, and armed robbery wouldn't pass a good crook's risk assessment."

"Armed robbery? American Bank and Trust in San Clemente, California?"

Noah nodded and grimaced. "It's been all over the news, for the cold-bloodedness of the killings alone. Dead security guard and bank manager. Sun has this idea that it's something other than a run of the mill robbery and talked Osbourne into letting her take it."

"Far be it from me to question anyone else's gut feeling."

Winter's tone was wry as she unlocked the door to her aging Civic. "But isn't there a field office in San Diego?"

"The FBI just isn't looking at bank robberies as hard as they used to, and San Diego is a busy office. They've got their hands full there. We handle robberies, of course, but since 9/11, they're handled more by the local LEOs, unless they're really bad. No one else is interested in or has time for this one right now, apparently. But Sun."

"And now me. Yay."

She slid into the front seat. Fat raindrops began to fall, splattering the windshield.

"Seriously, you're doing okay, right? Ready to jump into another case?" Noah held the door in a loose grip, his face concerned.

"I'm fine." It was true. The stitches in her arm had come out the week before, and she hadn't even used any of the painkillers she'd been prescribed. "I'm just lucky you didn't pull a move from *Speed* and decide to shoot the hostage."

She tried to smile at Noah with some reassurance, but it felt forced.

Sure, her arm had healed up, but she had a new recurring nightmare to add to her already-gory repertoire. One that featured the tiny, malformed bones of buried children and the hot barrel of a gun pressed to the base of her skull.

"How's Parrish doing?"

The question sounded like it had been wrenched out of Noah via torture. Winter couldn't help but smile. "I thought you weren't a fan of the SSA of the BAU."

Noah glowered. "Actually, I'm not a fan of the damned Supervisory Special Agent of the damned Behavioral Analysis Unit." His nose wrinkled as he said the words. "Can't stand the guy. He's an uptight prick, and I'm pretty sure he won't quit trying to get you to cross over to the behavioral analysis dark side. But any agent that can take two bullets for another and live to brag about the scars at least deserves some respect."

"I'll text you later and let you know how he's doing. I'm on my way over there now. Now, go away before you get struck by lightning." The rain had picked up, and the strobe flashes that lit the parking lot were getting more intense.

Noah didn't look happy that she was going to see Aiden, but he gave her a mocking salute and a grin before heading toward his truck at an easy jog.

Irritated by his attitude, Winter slammed her car door a little harder than was necessary. Noah Dalton and Aiden Parrish had a weird, petty rivalry going on, and both of them were annoying the hell out of her. When they'd all ended up working the same case together, Winter had to battle a near-constant urge to bash their heads together. If they weren't sniping at each other, they were ganging up on her.

She started the car and hit the window defogger, the red glow of Noah's new Ford's taillights shimmered through the humid haze that covered the inside of the windshield. Her phone buzzed with a text: *I'm not leaving until you do.*

She texted back a middle finger emoji.

A sad little yellow face followed almost immediately.

Sighing, she used the arm of her coat to wipe away most of the condensation on the inside of the glass. Noah's misplaced sense of chivalry was too deeply engrained to repair at this point. Trying to curb his protective streak was like beating her head against a very handsome brick wall. She put the car in drive and tried to ignore the big red truck exiting the parking lot at a polite distance behind her.

3

Lightning forked across the sky in a savage display of natural pyrotechnics as Winter hurried into Aiden's apartment building with a carryout bag of Chinese food. She could smell the crab rangoon inside, and her stomach rumbled. She was hesitant to work on her own investigation during work hours and skipping lunch had become routine.

Aiden's apartment building was in downtown Richmond, and a far cry from her single-level, one-bedroom apartment building done up in fifty shades of utilitarian beige. The lobby floor was marble, and looked more like a hotel reception area, with comfortable leather seating areas and a desk manned 24/7 by a security guard.

The uniformed woman on duty nodded at Winter as she passed through the entryway to the elevators. Winter had become a regular visitor since Aiden had been released from the hospital. She didn't like seeing her one-time mentor in a more human light, but she figured that for all the support he'd given her in the years following her family's deaths, she owed him. And in all the times she'd visited him, she'd never run into anyone else.

Besides, the bullets that had ended up in him had been meant for her.

He was a solitary figure. There was nothing in him to pity. Aiden Parrish was cool, sophisticated, and sometimes manipulative. He came off as the epitome of a polished professional. But over the last several months, she'd caught glimpses of the man beneath the veneer.

Aiden wasn't charming and easy to be around like Noah. He was sharp, sardonic, attractive, and unsettling.

She'd texted from the restaurant and didn't bother to knock at his apartment door. He was healing, but still had a hard time getting around without difficulty. The physical therapy for the wound in his leg would ensure that he'd get back to full mobility, but he wasn't there yet.

Like any normal man, he wasn't taking the restrictions forced on him with grace.

"I told you, you don't need to bring me dinner every night."

Winter set the bag on the counter in the kitchen, accustomed to the cold greeting. Aiden was stretched out in a chair in front of a large window, overlooking the city. He had his bad leg propped up on a black leather ottoman, and judging by the lines bracketing his mouth, the afternoon's PT session had been rough.

"It's not every night," she retorted. "You had to resort to ordering in from that fancy Italian place on Tuesday. What kind of wine goes with potstickers?"

"The kind that comes in a box," he replied in a flat voice, not looking away from the storm outside the glass. "In absence of that, pour me some of the Riesling, will you?"

She grabbed a bottle and two glasses and brought them to the low, glass coffee table. Aiden's apartment, like the man himself, was sleekly modern. It had none of the warmth and quirkiness of the vintage 1950s home her grandparents had raised her in, but it suited him right down to the ground.

"Just one," she warned, handing him his glass of wine.

"Of course."

Even at home, in recovery, and having been out of work for a month, Aiden was dressed in a charcoal cashmere sweater and dark slacks. "Don't you own any sweatpants?" Winter teased, trying to lighten the mood as she brought the brown paper bag to the table.

"No." Thawing a little, he looked at her, his blue eyes glinting. "And if you try to bring me any, I'll have them donated to charity before you even get to your car."

Winter shrugged and set two plates down, settling in the chair across from him. She leaned forward and pulled out a white carton of egg fried rice. "There goes all my Christmas present ideas."

She dished up their food and handed him his, with the little red paper packet of chopsticks.

"You know I have proper chopsticks in the kitchen, right? These…" he held up the packet, pinched between two fingers, "make everything taste like a tongue depressor."

She snorted indelicately and ripped open her own. "I own a single frying pan, and you have your own personal set of chopsticks. Admit it…they're solid white gold and engraved with your initials, aren't they?"

Aiden's lips curled in a reluctant smile. "Ho Wood and etched rose gold, actually. But no initials."

She'd gotten him out of phase one: irritation.

The storm outside had quieted by the time they'd finished their meal. Even though he hated her doing things for him, Winter brought Aiden his pain pills and a glass of water to wash them down. That was phase two.

She had his routine pegged. He'd be impatient and cutting when she got there, she'd feed him and he'd calm down a little, ready to relax afterward and more likely to take his meds. While she waited for them to kick in, she employed phase three. Shop talk.

"I got a new case."

Aiden's immediate shift into focused mode was fascinating to watch. "What are you working on?"

"Did you see the coverage of the American Bank and Trust robbery? Sun Ming requested the case, and Max put me on it. I'm apparently healthier and more likely to survive than Vasquez."

Aiden grinned. "Sun Ming? She's brilliant."

Winter kept her face carefully blank. "So I've been told."

"One of the best agents working in your unit."

"Uh-huh."

"You could learn a lot from her."

"The next person to tell me that is getting face punched." Aiden's grin widened, irritating her even more. She pulled out a verbal strike of her own. "Noah was the last person to say that to me."

The grin fell away like it had never existed, and Winter laughed.

"Seriously, she's not as hard as she seems." Aiden shifted back into a more comfortable position in his chair.

Winter tilted her head, dubious. "Spoken as a behavioral analysist?"

"Spoken as a man who dated her."

Winter would have been less shocked if Aiden had jumped to his feet and started yodeling. "You dated Sun Ming?"

"Don't look so surprised. I have a life outside of work, you know."

"Says the guy who just admitted to an interoffice romance. Not the best argument." Winter crossed her arms and leaned back in her own chair, narrowing her eyes. He stared steadily back, a half-smile on his lips.

She could have kicked herself. Of course Aiden Parrish had a life. He was good-looking, unmarried, probably only in his late thirties or early forties, which was always a jolt to realize since it felt like she'd known him so long. He had a successful career, a scalpel-sharp mind, and a restless nature. And, if you ignored her bitchy nature, Sun was gorgeous with her shiny black hair, creamy skin, and lithe build.

Aiden just seemed so solitary.

"I don't want to know any details," Winter replied. Her decisive statement made him chuckle, but she didn't care. She didn't want to picture the two of them together. It was too weird. "I have to work with her, you know."

"I wasn't going to share any. She's got more sharp spines than a cactus, but underneath, she's a good person. A good agent. Give her a chance. That's all I'm saying."

He closed his eyes for a moment, and Winter could see that he was getting tired. The pain meds he was on were strong ones. She gathered up their dishes and set them in the sink for his housekeeper, grabbing a bottle of water to set by Aiden's chair.

Before she could move away, he grabbed her arm in a light grip. "Thanks."

She laughed him off but stiffened a little. "For what? Getting you shot?"

His fingers tightened, and she could feel the heat of his palm on her forearm through the material of her shirt.

"For coming by like this, even when I insist you don't. And you didn't get me shot."

"I walked right into the line of fire." She had. The memory made her burn with shame just thinking about it.

"Get over yourself," Aiden suggested with mild rebuke. "Everyone makes mistakes, and you don't control my decisions. It's not your fault." When he finally let go of her arm, she moved to grab her coat and purse. "How are you doing? Any more headaches recently?"

It was a loaded question. He'd witnessed one of her "headaches." She shot him a look. He knew something of her abilities, but it wasn't like him to call her out.

"No. I'm fine."

"Would you tell me?"

Would she? After he'd pulled rank and tried to take her out of the VC unit, shit had hit the fan between them. They'd brokered a temporary truce during the past few weeks, but it was a tenuous one.

"Maybe," she answered with as much honesty as she could. "I don't know."

"Have you been working on The Preacher case?"

"That's blunt, even for you. Why do you ask?"

"No reason." He gave her a self-deprecating smile. "I've had a lot of time on my hands in recent weeks to think about all kinds of things."

The sketchbook in her purse seemed to get heavier. She could tell him that she'd gone through the house she'd grown up in, for the first time since she'd come close to being killed there. That she'd seen the face of her family's killer in a vision. Heard him apologize to her just before he knocked her into a coma. Remembered him saying that he was there for her baby brother—six-year-old Justin—and not her.

Aiden would believe her. But she couldn't be sure what he'd do with the information. He'd made it abundantly clear that he didn't want her in a position to be able to go after the serial killer alone the day he'd tried to pull rank and transfer her out of violent crimes to a safer desk job, within his realm at the behavioral analysis unit.

Winter gave him an assessing glance. "Maybe you could

use some of your spare thinking time to look back on The Preacher case. We could compare notes."

He looked at her for an intent moment before nodding. "Maybe I'll do that. Drive carefully. It's still raining hard out there."

"Always." She relaxed. The tension had dissipated.

"Let me know how it goes with Sun," he teased. Teasing from Aiden was rare. "Call me if you need a shoulder to cry on."

Winter smiled. With teeth.

"I'll tell Sun. She's more likely to need one than I am."

❄

IF ONLY SHE knew how much time he actually spent thinking about The Preacher case, Aiden thought as he watched Winter leave. It was worse, of course, now that he was confined to his apartment, suffering with just himself for company. She couldn't know how her request had sliced at him.

Aiden shifted his leg into a more comfortable position. Even with the meds, it still throbbed like a bastard.

The serial killer had been one of his early cases. Aiden had been fresh out of Quantico himself, partnered up with an older, more experienced agent. Cassidy Ramirez. They'd both come a long way in their careers since then. He'd taken over the Behavioral Analysis Unit, and she was Associate Deputy Director of the Richmond office.

They'd worked that case for over a year, following the Black murders. The Preacher, as he'd been dubbed—Aiden had always hated the moniker—had made his last kill on their watch. It had been over a decade, but he could still remember Winter's parents, Bill and Jeanette Black. The way they'd been found.

Bill, a quiet, thoughtful college professor, had been shot dead as he lay in bed next to his wife.

Jeanette, beautiful with her dark blue eyes and pale skin, a thick mass of silky black hair. She'd been brutalized next to her dead husband. The son of a bitch had then slit her throat and desecrated her lifeless body, then preceded to paint crosses and a Bible verse on the wall in her blood.

That was how the bastard had been dubbed The Preacher, and the behavioral unit thought he had been in the middle of writing something else on the walls just as he was interrupted by the arrival of the thirteen-year-old daughter. The daughter that now looked just like the mother.

The maniac had clubbed Winter over the head, hard enough to knock her into a coma that would last the next few months, leaving her for dead. Why she hadn't been raped and brutalized was still a mystery to them all.

It wasn't the only mystery of the case.

The bastard had taken Winter's little brother, Justin, with him. They'd never been able to find the boy. Aside from leaving Winter alive, that had been the only other variance in the pattern. In fact, it had thrown them off. Everything else fit The Preacher's M.O., but he'd never shown any interest in children. Or males, for that matter. Any females with spouses were either killed when the spouse wasn't home, or the male was simply shot in the head. Dispatched without any obvious emotion. It was humane, really, considering what would come next for the woman.

The whole brutal incident with the Black family was an aberration in the serial killer's profile. Aiden didn't like aberrations, especially those that he couldn't pick to pieces and puzzle out.

The Preacher had been tied to around forty murders, some of them tentative. It looked like he'd committed them over the span of thirty years, in scattered locations around the country. His M.O. was unpredictable, but somewhat consistent. He'd target a young woman between twenty and thirty-five years old, and they believed that he'd track her movements, sometimes for weeks or even months. There was no discernable preference in the woman's appearance, except that they were all attractive.

There had been Susan Illis, a librarian in Spokane. She'd been a petite brunette. Amber Valente, a red-haired nurse in Maryland. Mikaela Smith, an African-American woman from Grand Rapids, Michigan. Each woman had been single, living alone, and vulnerable to a killer. Later on, there had been a few married women. Never with children, though. The first man to be killed by The Preacher had set the pattern for any future men: single gunshot to the head.

The killings began in 1974, that they officially knew of, and ended with the murder of Winter's parents and her brother's disappearance. In the early days after the tragedy, the murder hadn't been connected to The Preacher. None of the previous victims had husbands or children. None of the women lived with anyone.

But what had been done to Jeanette Black had been unmistakable. The work was characteristic of The Preacher. Aiden thought he would have known it was the same man just from the brutality of the murder alone, but the crosses and Bible verses painted in the victim's blood left little doubt.

The question they'd never been able to answer was why the killer had deviated from pattern...and what had happened to Justin, the Black's six-year-old son. The Preacher had disappeared with the boy. None of the shaky leads on the case had panned out, and despite hundreds of hours of legwork, they'd made no progress.

The Preacher case was a sore spot for both Aiden, and now, Associate Deputy Director Ramirez. Never mind that the national murder clearance average was around sixty percent. In their unit, they'd prided themselves on beating that number. The failure to catch such a prolific murderer had been an embarrassment to them both. They'd failed to bring justice to the lone survivor of that bloody October night, along with dozens of others that had been killed over the years. And who knew how many more?

Aiden had kept in contact with Winter through her teenage years out of guilt. Back when he suffered from that emotion. Even now, he could still see her in the hospital bed. A thin and gawky teenager who had lain, almost lifeless, for three months before she finally came out of her coma, only to be told her family was gone.

Over the years, she'd gone from a devastated child to a determined woman, and now she wanted his help to dig it all up again.

Aiden levered himself out of his chair and started the slow, painful process of making his way through his own apartment. He never got out of his chair during Winter's recent visits. Call it male pride, but he despised the thought of her—or anyone else—seeing him as weak.

She was right, though. He had plenty of thinking time on his hands. He sat down at his desk and booted up his laptop, ignoring the ache in his leg. He'd scanned and transferred all of the old paper files and evidence photos from The Preacher case years ago.

It was time to go over them all again. Maybe he'd find something he'd missed.

4

"Not bad for a practice run." Heidi Presley eyed Ryan O'Connelly from across the scarred Formica table. "Two hundred and twenty thousand."

Ryan held a stack of hundreds, still banded, running his thumb across the edge, his face thoughtful. Or, it could have been an act. If he spent much time thinking, he didn't show evidence of it.

The bills made a soft whispering sound as they fanned over his fingertip. She watched him as he stared down at the money spilling out of the black canvas tote. Was it out of greed? Regret? She hadn't missed the way he'd looked when she'd dispatched the bank manager.

He'd looked too damned handsome.

The thought came out of nowhere, surprising her. Gritting her teeth, she pushed it away.

Heidi wasn't in the market for a man. After a disastrous attempt to rid herself of her virginity in college, she'd never had the inclination. Which was fine, because men never tended to look twice at her.

That suited her just fine. If men weren't paying her any attention, they were probably busy underestimating her. And that was the kind of man she liked...the dumb ones. Handsome was a bonus as long as their brains were made of rocks.

O'Connelly was good-looking in an old-fashioned way, like Cary Grant or Sean Connery. An old-time film star who would have played a cat burglar. Long and lean build, lightly muscled. Dark hair with just a little bit of a wave. A face that looked like it was carved from marble. Crystalline blue eyes that could be ice-cold or lit with humor, and changed as fast as lightning. And an Irish accent.

It pissed her off, that involuntary little flutter she got when he called her "love" in the mocking way he had.

Heidi steeled herself. She wasn't interested in Ryan O'Connelly for his looks, and sex wasn't anywhere in the plan.

He looked up at her, pinning her with his gaze. "Bank robberies?" he asked, the question blunt. "Heists? There's no money in it. Two-twenty is peanuts compared to what you could do with those computer skills of yours, and you'd never need to dirty your lovely white hands."

"I don't need to tell you why. I just need to know if you're in." Heidi folded her arms and stared back at him. "You can keep this take as a sign of my good faith."

His eyes didn't even flicker at her generous offer. He just continued to graze his thumbnail over the bundle of money. "I need to know what it is you have in mind for me. Details, love." His tone was hard, but his smile broke with a sudden brilliance that startled her. "I've had an illustrious career so far and have cultivated a bit of a reputation. I don't much care for the idea of putting my arse in the hands of an amateur." His grin widened with the innuendo. "So to speak."

Cocky bastard. Heidi didn't blink.

"You mentioned my computer skills," she responded. "Has it occurred to you that I found you with no trouble at all, when the authorities had no luck in tracking you?"

His eyes narrowed, but his smile didn't slip. "Tossing a bit of blackmail into the pot, are we? I hate to sound like I'm bragging, but I'm not sure you know who you're dealing with."

"And neither do you," Heidi shot back, keeping her tone level. "No one can disappear without a trace anymore. Trust me. Your digital footprints are a piece of cake to follow for someone who knows what she's doing. You do these three jobs for me and I'll erase your footprints so well that no one will ever find you again."

They were at a standoff, and she'd left him with no out, plus a fat, juicy carrot on a stick. She knew it. He knew it.

As if they'd been discussing nothing more unpleasant than the weather, Ryan winked at her. The move was unexpected. She didn't like unexpected.

"I guess I'm in, then," he said. "Three jobs."

"Three jobs," she affirmed, pretending for his sake that he'd ever had a choice. "I'll be in touch."

"Now, love," Ryan said, shaking his head. "There will have to be some give and take here. I need to know what it is we'll be doing."

"Something epic. That's all you need to know."

He shrugged, as if it didn't matter.

But she knew he was chafing at the control she was exercising over him. That was fine. As long as he knew who was in charge. She slid a burner phone across the table to him. "I'll text you with instructions."

He picked up the phone and slipped it into his jacket pocket. "I hesitate to ask, but I assume you've covered our bases with this little…'practice run?' I won't be walking into a police ambush when I leave here?"

Heidi nodded. "I've made sure no one will be able to pin us to the burglary."

"And the violence? Was that absolutely necessary?"

"Squeamish, O'Connelly?"

"Not at all. It just seemed excessive for our purposes." His tone turned just a hair toward condescending. "'No dye packs or I'll hunt down your fucking family?' Sounded like a line from a bad movie. And the killing after? We already had the money. There didn't seem to be a reason to shoot the bank lady. She was cooperative. Seemed…unsporting."

Heidi wanted to reach across the table and punch the smugness from his face. Every step of her plans had a purpose, and she hadn't brought him into this to question her at every turn of the road.

Her tone was cold enough to flash freeze him when she replied, "Those executions were a demonstration for *you*. You now know that I'm serious and fully committed to our little project."

He pushed back his chair and stood, scooping the money back into the bag. "A pinkie promise would have worked just as well. I'm a trusting sort, after all. No need to blow any more heads off to prove your point, love. I'd just as soon avoid messy bloodshed."

Ryan glanced around the shabby beachside bungalow she'd rented in cash, under an assumed name—chosen special for the occasion—and through several layers of security. "Will we be operating out of here, then?"

"No. I'll text you instructions on where to go next." She pulled a small bundle out of her bag, where it had been nestled in with her Ruger, and slid it across the table. "Credit cards and a temporary ID."

"I'm used to handling my own travel arrangements."

"You'll use these." *Best get used to it, boyo,* she thought. I *pull the strings here.*

"As you like."

"Do you have a way to get rid of the money?"

Ryan chuckled. "I'm no newbie at this. I won't be hauling it around with us, if that's what you're asking."

Heidi gave him a curt nod and then dismissed him without another word, pulling out her laptop. She heard him leave, and then the faint sound of whistling as he headed out to the car he'd rented. She knew he wasn't a newbie and wouldn't make any stupid mistakes.

She knew all about Ryan O'Connelly.

Besides, he wouldn't be allowed to make mistakes. She'd made sure of that.

※

THE WOMAN GAVE him the heebie-jeebies.

Ryan tossed the bag into the back seat of his silver Land Rover and climbed in the front, having already decided to donate every dollar of the blood money to a charity. He didn't want it. Didn't want to be cursed by it. He rubbed the spot where his Saint Dismas medallion should have been.

He was already cursed quite enough.

When he'd received a cryptic email a month ago, the sender's address a mess of letters and numbers, he'd written it off as spam. He had been flush with cash from his last job, an art gig, and spending some time with a sweetheart he'd met down in Jamaica.

The email had been terse, to the point.

I know where you are, Ryan.

It had struck him as weird. Kind of creepy, like that movie where the bad guy reminded everyone that he knew something bad they'd done. *I Know What You Did Last Summer.* But he had the luscious distraction of Ionie. A gorgeous Jamaican woman with a sweet personality, a wicked sense of humor, and an inventive imagination, she worked at the hotel he was staying at. It had taken some doing, but once he'd coaxed her into his room and out of her panties, neither of them had been able to get enough of each other.

Two days had gone by while he'd worked on tanning his pasty arse on the beach, drinking rum and smoking the native ganja, before he'd received the second email from the same encrypted address. This one just had a phone number.

They didn't call him The Cat for nothing. Not only was he undetectable when he wanted to be, silent on his feet, unpredictable…he was curious as hell. He'd debated for a bit, finally deciding to call the number and appease his curiosity. Now, he wished he'd never done so.

Curiosity killed cats. The reminder made him uncomfortable.

The woman on the other end of the line had introduced herself as Heidi. At first, she'd been flattering. He'd been just drunk enough to believe her when she told him how she'd been an admirer of his for the last several years, since he'd pulled his first high-profile theft. It had been an artifact from a collector in Brussels, for a minor Saudi prince who wanted the piece for himself.

The execution of that theft had been flawless—managed *without* bloodshed, thank you very much—and had put him in high demand with those who followed such things soon after. He'd been commissioned to do everything from liberating paintings and jewelry to the occasional job where he'd lift goods from safety deposit boxes tucked away in banks, hotels, or private residences. He'd risen fast from the ranks of petty thieves to a sought-after professional who operated all over the world—wherever his clients took him.

He had a healthy sense of self-worth, but in this, he didn't need to exaggerate. He was good.

He hadn't lied to Heidi. Ryan had an excellent reputation

and was at the top of his field. He'd never even come close to being caught, and he was well set-up enough to never have to work again in his life. He could afford to be picky, choosing only jobs that appealed to him or carried some sense of justice or irony.

He was ashamed to admit it now, but he'd flirted with her on the phone that day. Talked too much. Hell, her name was Heidi. With her low, sultry voice and that name, he'd pictured a stunner. Probably tall and blonde. Blue eyes were almost guaranteed. By the time their conversation was over, he'd imagined her as a cross between a Nordic princess and part-time lingerie model. And with her admirable computer skills, maybe she even owned a sexy little pair of black-framed, librarian-type glasses.

He'd been feeling a little too cozy with Ionie and had talked himself into falling for the imaginary goddess over the phone. Blame it on his romantic streak. And the rum.

After a few more conversations over the next couple of days, he'd agreed to meet her. He flew to the States, even though he'd sobered up enough by then to seriously question the wisdom of leaving Ionie, his gorgeous Jamaican playmate.

When he'd met Heidi at the airport in Bismarck, North Dakota, she hadn't been what he expected.

She was tall, but that was where the resemblance to his dream goddess ended.

Truth be told, she was a bit mannish. About his height, shoulders broad for a woman. About his age. Mid-thirties. Her hair was long, but a plain, dirt-colored brown that looked a little lank under the green and white trucker's cap she wore. She'd dressed in baggy jeans and a flannel shirt that hid any hint of the curves that might lie beneath them, and a pair of dusty brown boots. She looked like a cowboy.

Her face was all right. Strong cheekbones. Clear, tanned skin. Her eyes were a muddy brown. Lips wide and full on a downturned mouth that looked like it never smiled.

Ryan wanted to turn around and get back on the airplane. Even though he'd really had no idea what she looked like, he still felt catfished.

But he'd given her his patented, charming smile. Had even taken her hand and kissed her knuckles. Women loved his courtly manners. Except this one. This one had just stared at him with a cold, closed expression, like he was cow shite crusted at the bottom of her boot.

The burner phone buzzed, interrupting his reverie. Stopped at a red light, he picked it up, glancing at the screen.

It was a reservation confirmation. Instead of staying the night at the charming hotel he'd booked in Long Beach, it now looked like he'd be heading out on a red-eye flight from LAX. He tossed the phone back down on the passenger's seat and huffed out an irritated breath.

She couldn't have bloody told him that while he was there?

He didn't like any of this. Not at all.

After only a few minutes in Heidi's company, he recognized a trap when he saw one. She'd manipulated him with an ease that was disconcerting. She knew *everything* about him. As they'd sat in a dingy, anonymous little diner in Bismarck, she'd made it clear without saying straight-out that she'd turn all of that information over to the authorities if he didn't humor her in this mysterious little plot she'd cooked up.

If she were to somehow disappear, she had a kill switch in place. He'd still be caught.

But, to his mind, it was better to have a poisonous snake where you could see it than to know it was slithering around, but not exactly sure where. He and Heidi were partners…for the time being.

He'd play along with her game, but he wouldn't be played.

In the meantime, he had an errand to run.

5

Sun was going over her notes again when Agent Black came into the conference room at a quarter to seven. Sun had been in the office since five-thirty and had looked forward to Winter being late. She was mildly disappointed to find that her new "partner" was also an early riser.

"Sit down," Sun snapped. "We don't have a lot of time."

"Good morning to you too," Winter replied, her tone even. Her eyes were a calm, dark blue in the harsh overhead lights. She took off her jacket with deliberate movements and pulled a notebook and pen out of her bag. She sat down across the table and opened her notebook. "What do we have?"

"I'd like to lay down some ground rules first, *rookie.*" Sun had the satisfaction of seeing Winter's gaze fly up to hers, her eyes narrowing. "I'm the case agent on this. I want that to be crystal clear. This means that there will be none of the behavior you've shown on other cases since you've been with the department. You answer to *me.*"

Winter set her pen down and leaned back in her chair,

crossing her arms. "Would you like to clarify what behavior you're referring to?"

"I've watched you since you started." Sun ticked items off on her fingers. "In less than a year, you've shown a decided inability to participate within this unit as a part of the team. You have a hotshot mentality, going off on your own and breaking with protocol to apprehend a suspect. You put another agent in danger and nearly got him killed."

"Did SSA Parrish tell you that?" Winter asked. Her voice was quiet. Deadly quiet.

"He didn't have to," Sun replied. "I read the reports." It had been a calculated guess on her part, and her lips curled as she scored the point. "You will not go off on your own, and you will curb this immature need for attention you seem to have. You are an unseasoned agent. Fresh out of Quantico. You have untrained instincts, no law enforcement or military background, and no practical work experience to speak of. I have no idea why they hired you and still believe it was an absolute mistake."

She watched Winter as she said it, looking hard for any reaction. There was none. Winter had a helluva poker face. Sun had hoped for more of a fight.

"I don't like you," Winter responded after a moment. Her voice was flat, and she sounded almost bored. Her posture was relaxed, her fingers laced together on the table in front of her, loose and easy. Her face was like marble for all the expression she showed. "You don't like me either, but we have a job to do. I'd appreciate if you filed a complaint with Osbourne, requesting another agent to assist...*if* you can find one willing to come near you. Or you can get on with the briefing. I have no interest in your opinion of my conduct, and you're wasting my time."

"You'd like that, wouldn't you?" Sun kept a furious tremble out of her voice by force of will. "Let you off the hook on this so you can go back to working your way through every man in this office?"

Winter's eyes widened, and she burst into laughter. It rang through the small room, and from the corner of her eye, Sun could see other agents—John "Bull" Durham and Brian Camp—pop their heads over the sides of their cubicles to see what was happening.

"You're mental," Winter gasped out, sparing the other woman a rare grin. "Completely mental."

Conscious of their coworkers' stares, Sun stretched her lips into a thin smile. "You act like you're sweet and innocent, but I know how you got this job."

"Hard work? Excellent college credentials?" Winter suggested. "Tying with Dalton for the top of our class at Quantico? Get on with the brief. I'm having a hard time taking you seriously right now. I can't believe I heard you were brilliant."

Sun seethed beneath the thin veneer of calm. This was not going as it was supposed to. The bitch was laughing at her.

Sun pulled out the binder that held her case notes and slammed it down on the desk, hard enough for the sound to echo like a gunshot. "Armed robbery. American Bank and Trust in San Clemente, California."

"Two fatalities," Winter supplied, making no movement to even look at the file. "Security guard and branch manager. Suspects wearing Richard Nixon masks got away with two hundred and twenty thousand dollars. Three witnesses, no leads. Why did you request this case?"

If looks could kill, Winter would be writhing around on the floor in her death throes. Sun had lost the reins of the conversation, and she needed to get them back. Winter, in just minutes, had hit on something dangerous.

Sun reined herself in. Any display of additional temper

now would just make the rookie more curious. She'd already shown a tendency for making logical jumps that escaped others.

"Have you ever heard of the United California Bank burglary?" Sun bit out the words, modulating her tone a little.

"I'm familiar with it. One of the biggest bank robberies in U.S. history. Happened back in the seventies."

"You should be familiar with it, if your 'college credentials' are really that excellent. In 1972, at the United California Bank in Laguna Niguel, nine million dollars in cash and valuables were stolen by a group of professionals led by Amil Dinsio."

"Right. The guy wrote a book about it a few years ago."

Sun nodded. "The thieves were under the impression that Nixon's reelection campaign money was kept in that vault. It wasn't, but they managed to blow a hole in the roof of the place with dynamite and go back in over the course of the next couple of days to take most of what was in there. The banks were closed on the weekends back then."

"What's the connection between this robbery and the 1972 one? Besides the Nixon masks?"

Sun had been thinking hard during the conversation and had already decided what information to give Winter and what to hold back.

"The Dinsio gang didn't find Nixon's money, because it wasn't there. It was at a American Bank and Trust in San Clemente. I think the Nixon masks worn during the San Clemente robbery were a nod to the United California Bank burglary." Sun tried not to react to the way Winter was watching her with a steady, questioning gaze.

Winter put down her pen. "It's more than a stretch. These bank robbers didn't blow a hole in the roof with dynamite. The Dinsio gang didn't execute two bank employees. It didn't take these three days, and they definitely didn't make off with nine million. Plus, the Nixon masks could have just as easily been inspired by the movie *Point Break*."

"The American Bank and Trust robbery is just the first." It was hard to keep the excitement out of her voice, but dammit, this was it. This was going to be the case of Sun's career. "It's a practice run for what's coming next." Even just saying that out loud made her blood tingle in anticipation.

"How do you know?"

"Call it a hunch. You're familiar with those, I'm told," Sun added, sneering.

Winter shrugged. "Have it your way. When do we leave?"

She'd accepted it. Sun could let herself relax. A little.

"We check in for our flight at nine. We're meeting with local law enforcement tonight. I hope you don't mind, but there was only one seat left in business class. You'll be flying coach."

"Not a problem," Winter replied, matching Sun's tone as she gathered her things. "I'd never be a bitch over something as petty as an airplane seat. See you in San Clemente."

❋

SHE'D GOTTEN the last word in, for whatever that was worth.

Winter fumed as she swung by her desk to pick up her laptop. Sun was unbelievable. She knew the situation wasn't going to be a picnic. She didn't need any special abilities for that. But the reality was shaping up to be far worse.

"Hey." Noah was there, his usual grin in place. It faded a bit when he saw her face. "Not an auspicious beginning, I take it?"

Winter glared back and slammed her purse down on her desk. "Understatement," she gritted out.

"Got time for a cup of coffee? I know a little chocolate and caffeine always perks you up."

"I have to be at the airport at nine. Coffee will not fix this."

"It can't hurt." Without waiting for an answer, he picked up her bag himself. "Come on. We'll hit a drive-through on the way to the airport. I'll drop you off. You haven't gotten to ride in Beulah yet."

He kept chipping away at her with that annoying good mood of his, the entire way to the parking lot.

"Don't you have work to do?" she asked, after climbing into the impossibly high up Ford and buckling her seatbelt.

"Sure," he responded, his tone cheerful. "I'm part of a surveillance team later this morning, but I happen to have just enough time to chauffer you first. What do you think of Beulah?" He patted the dashboard with such transparent pride, she had to stifle a laugh.

"She's big." The truck could eat her Civic for breakfast and still be hungry. "What's my reputation like around the unit?"

Noah glanced at her in surprise at the non sequitur. "Um—"

"Be honest," she demanded. "I don't want any of your kumbaya bullshit."

"Okay," Noah drawled, and she thought he might be stalling for time. "I guess people think of you as kind of standoffish. Smart. Good instincts. I'm pretty sure Doug in computer forensics thinks you're cute. No one knows about your extras. As far as I'm aware, anyway."

"Sun said I'm working my way through the guys in the office."

Noah's jaw dropped for a full five seconds, processing that before he burst into laughter. "Darlin', if that's the case, consider me first in line. Did she somehow find out that we shared a hotel room in Harrisonburg?"

Winter scowled at the reminder. "There was nothing to that, and you know it."

"Yeah." His sigh was mournful, but his green eyes twinkled at her. "We would have had more fun if there *had* been something to it."

The tension in her shoulders eased, just a little, and she sat back farther in her seat. The truck was comfortable, not that she'd ever drive something as huge.

"I thought you were seeing that waitress from Louie's. The little blonde. Janet?"

"Jessie," he corrected with a wistful smile that showed the dimple in his right cheek. "It was a fun two weeks, but she dumped me for the bartender." He hit the left-hand turn signal and pulled into a Starbucks. "She said I was too old for her."

"You *are* too old for her. What are you? Thirty?"

"Thirty-one."

"Sun's holding something back from me on the case. Something important."

"Another non sequitur?" His smile widened into a teasing grin. "You don't even want to hear me whine about my broken heart?"

"If I wanted to hear whining about broken hearts, I'd just turn on your radio."

He tapped his thumb on the steering wheel. "So, is this a regular old hunch, some serious intuition, or did you...um, *see* something?"

"I didn't see anything."

That would be awful. To have one of her blinding headaches and wake up on the floor with her nose bleeding and Sun staring at her with those smug, dark eyes of hers. She shuddered.

"It's more of a strong feeling. Her reasons for wanting this case are flimsy at best and farfetched at worst. I'm thinking Max agreed just to get her across the country for a while and out of his hair. I'm just the sacrificial goat picked to go along for the ride."

"Darlin', it shouldn't have taken any special skill to figure that one out."

Once they had their coffee in hand, Winter filled him in on the case info Sun had given her. She left out the argument and the bitchy sniping. Not because she thought he'd pass it around—he was too good of a guy for that—but because she didn't want to sound like she was complaining.

"Just keep your head down, but your eyes open," he advised. "If you feel like there's something there, there probably is. And be careful."

At the airport, he pulled up in the passenger drop-off lane.

"Thanks for the ride. And the verbal valium."

Noah snorted. "Really? Verbal valium? Maybe that's why Jessie broke up with me."

6

It was agents like Sun that gave the FBI a bad reputation for bossing around local police departments. Winter wasn't a people person. At least it didn't come to her without effort, like it did with Noah. But when Sun put herself in the role of bad cop, it was clear that left Winter to have to pick up the slack and play damage control.

Sun had already pissed off everyone she'd come in contact with. Apparently, she didn't just save her attitude for her co-workers. She spread it around with liberal generosity.

"I need to interview the witnesses again," Sun said. "Whoever did this the first time shouldn't be allowed to wear a badge."

Shannon Marchwood, the San Clemente Sheriff, reddened under her tan. She was a slim woman in her forties with dark hair scraped back in a ponytail and a no-nonsense attitude. She wasn't tall, but she still topped Sun by two inches when she straightened up in a fury.

"Look, I already talked to two San Diego agents about this," Shannan spat. "They did their report, asked some questions, and promised to assist if we needed help. Same with the ATF guys. We didn't ask for assistance. My department has everything under control."

Sun scowled and started to speak, but Winter jumped in to referee the situation. "Sheriff Marchwood, we're here to serve as a resource, not a threat. We won't do anything to invalidate what you've done so far or jeopardize your investigation. Maybe what Agent Ming meant to say is that we'd like the opportunity to sit with you while you interview the witnesses again. To see if they've thought of anything else that might be helpful during the time since you talked with them last."

Sun hadn't missed the fact that the sheriff's name was on the interview reports. She was deliberately goading the woman.

Shannon took a deep breath and sat back down behind her desk, her posture stiff and defensive. "Of course. I'll make the arrangements for tomorrow morning."

"You'll make them—" Sun looked militant when Winter interrupted again.

"Tomorrow morning will be fine," Winter corrected. "We have the security recordings to go over, right?"

Sun shot Winter a warning look that promised retribution later.

Oh, well.

The sheriff took them to a conference room, where a TV had been set up. She pulled the video up on the laptop. "There's nothing here," she stated. "Whoever did this was thorough enough to hack the security system and erase the footage."

They studied the screen, where the sped-up recording showed customers streaming in and out of the bank. The security guard to the right of the entrance lounged at his desk and didn't seem particularly alert. The tellers all worked with practiced efficiency. There was no odd behavior or anything that stood out to Winter. Except for the timestamp at the bottom of the screen.

"So, they replaced the footage with the previous day's recording," Sun muttered.

"Right," Shannon replied. "I'll email you both the files, but we've gone over it all and haven't caught anything out of the ordinary. We've also checked out every employee and past employees, in case it was an inside job or a grudge thing. It doesn't seem to be."

They continued to talk, but the conversation blurred as something on the video caught Winter's eye.

Still playing, sped up, security footage was now showing the day after the robbery. The picture was in black and white, but a red dot shimmered on the screen, just below the teller cubbies. The farthest one toward the left. It flickered when people moved in front of it but stayed in the same place. It was tiny, maybe coin-sized.

Winter had seen this happen before.

Like in college, when a student had been holding people up for cash and jewelry, she'd found the guy out. Because the stolen items glowed so distinctly, she could see the light leaking out of his closed desk drawer in his bedroom, where he'd stashed them.

It hadn't been the last time something like that had happened. For some reason, sometimes things connected with violent crimes glowed with a crimson light that no one else but Winter could see.

By now, she didn't question it, but she couldn't very well tell Sun and the sheriff. At best, she'd be treated as a woo-woo freak. At worst, she'd be tossed into a looney bin...and treated as a woo-woo freak.

Winter felt enough like a freak on her own.

Sun was playing nicer now but still had an irritating,

condescending edge to her voice as she questioned Marchwood.

"Would it be possible for us to still see the crime scene today?" Winter asked as soon as she could get a word in without interrupting either combatant.

The sheriff nodded. "I can take you through it. You know how to get there from here?"

Sun, who'd insisted on driving, did.

The silence in the car was loaded and angry. After a few minutes, Sun spoke first. "Do we need to go over our talk from this morning?"

Winter bit back a retort. "Noted," she said instead. "But you'll never get anything out of the local LEOs if you don't tone down the attitude."

"I didn't ask for your advice. From now on, don't try to make me look bad."

Sun turned on the radio and cranked up the volume on the NPR station that was programmed into the rental car stereo, signaling the end of the conversation.

Nice talk, Winter thought as she looked out the window.

It was the first time she'd been to California. With the time difference, it was still only five in the afternoon. She was thankful that she'd swapped out her wool blazer for cotton before leaving Richmond because it was almost eighty degrees. The roads were lined with palm trees, and adobe-themed buildings with iron railings gleamed white in the sun.

The bank was on the corner of a road that saw moderate traffic, El Camino Real. It was housed in the same building as a Starbucks. There was a traffic light in front of the bank, and businesses around it. Hard to believe that there hadn't been any witnesses stepping forward to say they saw two Nixons leaving the bank with a big bag that morning.

Winter made a mental note to double-check whether the

local PD had looked at the traffic cameras or any outdoor security cameras from neighboring businesses. The suspects had opted not to double-park for their getaway but must have circled the block until they could pull into a spot with an easy exit. Since the bank was still closed now, most of the parking spots were free.

As they got out of the rental car, Winter saw one parking place, the painted lines looking brand new, directly in front of the building. It was striped over, as if the area was blocked off for a loading zone. The paint gleamed like it had just been done.

Maybe it had.

Sheriff Marchwood joined them in front of the building. Before she could unlock the door, Winter pointed out the space. "You live here," she said. "Can you remember if that spot has always been a loading zone?"

The sheriff's eyes sharpened. "That paint looks new."

Even Sun perked up. "Have you accessed the CCTV footage from the traffic cameras?"

Marchwood nodded but was already on her cellphone. "Davis, I need you to check the footage from the traffic light on El Camino in front of the bank." Winter could hear the new excitement in the woman's voice. "I know, but I want you to start with the day before the robbery. Let me know if you see anyone painting parking spot lines in front of the entrance."

"Good eye," she told Winter when she'd hung up. "I can't believe I didn't notice that." Her attitude had warmed toward Winter, but she was still freezing out Sun.

Inside the bank, it was freezing cold, like someone had left the air condition running on full blast. Congealed blood was still thick beside the counter where one victim had been shot. It had been tracked across the floor in places, likely by emergency personnel that had responded after the scene was cleared by police.

Then, Winter understood the air conditioning. There was enough blood that the coppery smell would have been over-powering had the temperature been warmer.

Based on the witness statements, they already knew about what had happened, but Sheriff Marchwood walked them through it again.

The suspects had come in during a lull in business hours, already wearing the masks. They'd approached the counter. The security guard had been in the employee restroom in the back. He'd just come out of the hallway, behind the tellers, when the female Nixon shot him. He'd fallen, blocking the branch manager's door. Everything had happened so fast, no tellers were given the chance to push their emergency buttons.

The suspects then ordered the branch manager to be brought out. She'd made a 911 call from her desk but left the phone off the hook when she left her office. Another teller, having escaped to the back offices, called 911 within a minute after that.

Officers were dispatched—the American Bank and Trust was only a minute away from the substation at San Clemente City Hall, just on the other side of the overpass—but they'd also had all units responding to two other emergencies happening simultaneously. The first two officers were en route and rerouted, but they didn't arrive until about nine minutes after the call had been placed.

Within five minutes, the suspects had the money in hand. Within another thirty seconds, the female suspect shot the branch manager, and the two suspects left the building. None of the tellers could say what happened after that. They were too traumatized by the murder of their boss to have looked out the window at that point.

When Marchwood finished her run-through, Winter went to the counter where she'd seen the glowing dot on the security footage. Wedged just beneath the trim below the counter was a religious medal of some sort.

It always irked Winter when police dramas had investigators grab an ink pen or some such thing to pick up a piece of evidence. Who knew how many people had already touched that ink pen, causing cross contamination? Taking a fresh swab from the evidence collection kit she carried, Winter tore off the paper and used the swab as a reaching device to pull the medal out. Despite the blood spatters all around it, the medal was clean, the silver shining in the overhead lights.

"What are you looking at?" Sun demanded.

"Anyone have a pair of sterile tweezers?"

"Will these work?" Marchwood crouched beside Winter and handed her a pair of needle-nose pliers. "The air conditioning switch in the cruiser I drove is broken," she explained. "Everyone who drives it carries a set of these if they don't want to roast."

Since they would clearly contain DNA, Winter wrapped the pliers with clean gauze, then used them to grasp the end of the medal and turn it over. There was blood on the bottom. The medal hadn't been there before the murder.

"Got an evidence bag in your pocket too?" Winter asked Marchwood.

With a half-smile, the sheriff pulled one out and handed it to her. "Who doesn't?"

Winter dropped it in, sealed the bag, and held it close to read the writing around the head of the saint that decorated the front of the medal.

"Saint Dismas," Sheriff Marchwood read. "Do we have any Catholics in the house?"

"Saint Dismas is sometimes called the patron saint of thieves, along with Saint Nicholas," Sun put in, her voice vibrating with excitement. She grinned at them, something Winter had never seen her do...unless it was at someone else's expense. The way it transformed her face was startling. "I watch *Jeopardy*," she admitted.

Marchwood's phone rang. She listened for a moment, and a grim look came across her face.

"I wasn't sure about you two at first," the sheriff said after she'd hung up from the call. "But now, I think you might just be my good luck charms. One of the traffic cameras was at the perfect vantage point to pick up footage of a man painting the lines on that parking spot on the day before the robbery. We even know who he is."

"You don't look happy about that," Sun pointed out. "Why is that?"

"Our units were split that morning between two calls when the robbery 911 came in. One was a possible homicide. Someone called in a report of a dead body on the beach. That body was Jack Hanley, our Picasso caught in the footage."

7

He'd have preferred California for the weather, but New York did have a certain level of charm in December. The Christmas decorations and lights, busy shoppers bundled up against the tit-numbing cold. A recent dusting of snow covered the smog-grayed banks and edged the icy puddles that struggled to stay frozen under the afternoon's bright winter sunshine.

Jamaica, Ryan thought, also had no snow. He wanted to be in Jamaica.

He reached to his collar, where his good luck charm normally hung. Saint Dismas, though, had fallen off somewhere. Not a good omen for his current business relationship. Dismas protected thieves.

The absence of the little metal disc and its chain sent a little chill of superstition up his spine. No help for it now, though. He'd have to find time to buy another. *If* he could find the time.

He glanced at the long list on his phone, complete with dozens of ridiculous details and instructions, and tugged his wool cap lower on his forehead. Sunglasses shaded his eyes.

His black down-filled coat was bulky and puffy—the kind that made its wearer look about fifty pounds heavier. The tip of his nose was numb, but beneath the coat, he was sweating.

The reasoning behind the instructions Heidi had given him was incomprehensible. It was like a scavenger hunt run by a schizophrenic squirrel.

Stash your luggage at an airport locker. Number 365, to be exact.

Visit the Metropolitan Museum of Art at precisely noon. Stand for three minutes in front of the Portrait of Madame X.

Take a taxi to the Empire State Building. Tip the driver ten dollars and fifty cents.

Go to Macy's. Buy one pair of a specific type of dress shoe, one-half size larger than your regular size.

And on, and on, and on.

What the bloody hell was he supposed to do if Macy's didn't carry the right size? If the Madame X portrait had been moved last minute to another museum?

The entire thing was a bloody waste of time. He'd been running, sometimes literally, all over town. He was exhausted. Nowhere on the list was *take a well-deserved break and sit down at a coffee shop somewhere for a cuppa.*

Now, he was hauling all the packages he'd picked up that day to the address of the hotel she'd specified on the Lower East Side. He was looking forward to getting off his feet, but this neighborhood did not look promising.

Ryan was laid back. Easygoing. Every man for himself, sure, but live and let live. At the first sight of the hotel that Heidi, the sadistic bitch, had booked for him, he felt complete and total rage.

It was a dingy walk-up above an appliance repair store that looked to be a leftover from the middle of the century. The narrow staircase smelled like spilled milk gone rancid. The check-in counter was caged behind chicken wire like the stage at a bad honky-tonk bar. The bored-looking clerk slid him a key across the desk when he gave his assumed name and didn't look up from the tiny television in front of her.

To top it all off, there were three flights of stairs to climb since the elevator was out of order.

He unzipped his jacket at the bottom of the third flight and would have sworn he could see steam billowing out into the unheated air. He tried not to think about the fact that he could be already kicked back on 300-thread count sheets at the Four Seasons instead.

Ryan made his way down the hall, grimacing at the sound of a couple two rooms over fucking with great enthusiasm. He used his key on the assigned door, though a half-hearted shove would have done the job just as well. But he paused, his hand on the doorknob, and sniffed at the air. Under the musty smell of the hallway carpet, he detected perfume. Fresh. Something musky and sexy and out of place.

Turning the handle, he let the door swing open with a creak. At first, he thought he'd been mistaken, and he'd gone into the wrong room. The woman sitting on the single bed was all leg.

Black high heels with ankle straps. She wore black tights, and a short, violently green skirt hugged her crossed thighs like a second skin. A black top, the neckline scooping low. Hair as red as an Irish sunset draped across her shoulders in loose, fat curls. Wicked blue eyes in a face that looked like Heidi's...but didn't. It was slimmer, somehow. More contoured. She'd done something with her eyes, too, with makeup, to make them dark and exotic-looking. Her Mona Lisa smile was slicked with red.

Ryan ignored the automatic tug in his groin and stepped in, closing the door behind him. It shut the sounds of the neighbors out, but not all the way. He dropped the bags on the floor beside him.

"Tarted yourself up good and proper, now, didn't you?"

As her now-blue eyes narrowed, he realized that he didn't know *what* Heidi Presley looked like—if that was even her real name, which he doubted. She wasn't the drab cowgirl he'd first met in North Dakota. She also wasn't the prim, buttoned-down businesswoman with the short, chestnut curls who'd robbed a bank in California in a Richard Nixon mask. He could likely pass the real woman on the street without a flicker of recognition.

She was slippery.

"You followed my instructions well today," she said. "Good." Her voice was the same. Cold and crisp.

"Up until now," Ryan corrected in a smooth tone. "If you think there's any way in bloody fucking hell I'm going to sleep on that bedbug-infested mattress in *this*—" He gestured to the room, not much bigger than the bed she sat on.

A mini desk fan was mounted in one corner of the ceiling, maybe an effort to stir the stagnant, musty air. There was no bedside table. Nothing but a rickety three-legged stool with a tiny television perched on top, positioned at the foot of the bed.

"You'd sleep in this bed if I told you to," she said. Her eyes glinted with a dangerous light, even though she used the same, patient tone one would use to chastise a beagle. "We're partners, but I hope I've been very clear about who is running this show. As it happens, though, your 'assistant' has already registered you a room at the Park Lane Hotel. Your luggage has been delivered to an executive suite with an excellent view of Central Park."

The stab of relief he felt was almost pathetic, and Ryan hoped it didn't show on his face. He'd come a long way from his underprivileged upbringing. This place reminded him too much of the flophouse he'd been raised in.

Something about the way she watched him told him he hadn't hidden the reaction deep enough.

"Then why the charade? Having me traipse all over and meeting you here?"

"Persuading you to participate was one thing. Assuring myself that you could follow directions without question was another. You passed the test."

"And what if I hadn't?"

She stood up and picked up the jacket she'd been sitting on. He forced himself not to recoil when she closed the space between them. The hooker heels made her taller than him, and he had to look up in order to meet her gaze. For all their pretty color, hers were cold and flat as a frozen lake.

"Let's go. Leave the bags."

Heidi slipped around him and into the hallway. Instead of heading toward the stairs he'd come up, she went to a set at the other end of the hall. It descended down four levels, where a fire exit opened out on to an alley at the back of the building. No alarm rang when she pushed it open.

A silver Lexus with dark tinted windows waited for them.

"You're Oliver Brown, a professor at Oxford on sabbatical," Heidi told him on the way. "There's a bag in the back seat. You'll look the part. I've instructed the staff that you're working on a novel and don't plan on leaving your room for at least a week. You don't require housekeeping or a nightly turndown service."

He reached into the back and pulled out a gray briefcase. Inside were a pair of tortoiseshell glasses, a package of colored contacts, a salt-and-pepper wig, and cheek padding. He'd used the same type before. It wasn't comfortable, feeling like a food-hoarding chipmunk, but the padding would fill out the slight hollows in his cheeks and make his face look rounder.

"How long *will* I be there?"

"No more than two days." She glanced away from the heavy traffic for a moment. "And you will stay in your room."

Irritation bubbled again. "Are you going to tell me what happens next?"

"No. You'll know as soon as you need to."

This was bollocks. Insane. If he'd had a gun, he'd have turned it on her in a heartbeat and damn the consequences. Ryan had never killed anyone before, but he'd be glad to make an exception.

Sure, he'd stay in his room at the Park Lane Hotel like a good boy. Hell, maybe he'd even start his memoirs since it appeared that anyone with a little computer skill could find out every damned thing about him. But the second he found an opportunity, he was gone.

Heidi either sensed his rebellious thoughts or had uncanny timing.

"I've left you a laptop," she said, sarcasm threading her words. "Be sure to read the dossier I've put together on you if you get a chance. I really think it's some of my best work."

He schooled himself to calm down, recognizing the area they were driving through. He'd stayed in the same part of New York when he'd been here on a job two years before. They were almost to the Park Lane Hotel, and he'd be able to at least put some distance between himself and his blackmailer.

He put in the contacts that changed his eyes from blue to hazel and added the glasses. The cheek pads went in, and he had instant jowls. An eyebrow pencil and some delicate shading, along with some sallow-looking powder aged him by about twenty years in thirty seconds.

He modestly considered himself gifted with disguises, and she must have known that, providing all of the gear he would have bought for himself. The wig was the finishing touch. The items went back in the briefcase, except for the

ID and credit cards that would make the transformation just about complete.

It was creepy what she'd done to his photo. It was a photo of himself, and she'd somehow computer-aged it. The resemblance to his Uncle Frank made him feel a little sick.

"Swap the puffy coat for the one in the back," Heidi instructed, pulling up in front of the hotel. "I'll contact you in two days," she reminded him. "Stay put."

Ryan shrugged into the black wool greatcoat, grabbed the suitcase and got out of the car. The freezing air that smacked him in the face was warmer than the inside of the Lexus had been, and for the first time since he'd found Heidi in his room, he felt like he could breathe again.

He nodded to the doorman as he passed. He had two days.

He would use them.

※

THIS WAS EASIER than she'd thought it would be.

Heidi pulled away from the curb without waiting to make sure that O'Connelly went in. She had other things to do before she checked in to her own hotel for the night, and he would do as he was told.

It was satisfying to see that she hadn't been off-base in her assessment of Ryan O'Connelly. Like most men—like most other *people*—he was weak.

She allowed herself a smile, remembering the way he'd looked baffled and angry when she'd checked in on him at the art museum. He'd glanced around, looked at his watch, glanced around some more. Those three minutes must have felt like an eternity, but he obeyed her instructions to the letter.

He looked and behaved like a throwback to the old days

when a professional thief was a mysterious, debonair figure, and cat burglars crept the silver screens. He was smart, quick, and could charm the average woman out of her panties in about twelve seconds, if he really put his mind to it. Handsome enough to do it in twenty, if he wasn't paying attention.

But it was all just an act. A persona he'd picked out when he was nineteen years old. Ryan O'Connelly was nothing more than a cardboard cutout.

And she wasn't an average woman.

She'd done her research. Patrick O'Connell was his real name, and despite the cultivated Irish accent, he'd been born in Chicago, in the slums. His mom was a stripper who'd discovered the joys of crack cocaine when little Patrick was just seven. His drunk uncle had taken him in at ten, when Chrissie O'Connell died of an overdose, but life didn't get any better. Uncle Frank was a belligerent asshole who'd liked to use his fists.

At least he'd taught little Patrick one valuable skill: how to steal and not get caught.

Most people would admire the way Patrick O'Connell had transformed himself into Ryan O'Connelly.

Heidi didn't give a shit.

It wasn't his moxie or his dimples that she was after. It wasn't even his handy thieving skills. She was capable enough to pull this off on her own, far better than Ryan could.

No, Ryan was just a prop. She needed The Cat's reputation, and nothing more. His apparent willingness to be manipulated was just an added bonus.

After watching him perform today, following her instructions to the letter, it appeared she'd chosen well.

She maneuvered the car through the busy streets with ease. Her experience driving in congested areas was limited, but being a logistical thinker served her well. As businesses thinned out to be replaced by cheap apartment buildings— probably still with sky-high rent—she kept an eye out for one in particular. With a quick, deliberate movement, she tugged her skirt up another inch to reveal more leg.

A young man was sitting on the stoop of one apartment building. When she pulled to a smooth stop in front of him and rolled down the window to give him a flirty little finger wave, he jumped like a trained seal. His face split into a grin as he headed for the passenger side door.

When he got a good look at her—the made-up face and skintight, slutty clothes that implied she was a rich woman with poor taste and questionable hobbies—his tongue almost rolled out of his mouth.

"Did you bring me what I asked?" Her voice had been modeled on Marilyn Monroe. High and breathy, promising to fulfill every one of the kid's most prurient desires without coming right out and saying so.

He held up a bulky canvas bag in one hand.

"Good boy." She gave him a slow, curving smile, knowing how she must look. *All tarted up*, like Ryan had said. She kind of liked that. "Hop in, and I'll take you wherever you want to go."

He did, with pathetic eagerness.

It was just too, too easy, she thought later as she walked away from the Lexus, picking her way through the rubble of the empty lot in Queens. The crackle of flames was just becoming audible.

So easy, that it almost took the fun right out of killing him.

8

It had been two days, and Winter had more questions
than answers about the American Bank and Trust
robbery. But after the heart-wrenching witness interviews
she'd sat through the morning before, she'd put aside any
thoughts of working on her own investigation in her scarce
moments of off time. She was all in on this case. If, for whatever reason, Sun was right and this was only the first in a
series of similar robberies, they had to figure out who did it
before more people died.

The body count was already up to at least three.

It looked like Sun had resigned herself to the fact that
Winter could be an asset, rather than a liability. Finding the
religious medal, in her opinion, had shown Winter had
beginner's luck. They'd interviewed friends and family
members of Jack Hanley the day before, and she'd even given
Winter the go-ahead to take the lead.

Robbie Carter was the one who had told them through
tears that Jack was only dead because he had answered a
Craigslist ad.

"He said he was gonna make an easy thousand dollars,"

Robbie told them, wiping away a bead of sweat from his dark skin. "All's he had to do was to paint some lines on the road without getting caught. When he was sober, he'd gotten good gigs like that there before, but nothing that paid so well."

Robbie had driven his friend to the "job" himself. They'd taken Robbie's work truck out at two in the morning the night they were supposed to and put out cones. Robbie painted houses for a living and loaned Jack a paint sprayer. Robbie waited in the truck while Jack did the job.

Jack, who'd been paid the first half up-front, took his buddy Robbie out for a beer afterward to celebrate. One beer had turned into six. Robbie dropped Jack off at another friend's house around five in the morning, where Jack had been couch-surfing. He'd even warned Jack not to oversleep, or he'd miss his meeting for the other half of his paycheck.

The next morning, Jack was dead.

Jack's friends, including the woman he'd been staying with, all showed genuine grief at the news of his death, from what Winter could tell. Sun, in her usual, abrasive way, had taken some effort to convince that Jack hadn't been killed by one of his acquaintances for the thousand dollars. Background checks on everyone showed no violent priors.

The San Clemente detective assigned to the case, Shelby Patterson, had dismissed her suspicions. There was no reason to disbelieve Robbie's story.

The Craigslist ad had been pulled. So far, support at Craigslist hadn't been able to provide any useful information. It appeared a computer glitch had wiped that ad and several others, and they had no record of it.

They didn't hit another break on the American Bank and Trust case until their third morning.

Detective Patterson had asked them to meet at the station at nine. He was tall and skinny, about fifty years old, with the face of a sad hound dog and a bald head that gleamed in the overhead lights. He was slow and methodical in both thinking and speaking, and he drove Sun up the wall.

Winter had to like the guy, just for that.

"So," Patterson began, his voice deep and slow. He adjusted a pair of bifocals as he looked at his notes. "We have a medal of Saint Dismas, a Craigslist ad, some Nixon masks...let me write this down."

He got up and moved to the whiteboard at the end of the conference table. His handwriting was neat and exact, and he seemed to be just as slow and thorough with it as he was with everything else.

Sun already looked annoyed.

"So, we think that the suspects likely placed the ad on Craigslist?" Winter asked, forestalling any snide comments Sun might make. "And then reported their own homicide in hopes that it would slow down the bank call response time?"

"I think so," Patterson agreed. He stopped writing to turn around.

Sun was gritting her teeth. The sound was audible.

"I'm just not sure about the Nixon connection, though," Patterson added, with an apologetic look at Sun.

"It's not a connection to Nixon," Sun burst out. Her pale skin was flushed, and her black eyes snapped. "The Nixon masks are a nod to the United California Bank robbery in Laguna Niguel in 1972."

"I just don't see it." Patterson shrugged, a slight lift of his shoulders, and turned back to the whiteboard. "Yeah, San Clemente's close to Laguna Niguel, but the whole operation was completely different."

"Let's work with Sun's theory for now," Winter suggested. "The suspects could have used names connected with that robbery for a car rental, a property rental if they were from out of the area, something like that."

The conference room door flew open, and Sheriff Marchwood burst in, her face lit with excitement. "We just got a call from a Catholic church in Laguna Niguel," she announced. "An anonymous donation in the amount of two hundred and twenty thousand dollars was found in a large tote bag outside of their church the day of the robbery. Apparently," she added with a wry smile, "there was a difference of opinion among the church leadership as to whether they should keep it or report it."

"They donated it? Why would they do that?" Sun demanded. "What sense does it make to hold up a bank, kill three people, and give away the fucking money?"

Marchwood shrugged. "Who knows why people do what they do. One of them wore a Catholic religious symbol. Maybe they felt guilty. Patterson, let's go talk to the priest."

He nodded and gathered up his things. "You two want to tag along?"

"Go ahead," Sun replied, already opening her laptop. "We're looking for the suspects, not the money."

Patterson arched an eyebrow at Winter, who made a sympathetic face. He was smiling when he left.

"I'll take car rentals," Sun ordered without looking up. "You call on properties. Ask about the names on the list I just emailed you. They're all members of the gang that pulled the robbery in 1972."

"Why are you so convinced it has anything to do with that?" Winter asked again. "If you get too focused on a theory, you might miss what really happened."

Again, Sun didn't answer straight-out. She deflected, and hard. "Who is the case agent here? The one with actual experience? Just do it, all right?" She was already dialing the first number. "Be sure to look for any townhouses near the bank, maybe in view."

Winter sighed and took a sip of her coffee. It was going to be a long morning.

She was wrong. The third property management company she called had booked a beach bungalow for the week for a James and Amelia Dinsio.

"You're fucking kidding me!" Sun crowed, jumping out of her chair, sending her chin-length black hair swinging around her grinning face. "Amil and James Dinsio were the brothers that masterminded the Laguna Niguel heist." She was already closing her laptop. "We need to get over there."

It didn't feel right.

"Why would the suspects still be there? They robbed a bank a few miles away and donated the money. None of this makes any sense. Call Marchwood and Patterson. This is their case. Find out what they want to do."

All excitement slithered from Sun's face. "We're FBI, *Agent Black.*"

"And we're *assisting* the local PD, Agent Ming."

"You can call them," Sun said, heading for the door. "On the way there."

A headache was starting to throb behind her eyes. Winter grabbed her things and gulped the rest of the coffee, hoping the caffeine would ease it. She could not have an episode in front of Sun. Could not.

She tried to will the intensifying headache away as she dialed Marchwood and followed Sun.

The sheriff answered on the second ring. "We've got the hideout," Winter said without preamble, getting into the passenger seat of the rental. She explained the name connection, and that the place was booked for the week before giving her the address.

Marchwood asked them to do a drive-by and try to see if it was occupied. Sun agreed with reluctance that they'd wait a short distance away until the sheriff, detective, and other San Clemente officers arrived.

The rental cottage was a little way outside of town, just

off the coastal highway. Closer to Laguna Niguel and convenient, say, if the suspects planned on heading to Los Angeles to catch a plane.

The farther they drove, the worse Winter's headache got. She dug in the glove box, and then her bag, looking for a paper towel or tissues. Her movements became more jerky and urgent as the seconds ticked by and the pain level rose.

"What are you doing?" Sun asked, glancing away from the road. Her hands tightened on the steering wheel. "You look weird. Are you sick?"

"No, just looking for a tissue," Winter lied.

"I have some in my purse."

She picked it up and rummaged around, feeling her own pulse beating at her temples. Her vision was starting to gray around the edges. Her fingers closed on the little packet of tissues. She dropped Sun's bag and ripped the tissue package open, crumpling several of them into a ball. She held it under her nose.

The car swerved to the right, and some part of Winter's brain heard Sun yell, "You'd better not puke in here!" Then, her vision went black as her headache peaked on a blinding crescendo of pain.

❄

SUN FLICKED on the emergency flashers and yanked the wheel hard, the tires crunching on gravel at the side of the road. Winter had slumped over, her hand falling to her lap. The tissues she'd been holding were splashed with red.

She cursed. This was going to look great on her record. Killing her partner after only a couple of days together.

She glanced in the side mirror to be sure traffic was clear, and jumped out of the car, rounding the hood to Winter's door. By the time she'd gotten it open, Winter was already struggling to sit up. Her face, pale on the best of days, was fully bleached of color, except for a line of blood that leaked in a sluggish stream from her right nostril.

Her dark blue eyes were unfocused.

"Winter!"

Sun didn't want to touch her. But she yelled in Winter's face and pushed her shoulder, hard. "Snap out of it. What the fuck is wrong with you?"

Winter shuddered once, a shiver that shook her entire body, and her eyes rolled back in her head until her seizure, or whatever it was, cleared. It was like she was coming out of a trance or something, and it was creepy as hell. Sun wasn't superstitious, but she felt like her Japanese *obaasan* at that moment. She almost wished she had an *omamori*—one of the little amulets in a silk baggie that the old woman would wear around her neck. She replaced it every year to ward off bad luck.

"Shit," Winter gasped. "I'm sorry."

She should be, Sun thought, still feeling uneasy.

"You had some kind of fit. What do you need? Water? I'm no good at this. Please don't puke."

"I'm not going to puke."

Winter picked up the pack of tissues and pulled out a couple more, dabbing beneath her nose. "What is your obsession with puking?" Her voice was weak, but her sarcasm was still going strong.

"Emetophobia. Fear of vomit. Ever since I was a kid."

The color was coming back into Winter's face in slow stages.

The crisis may have passed, but Sun's heart hadn't stopped racing.

Puke, blood, vomit...anyone else's bodily fluids basically wigged her out, causing what was officially known as a vaso-vagal syncope response. In essence, she likened herself to a fainting goat who got a scare. And it pissed her off. Years of therapy had helped the response, but she still didn't have full control. Which pissed her off even more.

She came into contact with bodily fluid sometimes in the field. Not often, or she might have had to consider a different line of work. It was that bad.

As a rule, she tried to avoid anything that had to do with even the possibility of other people's involuntary excretions. She was certified in CPR, according to the certificate she renewed every couple of years when it was required. The only reason she'd managed to maintain it was that she lucked out. The first time she'd renewed, she had a coach who saw how grossed out she was by the whole other-people's-body-fluids thing and rubber-stamped her certificate. She'd looked him up bi-annually ever since.

Winter closed her eyes and tipped her head back against the headrest as Sun watched her for signs of any sudden movement.

"Calm down," Winter said, not opening her eyes. "I get migraines once in a while. It's gone now, and I probably won't have another one for six months or more. And if I hear anyone back in VC mention what you witnessed today, I will make your life hell. Fake puddles of vomit on your desk. Spilled vegetable soup in the parking lot outside your driver's side door. I will *hire* people to puke in front of you. Now, get back in the car."

They weren't friends, Sun decided, suppressing a shudder at the mental images Winter had evoked as she got back behind the wheel. Sun hadn't joined the FBI to make friends and wasn't about to change that now. But they were closer now to co-workers, or competitors at least, than enemies.

Which was fine.

It was more satisfying to win battles when they were played on even ground. It was only fair that they each knew one of the other's weaknesses. That would keep things balanced.

Plus, Sun had to admire anyone who was as good as she was with threats.

✻

WINTER'S HEADACHE WAS GONE, like it had never existed. That was how it had happened in the past. She'd at least had more warning before this one hit. When she'd had her "migraines" before, she sometimes got as little as a few seconds of build-up.

But the experience was the same. Once she'd gone under, the vision had burst on her in vivid technicolor. The inside of the small cottage, decorated in a tired, beachy theme, showed signs of wear from years of careless tenants. A small living room, the plaid sofa leaking a little stuffing from the corner, was empty. Through an open doorway to the right, she could see an empty bedroom with a window that looked out on the ocean. A bathroom door opening off the living room, too, stood open.

She could see the kitchen to the left. Seventies-era, harvest gold appliances and dingy brown linoleum. A battered Formica table and four plastic-covered chairs. And a glowing dishwasher that bathed the room in ominous red.

And then it was over. She'd come out of it.

"You sure you're okay?"

"I'm fine. Like I said, don't worry about it."

Winter couldn't very well just segue into a warning to avoid all kitchen appliances when they reached the rental. She was already the weird kid on the block, and she didn't need to give Sun more ammunition against her.

But something was wrong.

She could feel it.

With her visions, the hazy red she saw indicated a clue... not a threat. But Winter felt the threat down in her bones.

How did she warn others without ending up in the looney bin herself? Be laughed at. Feared.

"Gut instinct" would only get her so far.

She didn't have time to think about it. Sun made the turnoff from Highway 1 onto a small side road where the faded green rental bungalow sat at the end of a short cul-de-sac. They were less than a minute away from the scene.

Parked in front of the home was a San Clemente cruiser. Sheriff Marchwood and Detective Patterson had arrived first. The front door stood open. Winter opened her mouth to tell Sun to hurry, but it was too late.

One side of the small house exploded, shards of siding and broken wood blasting outward as far as fifty feet. As if the structure had taken its last breath, half the roof collapsed in a crooked dive inward. They heard the impact through the rolled-up windows of the car.

Sun slammed on the brakes, throwing the car into park at a crazy angle to the police cruiser. They were out of the vehicle and moving toward the house when a figure stumbled through the open front door and crumpled to the ground.

"Shannon!" Sun yelled.

The figure didn't move.

They reached her at the same time, squinting against the intense heat of the fire that rolled off the house in waves. Was there a second bomb? Anything else that could detonate under the penetrating heat of the flames?

Winter had no time to worry about that.

Sheriff Marchwood's eyebrows and lashes were gone. Her face was already a painful red color, beginning to blister.

"Son of a bitch." Sun stared down at the woman in horror, transfixed.

"Sun!" Winter yelled. "Move. Call for backup."

She didn't react.

"Now!"

Winter didn't wait to see if Sun obeyed. She grabbed Marchwood under the arms and pulled her away from the house, toward where the cars were parked. She held her breath against the smell of cooked flesh and tried not to think about the damage she could be doing to the woman's burned skin. She also tried not to think about Detective Patterson.

It could have been them.

The fact that Sun had pulled over while Winter had her vision had kept them from getting to the house before the other two arrived. She flinched as, with a creaking, rumbling crash, the rest of the roof caved.

Working as fast as she could move, she slapped out any embers still glowing on the sheriff's clothing and held her breath as she checked for a pulse. As she heard Sun's voice in the background, higher than normal and shaky, she started CPR. Sun's voice faded away.

Everything else faded away too. Even time, as the seconds unraveled into minutes.

She was unaware of anything for a while except counting. Rhythmic chest compressions, the blowing of breath into another person. Aching arms, quivering with strain, but knowing that she couldn't stop. She was breathing for Shannon Marchwood. Pumping her heart. Sending oxygen through her limp body. Keeping her from having permanent brain damage when she was resuscitated.

If she was resuscitated.

Instead of thinking about that, Winter focused on the dull throbbing in her palms, where her hands, one over the other with fingers interlaced, pushed down on Shannon's sternum in a repeated rhythm, hard enough that she knew they'd be sore and bruised the next day.

Sometime later, Winter registered sirens in a vague way, but she kept going. There were voices, loud and questioning, but she ignored them. Hands finally pulled her away.

"Come on." It was Sun. Her face was grim, but she grabbed Winter's arm in a gentle grip and pulled her toward the car.

Winter felt lightheaded, the sun too bright, and blinked against the feeling. "We need to stay here. This is an active crime scene."

"There are officers, firefighters, and EMTs swarming this place. San Clemente's undersheriff is in charge right now, and the Orange County Sheriff's Department has more on the way. I've called Max Osbourne back at home. He's coordinating with the OCSD and the FBI office in San Diego in case they need more agents to assist. Things are covered here."

Sun steered Winter to the car with manual effort and opened the door for her. She all but pushed Winter in, holding her head down like she was loading a perp into the back of a cruiser.

She climbed in the driver's side, tersely instructed Winter to buckle up, and took out her purse. She dug out a small packet of hand wipes, some sanitizer, a half-drunk bottle of water, and a stick of peppermint gum, passing them over to Winter as she did.

Then, not saying a word, she drove them back to San Clemente.

9

Almost forty-eight hours to the minute after Heidi dropped him off at the Park Lane Hotel, Ryan received a brief text.

Floating Mountain Tea House. 6:30.

He'd read the dossier she'd put together on him. She had him well and truly by the balls. But he'd had a lot of time to think in the last two days. He was ready for her.

The tea room was about a mile and a half from his hotel. The sky was dark with impending snow, but Ryan opted to walk. Two days in one room was two days too many. He wanted a clear head when dealing with Heidi.

She'd gone for hipster this time, he noted. Black hair, loose and shoulder-length, except for a couple of small braids twisted back at her temples, and black-framed Buddy Holly glasses. Jeans, no makeup, and a thick, ugly green sweater added bulk to her slim frame.

She was already seated in an alcove near a window that overlooked 72nd Street, cross-legged on a flat cushion on the floor. What looked like a textbook was open on the low table in front of her, with a pen and notebook beside it. She could pass for a college student studying for an exam.

There were a few other artsy and pretentious-looking customers in the tea house. Most had earbuds in and were seated on the floor with their own books. A few couples spoke in low voices and had their own little tables farther away.

He ordered what he hoped was just a strong black tea with nothing weird in it and joined Heidi. Still in his Oliver persona—the professor to her student, he supposed—he sat down on the floor cushion with a little feigned difficulty.

Without speaking, she moved the small potted plant on the table to one side and slid the book across the table. She'd written in the top margin of the book in neat, precise handwriting.

The Phoenix Hotel, p. 263.

He looked up at Heidi. Her eyes were once again the normal nondescript brown behind her glasses. There was no expression in them.

The Phoenix was one of the most exclusive hotels in New York. He had an admitted weakness for luxury and had come across an article on the internet about the place. If a regular person wanted a room there, they could splurge on one for fifteen hundred a night. If a rich person wanted to stay there, they could get fancier digs for a few thousand a night. An insanely wealthy person could rent a suite for a half million a month.

The hotel had been around since the 1930s, renovated in the last decade or so, and a fortunate few were rumored to live there full-time. Their annual housing costs might feed a starving third-world country for a year.

He turned to page 263 of what looked like a textbook history of modern crime in New York and began to read about The Phoenix Hotel robbery.

By 1972, Samuel Nato and Bobby Comfort already had a successful string of high-profile hotel heists under their belts. Affiliated with the Lucchese crime family, they'd hit most of the shining jewels of New York City's luxury hotel hot spots, including the Sherry Netherland, the Regency, the Drake, The Carlyle, and The Saint Regis.

After organizing a hit on The Phoenix, they would top their careers off with the crowning achievement of ending up in the Guinness Book of World Records as the most successful hotel robbers in history.

One thing struck Ryan as odd. Despite the gang's heavy mob connections and the fact that their group included Ali-Ben, a professional killer from the Albanian mafia, they pulled off the heist with no bloodshed. They carried three dozen pairs of handcuffs and targeted the hotel on New Years' Day when staffing was slim, and most of the guests were hungover.

One by one, they politely cuffed security guards and hotel staff, lining them up on the floor of the registration area. They were careful to treat everyone well, leaving the cuffs off anyone who looked sick. They even went as far as to summon a doctor—a fellow hotel guest—for a man who claimed to be having a heart attack.

Then, they broke into dozens of lockboxes belonging to the wealthy guests whose names they recognized from the newspapers. A short time later, the group walked away, having lifted millions in stolen goods and cash after informing the handcuffed group that anyone who identified them would be murdered. That was pretty much the extent of the violence, and they could have been polite about it, he supposed.

Ryan had to grin at the last detail in the story. On their way out, the gang presented a twenty-dollar tip to each staff member of the hotel. Coincidentally, not one of them were able to provide any identifying information on any of the gang members later when questioned by police.

You had to appreciate manners, class, and a willingness to reward cooperation.

He looked up at Heidi, considering. If she wanted to pull another stylish robbery like The Phoenix, he could get behind an idea like that. For the time being, he had to work with her until he found another way out. And this was a hell of a lot more appealing than the thought of another violent bank robbery.

He thought about the bank manager, sprawled out on the floor of the lobby, a surprised expression on what was left of her face. That wasn't his kind of job, and it left a bad taste in his mouth. He preferred finesse over brute force and blood.

As his mind played through the upcoming events, Heidi sipped her tea, watching him. Waiting for a response.

"Just two people?" he asked in a voice that wouldn't carry.

Heidi shrugged. "That's all we'll need."

"New Years?"

"Tonight."

Ryan's palms went damp at her flat statement, and he gripped his mug more securely before it could slip from his grasp. He was good—an experienced and accomplished thief with a natural cleverness and aptitude for the work—but bloody hell.

She was insane.

10

In a neat black suit that hugged his portly middle just
enough to not be tacky, Oliver Brown, a middle-aged
professor on sabbatical from Oxford University, walked in a
slow, sedate way across the checkerboard-patterned floor of
the lobby of The Phoenix.

His eyes, behind the clear glass of tortoiseshell frames,
appeared to take in an appreciative view of the lobby's rich
gilding. The sumptuous chandeliers, dripping with crystal.
The velvet-upholstered furniture that picked up the green
accents in the silk that hung on the wall behind the reception
counter.

But canny Ryan O'Connelly studied the exits, the hall-
ways, and the number of employees that moved through the
lobby with brisk and efficient purpose. They were all dressed
in formal white-gloved, black and white uniforms. He
guessed that Heidi would take advantage of the standard
uniforms as a way for them both to blend in. He wouldn't
have to worry about maneuvering Oliver Brown's bulging
belly out of any tight spots.

Behind the concierge desk stood two men, one of them

security judging by his graying crew cut, heavy build, and alert gaze. That gaze skimmed right over the well-dressed, unassuming professor.

Near a claw-footed mahogany table stood a blonde, just this side of overweight. The older woman had the contented, well-fed look of a sophisticated society matron. In a plum-colored pantsuit, with discreet winks of gold at her ears and wrist, she waited for the professor, fingering the leaf of an exotic bird of paradise flower spearing out of a decorative gold urn. The absent way in which she performed the small movement was probably as calculated as everything else she did.

Not for the first time, he had to admire Ms. Presley's skill at disguise. She was possibly even better than he was. If he hadn't been expecting it, he might have walked right past her, and he was an observant sort by nature.

She was a chameleon.

"Oliver," she called out, crossing in front of the concierge desk. "So good to see you." She gave him a seductive smile that made him want to gag as she held out one French-manicured hand.

He took it with an obliging, obsequious flourish. "My dear Constance, the pleasure is mine," he replied, bringing Heidi's cold fingers up to brush against his lips with exaggerated gallantry.

"How has your stay been so far?" Heidi purred, all simper and good manners.

"Excellent. I at last found the time to finish that chapter that's been plaguing me for two weeks. You're looking the very picture of loveliness, as always. Shall we go get a drink?" He smiled in a wolfish way, the way a slightly older man with thick jowls and a paunch might at a passably attractive female who showed lukewarm interest. "I look forward to renewing our acquaintance."

It was like performing a very boring play for an audience who paid no attention.

She laughed in a dutiful trill—ha, ha, ha—tucking her arm through his.

Exit stage left.

They visited the Rotunda, with its spectacular curving staircases and exquisite murals. They ate a high-priced dinner at Perrine, and then moved on to the Two E, a chic lounge that featured excellent live jazz in the evenings.

Then, Constance Foster and Oliver Brown went up to her room together, an expensive suite on the forty-first floor.

There, Constance disappeared into the bathroom to shed her plum-colored pantsuit in favor of something more comfortable. However, instead of donning lingerie, Heidi came out in a crisp, black and white uniform, a tidy brunette wig, drawn back into a bun. She wore pristine white gloves on her hands and low, rubber-soled black boots instead of dress shoes.

When Ryan left the suite's second bedroom, having changed into his own matching uniform, keeping the wig in place at Heidi's request, Heidi was screwing a silencer on to her pistol.

"Yours is on the bed," she nodded, eying him.

Her scrutiny made him uneasy. He'd done his best to change his attitude. The charming, devil-may-care Ryan was back, at least on the surface. Not the trapped rat that had spent two days pacing his small room at the Park Lane Hotel, trying to figure out a way to escape this mess. He'd been ready to gnaw off his own arm.

He hated feeling trapped. Always had. That was one reason Heidi's threats held so much weight. He'd rather kill himself than go to prison.

But he realized his mistake in those two days. He was

letting on that he was intimidated. He needed to bluff his way through this.

He grinned at her. "Thanks, love, but where are the handcuffs? Not sure how you plan for just the two of us to carry three dozen pairs, but I'm game if you are."

She narrowed her eyes, unamused. "Handcuffs aren't efficient. Bullets are."

His gut twisted, but he didn't let his smile slip.

"Maybe you should fill me in on the plan, since it appears to be about go-time. I had the impression we'd be working in the spirit of the original heist."

"You were wrong." She set her gun on a nearby table that already held an open laptop facing away from him and sat down in a chair within arms' reach of the weapon. "The original heist could have been handled in a much more effective way."

"The security cameras on floors forty-one through forty-four are set to loop, starting at 2:36 a.m. At that time, the hotel elevators will stop working above this floor. The corresponding stairwell door locks will only open with my card key. We'll have about fifty-two minutes to hit three targets."

Ryan struggled to keep his posture relaxed, his tone unconcerned, but his anxiety had come back full-force. "And those targets are?"

"Qaaid Al-Muhammad is first. He's a minor Saudi prince. He's also wealthy enough to have the entire forty-second floor completely reserved. A man like that will have cash, without a doubt."

Ryan was appalled. "But will he be alone? A high-profile guy like that wouldn't be. There's no way."

"He has bodyguards," she snapped, clearly impatient. "But only two in his rooms at any given time. He doesn't like to feel crowded. They rotate shifts."

Great. Bodyguards. Probably trained to assassinate anyone who tried to assassinate their employer.

"On the forty-third floor, Richard Covington. He's a financial genius, on the fast-track to be the next Warren Buffet. At last check, he was worth upwards of seventy billion."

And probably had a security system to match, Ryan thought. It was madness to think they could do this successfully on such short notice.

"On the same floor, our last target is Charlotte Edwards. She's ninety-six years old and the only surviving heir to an industrial magnate who made his fortune in the early part of the last century."

Now, he wanted to drop his head in his hands. An old lady. They were going to kill an old lady. He kept the disgust off his face through sheer force of will.

Still, Heidi sensed his disquiet. Her lip lifted in a slight sneer. "You'll be handling that one. Just smother her with a pillow, since you're squeamish. We'll do the prince first and then split up."

Not an old woman. He couldn't.

Ryan was back into trapped-rat mode, trying to figure a way out of this. Heidi gave him no opportunity. With one hard look, she had him trailing her, following her lead.

The whole experience was lowering, for a man of his talent. And then, it got disturbing.

Ryan was sickened by just how "efficient" Heidi proved herself to be. At the door to the prince's rooms, she produced a master key. She let herself in as he followed. Two men—the bodyguards, he assumed—were lounging in a luxurious, well-appointed sitting room, watching television.

Before either of them fully realized they weren't alone, there was a mass of gore where both their throats had been. The silencer muffled Heidi's two rapid shots so that they weren't much louder than a staple gun. His stomach heaved, and he looked away.

"Make sure they're dead," she hissed at him and moved at a rapid clip toward where he assumed the bedrooms were.

He couldn't bring himself to look at what had been done to them, much less feel for a pulse on either man. He didn't have to. It was pretty obvious that Heidi hit what she aimed at.

Two more muffled pops came from another part of the suite. Moments later, Heidi appeared in the doorway with two small briefcases. "We're done here."

Back in the hallway, she loaded the take onto the room-service cart she'd pulled out of a utility closet, tucking them under a white tablecloth. A silver tray rested on top, adding to the convincing look of the setup.

He didn't bother to ask how she'd arranged for it to be there. Or where she'd gotten the master keys and uniforms. She'd planned everything down to the last detail, and he pitied the person she'd gotten her supplies from.

Come to think of it, that could have explained the reasoning behind her slutty outfit when she'd showed up in his room. It hadn't been for his sake, for which he was grateful, both then and now.

He'd seen enough of her to know that she discarded her tools when they were of no more use to her.

He steeled himself against the thought of what came next. Not only in the next few minutes, but when this was all over. When his obligation, or blackmail, or whatever this was, was complete. He couldn't think about it.

Now, it was just time to play his part and try to land on his feet like he always did, when all was said and done.

Entering the reclusive, elderly heiress's apartments wasn't difficult. He'd been given a key. He hadn't expected the woman to be sitting up in her dining room, playing a game of solitaire. Ryan fumbled for his gun, hating the weight and feel of it. The metal was cold, even through the thin white gloves he wore.

Charlotte Edwards was a tiny wisp of a woman, with sharp green eyes that snapped wide when she saw him in the doorway. She wore a quilted, lavender silk robe that hung on her thin frame, and little half-moon glasses that hung around her neck on a beaded chain. Her hair was thin and white, standing out around her wrinkled face like the fluff of a dandelion. She was no bigger than a ten-year-old child.

She set her cards down in a slow, deliberate way on the table in front of her. "I suppose I don't have to ask why you're here. I don't get many visitors." Her voice was as thin and insubstantial as the rest of her, but it was threaded with resigned humor.

"I'm sorry to disturb you," he said, using his most gentle tone. "Can I ask you to move to the living room, please?" He gestured with the gun, and she stood, her movements shaky, reaching for a three-legged cane that rested to one side of her chair. Her progress was painful and laborious, and he wanted to yell at her to hurry.

The living room, decorated in heavy and ornate carved wood furniture, was lit only by a glass-globed lamp on a side table. Its rosy light illuminated Persian rugs with subdued patterns in deep, rich burgundy and blue. Oil paintings in gilded frames graced the biscuit-colored walls. The room was like a shrine to Victorian-era elegance.

Charlotte sank down on the couch. "You'll find my safe behind the Matisse. It's on a hinge. Swings outward to the right."

The woman looked like a hard sneeze would be fatal, and he was supposed to shoot her? He moved fast, heading to the painting she pointed out, disgust at himself twisting in his belly.

She recited the combination. Inside, there were neatly stacked metal boxes.

"The top one is cash," she offered, sounding like she was trying to be helpful. "The smaller boxes are jewelry. If you plan to kill me, you might as well take them all. If you don't, please leave the smallest one. It's a necklace my father gave me on my seventeenth birthday, and I'd planned to be buried in it. It's worth nothing except in sentiment."

He took the large one and a few of the smaller boxes. His mind raced as he set them on the floor. "Listen," he said, turning around. He tucked the gun away and moved to the couch. "I'm a thief."

"I'd ascertained as much, young man. I'm old, not stupid. And despite that bad wig you have on, you *are* a young man."

He grinned at the acid in her tone. She was spunky.

"I should have said I'm a thief, not a killer. This is not the kind of work I normally do. Sneaking in and lifting that pretty Matisse on behalf of a client of mine in Germany who happens to be a collector, maybe. But not bang, bang, take your money. Tonight, though, I'm supposed to kill you." As he gazed into her bright eyes, his decision became concrete. "I'm not going to."

Charlotte folded her gnarled fingers together neatly in her lap and cocked her head, her eyes bright with curiosity. "Do you give your backstory and a rationalization like this to everyone you burglarize?"

He couldn't help laughing. She was a delight. She'd completely lifted the black mood he'd fallen into this evening with her sparky personality.

"Long story short, my associate is vicious and thorough, and I don't have a choice when it comes to participating in this. But you seem like a very nice lady, so I'm going to shoot one of these nice chairs of yours in case she checks to see if my gun's been discharged. She *has* to think I killed you. If not, she'll come back here and do it herself. I'm also going to take a few of your boxes, and I'm sorry about that."

Charlotte nodded and eyed him, her eyes sharp on his face. "So you're not toying with me. You're really not going to shoot me."

"No, ma'am."

"Good." She gave him a wide smile and pulled a small pistol out of the folds of her night-robe, setting it down on the cushion beside her. "Then, I won't have to shoot you first."

"Charlotte," Ryan said, reaching out to squeeze her small hand. "I think I like you."

"Oddly enough, the feeling seems to be mutual. This is actually very exciting. Much better than solitaire." Charlotte pushed to her feet. Leaning most of her weight on her cane but moving with a little more pep to her step than she had when he'd first arrived, she headed away from the living room toward the back of the apartment. "If you're going to pretend to kill me, at least do it in the bedroom where I can be comfortable until someone finds my not-dead body."

"By all means." Ryan was charmed by the little old woman, but nerves tingled beneath his skin. Time was running short, and he'd been here too long already. Heidi would have already finished with her finance guy. It was time to move things along.

Charlotte climbed into a high, four-poster bed using a kind of small ramp with a railing on one side. "The joys of aging." She wrinkled her nose. "Next thing you know, they'll want to put rails on my bed like a baby's, so I don't fall out at night."

"Ma'am," Ryan said, raising the gun as she settled herself beneath the brocade comforter. "It was a pleasure to meet you, and I do apologize for all of this."

He waited for her to hold her hands over her ears and

then fired twice at an overstuffed ottoman in the corner. Stuffing flew, and Charlotte giggled. "I never liked that chair." She fell backward dramatically onto her pillows, one arm outstretched, one fist clenched over her heart. "How's this?"

"That's perfect, love. I'll lock the door behind me. Take care, Miss Charlotte, and I hope you live to be a hundred and twenty."

11

Heidi had never lost control.

She looked around at the mess she'd made and grimaced.

Richard Covington was very, very dead.

She'd marked him as a target, not only because of the proximity of his rooms in relation to the other two targets, but with the expectation that he'd have plenty of cash and valuables on hand. He was a last-minute addition to the plan. She admitted to herself that she hadn't done her full due diligence on him. But she hadn't expected him to laugh at her when she'd woken him up and demanded money.

She didn't like being laughed at.

And now, she thought with a little shudder, she'd broken from her plan. Had blacked out a little, actually, when it came to the kill.

Heidi let herself out of his rooms, trying to shake the uneasy feeling that had come over her. She'd deviated from her own plans. It was unthinkable.

Down the hall, Ryan was coming out of the old lady's

rooms. He had his hands full of metal boxes and jumped, looking almost guilty when he saw her coming. As she drew closer, his eyes widened.

She looked down at herself. No stains showed on her black uniform, but her gloves were spattered with red.

"Everything okay, love?"

"Shut up." She glanced at her watch. No time to check Ryan's handiwork now. That, too, wasn't part of the plan. "We have three minutes to get back to the room and turn the elevators back on before security makes their next round."

"Ah, you seem to have left a trail," he pointed out.

Behind her, on the beige, tastefully patterned carpet, were bloody footprints.

Son of a bitch.

"Let's go."

After slipping off her shoes, she moved fast, her brain squirreling around to recalibrate the situation.

The original plan had involved them going back to the suite. She'd paid the same person, who had left a cart in the supply closet for her and snagged the master keys, to bring her a hotel comforter. It had gone into "Dr. Foster's" rolling suitcase ahead of time. She'd planned on leaving it behind in the room—less obvious than a pile of clothes—and repacking the suitcase with their take. Then, they'd check out first thing in the morning, before the bodies were discovered.

That wouldn't work now.

She opened the door to her suite. "Change of plans. We're going to have to leave fast."

That was an understatement.

Heidi moved to her computer and rebooted the elevators and cameras. The one for Richard Covington's floor, she left on loop. The timestamp might be noticed, but not as quickly as the set of bloody footprints trailing down the hall from his doorway. She'd planned on them having plenty of time to check out and be gone. Depending on circumstances after that, they could have had a head start of hours. Maybe days. Not now.

Again, she felt apprehensive. She'd planned this all for so long. Control was everything. She had control of the situation, control of Ryan O'Connelly. But control of herself? Maybe not.

"Unload the rolling suitcase," she instructed Ryan, not sparing him a glance. She tapped into the security system to monitor the movements of the guards. "Take the blanket out and load the briefcases and containers inside."

"What about the stuff from the Covington guy?"

There was no Covington money. Richard Covington had lost it all in a stupid Ponzi scheme. So much for being the next Warren Buffet. He was broke, on the verge of eviction from the hotel. A complete waste of time. And he'd had the nerve to laugh when he'd told her.

Well, he hadn't laughed for long.

She turned on Ryan, her voice a furious undertone that warned him to tread lightly. "If I wanted you to put more in there, I would have told you. Don't fucking question me."

He looked at her, his eyes speculative, but didn't argue.

Good. If he *had* argued, she might have changed her plan and ended his involvement right here and now. It would mess up her last scene, but she was tired of him, and her temper was frayed, to say the least.

"Change out of those clothes. Put the uniform in the carry-on bag."

Keeping silent—a wise move—he began loading the suitcase, not knowing how close he'd just come to being dispatched early.

She checked the cameras again. The regular security guard, a tall, muscular man she'd identified already as Andre, was on the thirtieth floor. He appeared to be chatting it up with the employee who ran the elevator. They had time.

Her fingers flew over her phone as she ordered an Uber.

She stripped off her bloody clothes in the suite's second bathroom. Wadding them up into a ball to shove in the carry-on she'd brought to hold her costumes, she looked in the mirror. Blood was spattered across her cheek. It had dried into tiny, crusty flecks. Wrinkling her nose in distaste, she pulled off her wig and scrubbed her face hard with a washcloth.

Heidi didn't bother to worry about DNA evidence on the hand towels or stray hairs that could be picked up by enterprising forensics specialists. She'd been diligent about wiping prints, but the FBI could try and identify her and succeed, for all she cared. They'd never dealt with anyone like her before. She wasn't planning on getting caught. And when she finished what she'd started, she had an exit plan in place. No one would find her where she was going.

Moving fast, she dressed in one of "Dr. Foster's" outfits—another pantsuit, this one in brown. She pulled on the frosted blonde wig and quickly did her makeup. With any luck, the security guard would stay occupied with the elevator operator for a while, buying them a few more minutes. Luck, though, had not been on her side this evening. She wasn't holding her breath.

When she came out of the bathroom, Ryan was already dressed and ready to go, his stomach and cheek padding in place. His face was aged and wrinkled-looking from the makeup he used, and he looked exactly how she wanted him to look. A middle-aged professor, no threat to anyone except his tailor, who had to account for his expanding waistline.

She did a quick check of the room—no booby traps for this one—to make sure nothing had been left behind.

Checking the camera views on the laptop, she saw that the guard was halfway through his loop on the thirty-fifth floor.

If they went now, they'd miss him on the elevator.

They left the room, as serene as if they weren't carrying stolen goods. She walked the short distance to the elevator and pushed the down button.

She could feel the weight of her Ruger in the underarm holster she'd stashed under her blazer. If she had to, she'd shoot her way out of there.

Ryan/Oliver, as if sensing her tension, gave her a reassuring smile just as the elevator doors slid open.

"Now, now, dear, there's no reason to be nervous." His eyes glinted at the irony of his words, behind his hazel contacts. "I know you absolutely hate to fly, but you'd think you'd be an old hand at it by now, with all the traveling you do."

The elevator operator, a pimple-faced kid who couldn't have been more than twenty, smiled with the polite distance of a bored hotel employee who'd seen everything. "Early flight?" he asked, making an effort to put cheer into his voice. Angling for a tip.

Heidi gave him a curt nod.

"Oh, yes," Ryan groaned. "I absolutely despise getting up before dawn. I can't imagine working an overnight shift. How do you stand it?"

The young man smiled as he pressed the button for the ground floor. "It's not so bad. Pretty quiet. Kind of boring. Sometimes, I wish something exciting would happen to break up the routine," he added in a stage whisper. "Just don't tell my boss I said that."

The elevator dinged on the thirty-fifth floor, and Heidi stiffened.

They descended a few floors, and the doors slid open again. Andre, the security guard, entered. He looked surprised to see anyone else in the elevator. It was just after four in the morning.

"Early flight," the elevator operator explained.

"Too early," Ryan said in a dark tone.

The other man smiled, commiserating. "Got to love those red-eye flights. Where are you folks headed?" he asked, leaning against the side of the elevator.

"We're going to Germany for Christmas," Ryan answered without skipping a beat. "Dusseldorf. Constance is going to show me the sights. You've been there dozens of times, haven't you, Connie?"

She wanted to scream at him to shut up. He didn't need to make conversation. They just needed to get out of the hotel and away to the safe house she'd set up. Her plans depended on speed and accuracy.

She was going to leave the police and FBI chasing their tails in circles.

"Darling?"

She dragged herself to the present. Control.

"Yes, of course, sweetheart." She smiled, her lips a tight seam. "Dusseldorf is beautiful this time of year. There's a little pub on the Rhine that you'll just adore. You know how much you like to drink."

"She's not a morning person," Ryan muttered to the security guard, who stifled a chuckle.

They finally reached the main floor just as her cell phone buzzed. Their Uber had arrived.

"Have a nice trip," the elevator operator offered, disappointed that a tip didn't appear to be forthcoming.

The security guard, though, watched them as they left the elevator and headed toward the exit. She could see him in the little rearview mirror of the glasses she'd planted on her nose.

His scrutiny pissed her off, scraped at her nerves. Even

without the glasses, she felt sure she could feel his stare on her back. After what felt like hours, she heard the elevator doors swish closed again.

Beside her, Ryan let out a long breath.

They'd made it halfway across the lobby, moving quickly across the checkerboard floor. The registration desk was darkened and empty, pre-morning shift. A silver minivan sat out front, illuminated in the lights from the hotel. They just needed to get through the revolving entrance door, and they would be out.

And then the elevator doors opened again.

The security guard stepped out. "Excuse me!"

Heidi stiffened and turned, her hand slipping inside her jacket. Her fingers closed around the butt of the gun, nestled under her left arm.

"Yes?" Ryan called out with manufactured calm, putting a casual, restraining hand on her elbow.

She subtly tried to shake him off, but his fingers tightened.

Andre quickened his pace to a light jog as he crossed the lobby, holding something out in front of him. "You dropped this."

It was Ryan's burner phone. The cheap little black throw-away she'd picked up a half-dozen of from a Walmart in Topeka. It wasn't the type of phone a middle-aged professor at Oxford would carry.

"Thank you," Ryan said, taking it and slipping it into his pocket. "I almost wish you wouldn't have found that." He heaved a regretful sigh. "My secretary hasn't stopped ringing it since I left for my sabbatical two weeks ago."

"Ma'am," the security guard said, looking at Heidi hard, his eyes narrowed. "You have something…" He gestured vaguely to the left side of his neck.

She put her hand automatically to where he'd indicated.

Her fingertips came away dark with a sticky, half-dried smear of Richard Covington's blood. She looked back up at the security guard just as his hand went to the inside pocket of his jacket.

Behind him, across the long stretch of the lobby, she saw the elevator operator's eyes widen as she wrenched loose of Ryan's grip and pulled out her gun. She'd taken off the silencer, and the report of the weapon echoed at full volume in the marble-accented lobby.

The elevator operator had disappeared to the side, likely punching buttons, praying for the door to close as his co-worker collapsed to the floor with two holes in his chest. In the guard's outstretched hand, he held a tissue, slightly crumpled.

She started to move toward the elevator, eliminate the other witness, but Ryan caught her arm again.

"No," he demanded, his face pale beneath the makeup. "The car is waiting."

She recoiled from him in disgust and fury and turned back to the elevator. She didn't have time for weakness.

The elevator doors had closed again. She'd missed her chance.

Heidi rounded on Ryan, grabbing a handful of his shirt and pressing the barrel of the Ruger against the underside of his chin.

Her breath came in short, furious gasps. "I'm in charge. Not you."

He nodded, flinching as his skin met the hot metal. She knew he was scared as piss, and she reveled in that, but he didn't break eye contact. "You're in charge, but our ride is right there. You could kill the elevator guy, but someone else would come, and you'd have to off them too. It would take more time we don't have. Let it go."

She hated it, and him, but he was right.

She let him go and grabbed the handle of the rolling suitcase.

It was time to head to the safe house. Recalibrate again, if necessary. The next phase couldn't go like this. It had to be perfect.

She took a steadying breath. It was all about control.

12

Sun left Winter in her hotel room, shutting the door quietly behind her. Winter had been silent the entire way back to San Clemente, and Sun didn't blame her. She didn't feel like talking, either.

There was no word yet about Sheriff Marchwood's condition. She'd spoken with the undersheriff when they'd returned to the hotel. The sheriff had still been unresponsive when they'd taken her to the hospital. Thanks to Winter, though, her heart had been beating again, and she'd finally started breathing on her own. She'd been taken to the hospital in Los Angeles with a state-of-the-art burn unit. Detective Patterson was missing, presumed dead.

She'd call later for more updates, she decided, and put the casualties aside. Right now, she was busy wallowing in self-disgust. She didn't tolerate weakness in others, but today, she'd been failed by her own.

During her time with the FBI, Sun had cultivated a deliberate reputation as a take-no-prisoners bitch with a temper, but also with a sharp mind and an even-headed approach in all circumstances. Today, she'd lost that. She'd been as ineffectual as a fresh-out-of-Quantico rookie agent in training.

Actually, worse than that. Winter, the rook, had stepped up and handled everything while Sun had been frozen in indecision. At least she hadn't passed out, she thought grimly.

It was lowering to admit. And even though she was beginning to respect Winter as a capable agent, a larger part of her was jealous.

Sun grabbed the remote from the bedside table and flicked the TV on. A mindless sitcom blasted out, and she punched the sound down with angry jabs at the volume button. Flipping through the stations to CNN, she lay back on the pillows. She'd give Winter some time to recover, and then they'd get back to the case. With any possible clues destroyed in the house explosion, they needed a breakthrough at this point.

Maybe her wunderkind partner would provide something, she thought bitterly.

While Jake Tapper rambled on about the latest scandal in the White House, she read the ticker tape of breaking news at the bottom of the screen without really paying attention. There was always breaking news. The media didn't even deal in non-breaking news at this point.

But the next chyron caught her attention.

The Phoenix Hotel in New York City had been robbed. Several were dead, including two hotel guests and a long-time resident. Two bodyguards and a security guard had also been killed when two suspects had attempted to leave the building before dawn. They'd gotten away.

The Phoenix Hotel. Site of another high-profile robbery back in the 1970s. Her stomach clenched as she muted the TV and pulled up her laptop. She pulled up her personal Gmail address. Just as she'd expected, there was a message waiting for her. Sent from an encrypted email, just like the one she'd received right after the San Clemente robbery, it contained just a few terse words:

Oops. Too slow.

Furious, she called Max Osbourne.

"Sun," he answered right away, his gravel-rough voice more grating than usual. "I was just picking up the phone to call you. What's the status there? Any word on Sheriff Marchwood?"

"Not yet. But I'm calling about something else. The Phoenix Hotel robbery. Did you hear about it?"

"Yeah," he answered. "Sounds like one of the guests killed was a minor Saudi prince. They think it was a politically motivated attack and the other guests were killed to make it look like a robbery."

"It's not." Her tone was urgent. Tight. "We're dealing with the same killers. It's tied to this case."

"That's a big stretch," he answered, his tone skeptical. "Just like it was a big stretch to say that the San Clemente robbery was some tip-of-the-iceberg thing."

Sun had already gotten off the bed and was throwing things back in her suitcase. "No. This just backs up my theory," she insisted. "The Phoenix was burglarized in the seventies. The thieves had a record-setting take, and it went down in the books as the biggest hotel robbery of all time. This is not a coincidence."

She couldn't tell him about the encrypted emails. She needed this win. She'd be on the fast-track up the FBI corporate ladder, not stopping until she reached the top.

It took ten more minutes of fast talking to convince Max that she had a connection, flimsy as it might sound. "So you just want to leave things there?" He was incredulous. "You've been there for three days now, working this case. Now, you have one dead cop and another who might well be dying, and you just want to pack up and fly to New York?"

"Look, I know it sounds crazy," Sun tried to keep her voice even and persuasive, "but I know I'm right. You've never had reason to doubt me before. Things are covered here. Let me..." She paused, correcting herself. "Let *us* follow up on this. I promise you, I'm right. Agent Black agrees with me and is fully on board."

In her imagination, she crossed her fingers at the lie. But, in the grand scheme of things, it wouldn't matter anyway.

He was silent for a long moment.

"Fine. Book a flight out. I'm assigning you two more agents. The San Clemente robbery was bad, but this one is huge. You'll have to work things out with the NYPD. They're expecting Feds, but they're still not going to be happy when you show up with wild theories. This is a potential political hotbed. Relations with Saudi Arabia aren't good right now anyway, and the prince's murder will only add more fuel to that fire. Come back here to regroup first, and I'll have Dalton and Durham briefed and ready to assist."

"Thanks, Max."

She hung up and grabbed her hastily packed suitcase, heading next door. Winter needed rest, but Sun decided that the rookie could get it when they were in the air. She'd been given a second message, straight from the suspects. She was smart enough to handle it. This was going to *make* her.

Winter was still in bed, looking exhausted when Sun entered the room, but she sat up fast.

"What's going on?" she asked. "I heard you talking to Max."

"We've got to go. We're heading back to Richmond and then New York. There's been another hit, and I'm positive we're dealing with the same people."

Winter didn't question her, which Sun was grateful for.

She was going to have a hard enough time getting everyone else on board. But she knew in her gut, with absolute certainty, that this was just the second hit. New York was where their suspects were. They had to find them before they moved on to their next target. Or figure out what they had planned for their next move. No more reactivity. They had to get ahead of them.

She was going to bring them down before they had a chance to send a third email.

※

WINTER WAS EXHAUSTED. She'd wanted nothing more than to lay in bed and sleep until she could get the incident with Shannon Marchwood out of her mind. But Sun hadn't been willing to take no for an answer. She'd been frenetic. Intense. There'd been no more awkward sympathy. Even the growing feeling of camaraderie between them had disappeared.

The old Sun was back.

Winter had to wonder why. Why the sudden urgency? Why the complete one-eighty in the woman's attitude? There was something wrong with Sun's relationship to this case, but she was too tired to figure it out now.

The wait at the airline had been blessedly short, which had worked in Winter's favor. In addition, Sun had been bumped from business class, and it was fun to see the airline employees not even bat an eyelash at Sun's temper tantrum.

Not in Winter's favor was the fact that they were seated together, and Sun had demanded the window seat. Any other day, Winter would have taken that challenge head-on and told her aisle or latrine and made her pick one.

For the sake of her own sanity, she'd let Sun have her way, hoping the woman would just leave her alone.

Once they'd boarded, taken off and hit cruising altitude,

Sun pulled up her laptop and went to work right away. Winter had just lain her head back on the seat and closed her eyes. After a few moments, though, Sun jostled her arm. Her eyes were bright and sharp.

"Look," she said, pointing to the screen. "The Phoenix Hotel Robbery. Biggest U.S. robbery in the history books."

Sighing, Winter read over her shoulder for a moment. Long enough to get the gist of the story. She resigned herself to the idea that sleep wouldn't come for her until Sun got whatever she had to say out of her system.

"Okay. Like the San Clemente, I can kind of see it. But how did they get across the country and arrange to rob one of the most luxurious hotels in New York City in just a couple of days?"

Sun shrugged. "Advance planning. This is just the second step. We have to figure out what the third one is and be waiting for them. That's going to be the tricky part."

"So, we just look at the highest-profile heists of the twentieth century and post up officers at every possible location they could hit? I don't know how feasible that sounds. Especially in just a couple of days."

"Max is giving me Dalton and Durham to add to the team. John Durham's a useless sack of shit who should have been fired years ago, but Dalton could be helpful."

Noah would absolutely be helpful. Winter didn't know much about John Durham. Bull, they called him. She'd never spent any time with the guy before. All she knew about him was that he was older, close to retirement, and built like a fireplug with a bald, bullet-shaped head. That, and he liked to tell dirty jokes and look at girls' legs while damning the entire concept of political correctness.

At least there would be two more people to blunt Sun's attention. And Noah was one of them, which meant she'd have an ally.

"Whatever. Your case," Winter reminded her. There'd never been any ambiguity about that. "I'm going to sleep. Wake me up when we're almost there."

Sun didn't reply. She was back in laptop land.

Winter closed her eyes again, trying to tune out the sound of a crying baby a few aisles behind them. And the fingers hitting the keyboard next to her with machine-gun speed. Her head was pounding, but not in a migraine way. She winced at the wet-sounding cough of a woman in the center aisle.

She just wanted to crawl under the covers of a bed somewhere and stay there for a week. In the absence of a bed, she wanted to sleep the rest of the non-stop flight to Virginia.

❄

I'D BEEN THINKING a lot about my girlie lately. I took a swig from the bottle next to my La-Z-Boy armchair. The liquor felt good going down. I'd liked seeing her in Harrisonburg. And now that I'd had some time to reflect upon the matter, I liked knowing that she'd grown up and gone into the FBI.

It was almost like I could take credit for that. If I hadn't chosen her mother for retribution and saved the brother from a life of sin, my little girlie would have likely grown up to be a hairdresser or model, or entered some other useless female career. In fact, you could say I'd done her a favor.

Created her. Shaped her. Molded her.

I held up my hands. Hands that had molded many, many lives.

Hands that had righted the world.

The talking heads on the TV chattered back and forth, arguing about the new tax bill Congress was trying to push through. Damned heathens, always trying to bleed the little guy dry. As if the government didn't take enough of our hard-earned money.

The news story changed without warning, focusing on a breaking story out of New York. A robbery at some hoity-toity hotel. A bunch of rich people killed. Sons of bitches probably deserved it. Spending all kinds of money to stay at a fancy place like that. One room likely cost more to rent in a night than my house payment used to cost for the whole month.

Rich people didn't deserve to live anyway. A few gone was no big loss.

You cannot serve God and money, the good book said. I'd written it precisely to warn these foolish people. But did they listen? No. They did not. It seemed they never did.

I perked up a little when they said some middle-eastern prince had been killed. That was interesting. I didn't care much for foreigners and could care even less about a dead Arab guy, but a big international incident like that? So close to Virginia where my girlie was working? Maybe she'd get assigned to the case. She was a good FBI agent. Real smart.

Because of me.

Maybe she'd do a press conference, like for the thing in Harrisonburg, and I'd get to see her pretty face again. She hadn't talked the last time, just stood in the background with that serious look on her face like she always had. But she looked good on TV. All serious and sober in her black FBI suit, with that long black hair tucked back in a braid, and those spooky blue eyes of hers taking in everything that was going on around her.

Yep, my girlie was a picture, all right. Pretty as anything, just like her momma had been.

Was she a sinner too? She had to be. They all were. Anger stirred inside me as I wondered how many of my commandments my little girlie had broken.

Or maybe she was just too busy to get in much trouble. So busy, it almost made me feel lazy. I'd been retired now for more than ten years...not from the work that paid the bills, but from the work that made up my calling. Maybe it was time for me to get back to it.

Yeah, I thought, watching the coverage of the hotel robbery. Maybe it was time to begin ridding the world of sin once again. Do some good. I'd gotten complacent.

Even as the thoughts of issuing my warning to the world stirred inside me, the hunger for sin cleansing grew. My girlie wouldn't understand my calling. She, like all the other ones who followed man's laws, didn't.

She'd think I was wrong. She'd want to catch me.

Maybe I'd let her. That could be fun.

It'd be nice to see her again, face-to-face, all grown up. After all these years, I was sure she had some questions that only I could answer. If she behaved real nice, I'd maybe share some secrets she'd probably wondered about. We could have a little one-on-one time, and I could see all that pretty white skin of hers, with that dark hair spread against it, just like her momma's.

Then, I'd rid her of her sins too.

Mother.

Daughter.

It would complete the circle, and maybe this time, the world would listen to my message.

Listen to me.

13

Noah had been thinking about Winter the last couple of days, wondering how she was getting along with Sun. When the two of them walked into the office, Sun laser-focused and waspish, Winter looking tired and pale, he figured he had his answer.

"Dalton, Durham, in the conference room, now." Sun was strident, heading for the briefing room without stopping.

Winter trailed behind her, giving him a small smile and a wave as she passed. It was a smug smile that clearly said, *Now she's your problem too.*

He grabbed his notebook and followed Bull Durham's stocky frame.

"All right," Sun said before they could even sit down. "We've got a related case. Our suspects from the San Clemente bank robbery have moved on to The Phoenix Hotel in New York. Several people are dead, two of them robbed."

Her eyes lit with glee, which struck him as wildly inappropriate, considering her previous statement.

"One detail is being kept from the press. We have a witness. Charlotte Edwards, an elderly woman who has been staying at the hotel for years, survived. We're going to New York now to question her. Anyone have anything to add?"

Noah raised a finger. "How do we know the two incidents are connected?"

Sun's eyes warmed just a little as she looked at him.

Damn. He wanted to groan. He'd been picking up a few vibes that she was interested in him but hadn't done anything to encourage her, hoping he'd imagined them. His interest just didn't lie in a workplace romance. He glanced at Winter. Mostly.

And, privately, he was afraid if he tried to turn down an advance from Sun, she'd castrate him. The woman was terrifying.

"The two incidents are connected. Trust me on this." Sun moved on, and he could breathe easier. "Bull? You have any questions?"

"The local LEOs think this has to do with the Saudi prince." Bull picked at his teeth with the cap of his pen. "You sure it doesn't?"

"I know what I know," Sun pronounced. "Let the other law enforcement officers chase the wrong tail. We'll be on the right one. I've got us four flights leaving at noon. Let's roll."

Five minutes later, they'd piled into a Bureau vehicle and were on their way. Sun drove, and Noah let Bull take shotgun. He rode in back with Winter, sacrificing leg room for distance. There was no way he was going to encourage Sun in any way if he could help it.

He waited until Sun and Bull were arguing over Bull's choice of a classic rock station to check in on his one-time partner, former Quantico competitor, and good friend. She had bags under her eyes and looked like she was carrying every worry in the world on her narrow shoulders.

"You okay?" he asked in an undertone.

She nodded, but he wasn't convinced.

Instead of elaborating, Winter pulled out her cell phone and dialed a phone number, fast, like it had been memorized. Was something wrong with her Grandpa? Noah knew he'd been sick.

Her face was tense as she waited for an answer. When someone picked up on the other end, she immediately apologized, which was unlike her.

"This is Agent Winter Black. I'm sorry to bother you again. I know you've got your hands full. Have there been any updates on Shannon Marchwood?"

Ah. The San Clemente Sheriff who'd been injured in an explosion. He'd already heard about the heroic effort Winter had put into saving her. Of course, she would be concerned about the woman.

He watched as the tension in her face grew, and then evaporated.

"That's fantastic. Do me a favor, will you? Save my number so you can text me. Keep me updated, and when she's ready for visitors, please let her know I'm—we're—pulling for her."

Then she blushed. That was interesting. Winter didn't do that often.

"Stop," she blurted into the phone, looking even more uncomfortable. "Anyone else would have done the same thing."

She disconnected the call and gave Noah a stronger smile. The difference in her attitude was palpable.

"Marchwood going to pull through?"

Sun was listening. Noah caught her eye in the rearview.

"Yeah. She's got a bumpy road ahead of her," Winter said,

letting out a long breath. "They're concerned about lung issues after the concussive blast she was exposed to. Plus, she's pretty badly burned, a number of second and third degrees. She's in good hands, though. They're hoping she'll make a full recovery."

Bull poked his bald, bullet-shaped head through the gap in the front seats. "You talking about the cop that was in the explosion in California? I heard Max saying you saved her life."

Winter started to protest, but Sun spoke up, the irritation in her voice obvious. "Focus, guys. I need your brains on the East Coast," she snapped. "San Clemente isn't our concern right now."

Harsh, Noah thought, considering a fellow law enforcement official's life hung in the balance. Sun was coming off as a little insensitive, seeing as how she had witnessed the sheriff's near-immolation firsthand.

Winter met Noah's eyes. She rolled hers and shrugged. Through the gestures, he could almost hear, *You see what I've been dealing with?* coming from her mouth.

❄

THE PHOENIX WAS CLOSED to incoming guests during the active investigation. Most of the guests already staying at the hotel were waiting to be interviewed by police before either leaving town completely or having their reservations transferred to another hotel. The street outside was crowded with reporters, hovering around the crime scene tape and barriers that had been put up to keep them back.

Winter kept her head low. Reporters shouted questions and raised cell phones to record them as they bypassed the yellow crowd barriers erected out front and entered the restricted area in front of the building. Dozens of bystanders chattered, sharing theories on what the heavy police presence might mean.

It was a circus.

She scanned the faces in the crowd out of the corner of her eye. The killers could be among them. It wasn't uncommon for criminals to visit the scene of their own crime, view the chaos they'd created firsthand. Thieves, though, didn't usually subscribe to that kind of behavior.

She focused instead on the task ahead of them.

Sun flashed her badge to the street cops, and their small group was waved through. She strode through the lobby like she owned the place, unerringly finding the sergeant in charge. He stood in deep conversation with another man wearing a nametag on his expensive-looking suit. Probably the hotel manager.

Behind them, evidence markers were laid out in different areas, and a pool of congealed blood marred the pristine perfection of the marble-tiled floor.

"Agent Ming, with the Richmond FBI office," Sun interrupted, thrusting her hand out to the sergeant while ignoring the hotel manager. "Is there a place where you can brief us? How soon can we get in to see the witness?"

To Winter's relief, Noah stepped in when the man's face reddened. The guy was practically sputtering. He looked like he was about to tell Sun exactly where she could go and get briefed. Sun needed to pass the public relations role over to Noah. He was better at it.

"Sergeant," Noah interrupted, giving the harried man a commiserating smile. "FBI. Richmond office. Sorry for the interruption. We're here to assist in any way we can. We'll be over there…" he indicated a small group of tables, "whenever you have time for us."

Before she could sputter some retort, he grabbed Sun's

elbow and steered her away. Winter and Bull followed behind.

"You need to cool it," Noah hissed. "You cannot just walk in here and stomp all over everyone's faces, expecting them to turn around and be ready to let you in on what is already their investigation."

Sun's face reddened with fury and embarrassment. For a second, Winter felt sorry for her. Only for a second.

"I'm sorry," Noah said in an undertone. "I know you're the case agent, but you should know better. Scale it back, Ming."

Lucky for Noah, the sergeant joined them before Sun could get a chance to pound him into the ground.

"Agents," he said, addressing Noah as he shot a wary glance at Sun. She wisely kept her mouth shut and let Noah take the lead. "I'm glad to see you all, actually. We've got a clusterfuck on our hands here and appreciate any help we can get. Come with me, and I'll show you what we're dealing with."

The sergeant moved to the bloodstains on the floor, first. "We're working in backward order right now, of course. This is where the night security guard was killed. Two shots to the chest. According to our witness, he was taken down without warning, trying to return the cell phone to a man who was leaving with a woman around four a.m. They'd all ridden down the elevator together. The elevator operator saw the whole thing. The rest of the murders took place higher up, on the forty-second and forty-third floors."

On the forty-second floor, he took them first to a sumptuous suite. The entryway opened into a living room, which was undisturbed by any signs of struggle. But the couch had obviously been the site of two shootings. Dark stains marred the expensive, cream-colored upholstery.

"This was their first stop. The suspects came in the front

door. We assume they had gotten ahold of some kind of master key. They shot the two security guards here."

"And the prince?" Sun asked, her voice still clipped but softer. She had grown paler, Winter noted. Bodily fluids. How had the woman ever gotten a job in law enforcement with such phobias?

The sergeant waved an arm and continued down the hallway at a fast clip. He stopped in front of a bedroom door. "Prince Al-Muhammad was killed here, while he was sleeping. We're trying to figure out if any valuables have been taken, but there's no one to ask," he went on in frustration. "His remaining security guards are at the consulate. He didn't check anything in for insurance purposes. Who knows what they could have gotten away with."

He took them to the next floor up, and Winter was careful to bypass the bloody footprints still dotting the floor.

"The pattern varies up here." He led them to the first door, grimacing. "This was the apartment of Richard Covington, a wealthy finance guy. He didn't go easy, like the others. I hope you're not squeamish."

"They left footprints?" Bull sounded astounded, staring at the floor. "Who the hell splashes around in a bunch of blood and doesn't wipe their feet?"

He was right. The trail of medium-sized, bloody shoe outlines were everywhere, moving from one door toward another before fading into more indistinct smudges as they went down the hall. Any sane person would have at least taken their shoes off before stepping into a public area.

Sun glanced at them. "A small man or a big woman," she decided. "Show us Covington's apartment."

In contrast to the prince's apartments, Covington's room looked like a slaughterhouse. He, too, had been killed in bed, but that's where the similarities ended. There was blood everywhere. Arcs of it had been thrown across the ceiling, the bed was drenched. The walls were spattered with it, and there were footprints all over.

"Why the deviation?" Winter wondered out loud. "It's like the others were done by a careful professional, and this one...the person who did this was in a blind rage."

"I agree," the sergeant said. His face had paled just a little bit since they'd entered the room. He, apparently, was the squeamish one. "This was not a premeditated act. Whatever happened in here was a result of pure, unadulterated fury. Not only did the suspect shoot Covington several times, they came back with a knife from the kitchen. I've seen a lot, but the mutilation that took place in here...I just hope the guy was already dead before they started."

They all stood in silence for a moment. Winter felt light-headed. The macabre scene in front of them seemed even worse with the additional information. And for her, it brought back unwelcome memories.

The sergeant cleared his throat. "While one suspect was in here, freaking out, the other was doing something different in the next suite over."

He led them out and down the hall.

He put his hand on the doorknob. "Before we go in, you need to know that this woman is supposed to be dead. You need to be careful when you question her, and you need to make sure it goes no further than here. Until we apprehend these suspects, Charlotte Edwards was *killed* during this robbery. Do you understand?"

At their agreement, the sergeant opened the door. Inside, two uniformed officers sat at the table in the dining area, playing cards with an elderly lady. She looked up as they entered, her eyes bright and curious, bird-like. She wore a nylon tracksuit, in purple and green. She looked like the 1990's version of someone's fashion-forward grandmother. Not like the wealthy heiress of a long-dead industry titan.

"Welcome," she sang out as they entered. She didn't look like a woman on the brink of death, after suffering at the hands of a brutal armed robber. Instead, she seemed to be blooming under all the attention and excitement.

"I haven't had so many visitors in years! Would any of you like something to drink? Something to eat? I made up some appetizers earlier. Just some cheese and crackers, and those little cocktail weenies, but they're very tasty."

The sergeant smiled at her. "No thank you, Ms. Edwards. I want to introduce you to our FBI agents. They've come from Richmond to help us out."

The old woman stood, a little awkward and slow, and took her cane in hand, hobbling around the table to meet them. After shaking everyone's hands, she called back to the uniformed officers, "We'll have to continue our game later. Come into my living room and make yourselves comfortable. And, please, call me Charlotte," she insisted.

"Miss Charlotte," Noah drawled. "You certainly look well for a dead woman."

Winter had to smile at the elderly woman's reaction to that.

Her face lit with humor as she made herself comfortable in a spindle-legged antique looking chair. "Thank you, young man. I'm feeling exceptionally well for a dead person too."

"Would you mind telling them your story again, Charlotte?" the sergeant asked, his tone deferential. "I'm sure you must be sick of sharing it at this point..."

"Oh, heavens no," she said with a bright laugh. "I'd be happy to."

Noah, turning on his Texas drawl, said, "Very much appreciated, Miss Charlotte."

Beaming under the attention, Charlotte batted her eyes at the handsome agent before setting her cane beside her chair and folding her hands in her lap. "A man came into my apartment in the middle of the night," she began. "He was very polite, apologized for the intrusion in a most charming Irish accent, I should add. He told me he was there to rob and kill me."

"Can you tell us what he looked like?" Sun demanded.

Charlotte waved a hand at her. "Let me tell the story without you interrupting. You can ask me questions when I'm done."

Sun sat back in her chair, tight-lipped in irritation.

Winter couldn't help it. She chuckled.

"At any rate," Charlotte went on. "He asked me to come to the living room. I told him where the wall safe was and gave him the combination. I didn't tell him I had a pistol stashed between my couch cushions. As a matter of fact, you—" she pointed at Bull, who was perched on a Victorian love seat, "be careful squirming around, or you might find a bullet in your rear end."

Bull stilled immediately, and the sergeant laughed out loud. It was clear why he'd been so protective of the woman. She was great. Gramma Beth would love her.

"Anyway," she continued, "before I could inform him of that fact, he turned around and gave me the most unusual story. He told me he was supposed to kill me, but that he didn't want to. We had a little chat about how terrible his partner was, and he asked me...very politely, mind you, to go into my bedroom. He was going to kill me, and he wanted me to be comfortable. He waited for me to get into bed, shot my chair twice, and then left."

"Wow..." Noah murmured.

Winter found herself nodding in agreement.

Charlotte slapped her hands lightly on her knees in delight. "He even locked the door behind him, as if other enterprising thieves might come in after he'd left. When I got up this morning, I went and checked. The sweet thing didn't even take all the money! He only helped himself to a little bit, and only took two boxes of jewelry. The smallest ones."

"Sounds like you like him," Sun said, her eyes narrowed.

Unabashed, Charlotte beamed. "He was a scoundrel, but oh, I did like him. A great deal."

14

"I know who one of the suspects is," Sun announced. She paused for a second, letting the suspense build. The faces around the small table weren't showing nearly enough of a reaction to be satisfying. She almost vibrated in her chair with excitement. She'd solved part of the puzzle.

The hotel staff had given them a small room to confer in, and they were gathered around the table. They'd also been given rooms for the night. The hotel had a lot of unexpected vacancies, and comping rooms was in their best interests. They wanted to wrap the case, control the publicity, and get back to normal business as soon as possible.

"I can't believe none of us saw it before. One of the suspects is Ryan O'Connelly." She looked around the table, half-expecting applause at her announcement. "Come on, guys. Ryan O'Connelly? The Cat?"

"Vaguely rings a bell," Noah commented, but his tone held doubt.

"He's known all over the world," Sun went on, feeling her impatience rise with every word. "He's Irish, and probably Catholic, which would explain the Saint Dismas medal and the donation of the robbery money to the Catholic church in California. From reports, he's handsome and well-spoken, which jibes with what Ms. Edwards told us."

Noah lifted a shoulder. "Maybe."

Winter wisely kept her mouth shut.

Sun pulled up her computer and read a description off to them.

"He's slippery and has been on the radar of the FBI, Interpol, and all kinds of international police departments. He's said to work for the highest bidders, slipping into his targets' homes and removing what he's after before anyone is the wiser. He gets around alarm systems, gets out of tight situations. He escaped through a chimney once in Lourdes. No one has managed to come close to getting him."

"I know who you're talking about now," Bull put in. "I saw a *Dateline* special on him once. But he doesn't kill people, does he?"

"Not so far," Sun admitted. "He's been strictly nonviolent. Almost a criminal passivist."

"That part doesn't fit," Bull said, scratching his cheek. "Maybe it's someone trying to make it sound like they're Ryan. Using a fake Irish accent and planting the details in the story he gave Charlotte Edwards."

"No," Winter put in. She'd kept quiet, but she was in agreement with Sun. "It fits. We're dealing with two people here. O'Connelly told Charlotte Edwards he didn't want to do it, but his partner was vicious, and he was under orders. For whatever reason, he's teamed up with someone who doesn't have any qualms about killing."

Sun nodded, glad for the backup. It irked her, but now that Winter had put her seal of approval on the idea of one of the suspects being O'Connelly, the other two were closer to being on board.

"So, we need to look at the accomplice," Noah said. "Are

there any profiles out there that fit so far? Have we talked to anyone in the BAU yet about putting something together?"

Winter scrawled something in her notepad. "I'll text Aiden. He can coordinate with whoever's in charge in his absence. In the meantime, it'll give him something to puzzle over at home," she added with a wry smile. "He's going stir-crazy."

Sun looked at her sharply, the case forgotten for the moment. "'Aiden? Since when are you two on a first name basis?"

Winter looked up. There was an expression on her face that almost looked like guilt. "What do you mean? I've known SSA Parrish for years."

Something in Winter's eyes was hard to read. They stared at each other for another few seconds before understanding dawned…Aiden must have told Winter that he and Sun had once dated.

Sun could feel her face growing hot and rapidly looked back down at her notes. What was it with this girl? Noah, who she'd toyed with the idea of approaching, was super protective of the rookie. And Aiden Parrish…had they *talked* about her? Anger started to simmer beneath her skin.

Sun had been right in her initial assessment of Agent Black. She was an opportunist. A manipulator. She'd used her connection with Aiden to get into the office, and now she was using her wiles to keep herself there. Sun could feel something inside herself shutting off.

"Yes," she finally answered. "You have known *Aiden* for a long time, haven't you? Please do let him know, if you will, that I would appreciate his insight on this."

She turned away from Winter. Dismissed her. Physically, at least.

"At least we know now that we're dealing with the same people," Sun said, forcing herself to focus. "The video footage, being replaced by the footage from the day before and looped, fits with the first robbery. The fact that most of the kills were quick. Passionless. The Covington murder was an anomaly, but we should be looking for booby traps, as with the first job. We should also check out how the suspects were able to get a master key. We need to check out all employees, find any that might have gone missing recently. These people are thorough. They wouldn't leave a loose end around that could implicate them. They'd kill them like they did with the guy that painted the lines in front of the bank."

"I'll handle that. I like legwork," Bull offered. He wiggled his thick, gray eyebrows. They looked like hairy caterpillars. "I'm a leg man."

Sun looked away from him in disgust. "Noah, you and I will look at possible next targets. And, Winter…"

She looked over at the other woman, but Winter had gone white, her eyes looking a little wild. "Excuse me," she muttered, pushing back from the table. "I'll be back in a second."

Noah half-stood in concern.

"Sit down, Dalton," Sun snapped. "Winter's a big girl. She can go to the bathroom by herself."

Noah shot Sun a look of reproof at her nasty tone.

Did Sun care? Not one bit.

❄

NOT AGAIN. Not already.

Winter stumbled into the hallway, the headache pulsing at her temples, behind her eyes. The hallway seemed to narrow, blur, focus and then lengthen, and she felt dizzy.

A few doors down were the restrooms. If she could make it there.

She pressed the back of her sleeve against her nose and

started moving. One foot in front of the other. She had to focus.

Her hand was on the doorknob, turning it, when her vision started darkening around the edges. This one was coming fast. No slow build-up like the last one.

She got into the room just in time and hoped it was empty. She felt herself going down, hitting the floor.

❄

NOAH ITCHED WITH IMPATIENCE. He wanted to go after Winter. It looked like she had another of her episodes coming on, and he knew how devastating they could be, even if they were only brief. Five minutes went by, and he started getting more and more concerned.

Finally, he interrupted Sun, as she talked about another robbery that could have the potential to be their next copy-cat. She was spitballing at this point, in his opinion, and he wouldn't be missing much.

"I'll be right back," he said, his tone short.

In the hallway, there was no sign of Winter. No blood droplets indicating that she'd had another bloody nose. But he saw that the bathrooms were just down the hall and closed the distance with quick steps.

"Winter?" he called, knocking on the door. There was no answer, and he pushed it open. Hoped no other females were in there.

She was sprawled out on the tile floor, face down. "Winter!"

At the sound of his voice, she shuddered. Crouching down beside her, Noah rolled her over. He grabbed a paper towel from the dispenser above them and gently dabbed at the blood underneath her nose. Some of it had smeared on her cheek.

Her eyes snapped open, and she sucked in a breath. "They were all dead. All of them."

His stomach tightened. "Take it easy, darlin'. Who is dead?"

Color was coming back into her face, and she struggled to sit up.

"Hold on. I'll help you." He stood, grasping her cold hands to help her to her feet.

"There was a pile of men in uniform," she said. Her voice was halting. Slow. She went to the mirrors in the bathroom. She ran the paper towels he'd given her under a stream of cold water, but then just stared at her own reflection. Lost for a minute.

It spooked him.

When she first confided in him about this…ability, or whatever it was, he'd thought having those types of insights would be a blessing for any law enforcement official. But these visions weren't good for her. He knew it deep in his gut. She was going to have an aneurysm or something if she kept on like this.

What he'd first thought was a blessing had become Winter's curse.

The hair raised on the back of his neck.

"Uniforms? Like police officers?" he prompted, shaking away the dark thoughts.

"No." She shook her head and dabbed the wet cloth underneath her nose. "Not police. Security guards, maybe? There was a pile of weapons too."

"Do you know how many there were?"

Frustrated, she shook her head. "No. It was just a snapshot. Ten. Maybe more. But they were dead."

"Okay." He put one hand out and rubbed her back for a moment. This couldn't be healthy for her. He had to find out more about her condition. He needed to know what caused it and whether the repeated episodes could cause any permanent damage. "But are you all right?"

Blood gone, she wadded up the paper towel. "I'm fine. But we need to figure out the next target, or a lot more people are going to die."

"That can wait a second." When she moved to bypass him, to leave the bathroom, he stepped in front of her. "Winter," he said, concerned. "We need to figure this out."

"I know. So step aside."

He didn't. "Not the security guard thing. Your migraines. Visions. Whatever the fuck they are." Her eyes widened at the outburst, and he softened his voice. "You need to see a doctor."

Her eyes fired, her jaw setting with grim determination. "The hell I do. Butt out, Dalton."

No way in hell would he be doing that.

"Every time this happens to you, aren't you afraid you're not going to come out of it? What if you're driving? It's almost as bad as epilepsy. You can't control these episodes!" He stopped. Tried to calm himself. His voice had echoed off the walls. "This could be dangerous. Every time it happens, you have nosebleeds. You pass out. This isn't normal."

"I know it's not normal. Hearing that is nothing new."

Dammit. Now, she looked hurt.

He wanted to pull her into his arms but didn't look forward to the kidney punch he'd receive for his efforts. "Don't try to play this off like I'm telling you you're some kind of freak of nature. You know that's not what I mean. You need to see a doctor."

"Don't do this. Don't try to take advantage of our friendship," she warned, her voice low. "No one knows about this, and I'm trusting you to keep it that way. I've seen doctors. I'm not going that route again."

"Well, you need to figure this out. I don't care if you've

had a bad experience with a doctor. You can see another one. I'm not going to let this go."

"Back. Off." She shoved past him, dropping the paper towels in the garbage. Her hand on the doorknob, she stopped again. "I mean it, Noah. I can handle this. Just let it go." Even though her tone was stone-cold, her eyes were pleading.

Shit. Damn. Hell.

After she escaped into the hallway, he had to take a minute to calm down. It mattered far too much to him that she could be doing permanent damage to herself every time she ignored the physical toll the visions took on her. She called it taking advantage, but he saw it differently. Grimly, he knew that he might have to risk their friendship to do some more digging.

Winter was seated at the conference table again when he came back. Sun gave him a narrow look but went back to what she was doing on her own computer. Bull, the goof, didn't seem to pick up on the tension that was thick enough in the room to choke a horse.

"Noah," Sun said. "Sit by me. I have a couple of possibilities I want to go over with you. Get your take on them." She looked up at him, her dark eyes liquid. "I value your opinion."

She lowered her lashes and Noah saw Sun send a quick look at Winter to gauge her reaction to the little display of open flirtation.

Just perfect. Noah wanted to slam his head on the table. He was stuck between a pissed off friend and a co-worker who'd decided for whatever reason she wanted to make him incredibly uncomfortable. Probably just to get under Winter's skin.

He sat down next to Sun, holding himself stiff in his chair, angled away a bit. It didn't help. She just scooted the computer over so that it was half in front of him and leaned up close enough that her small breast brushed against his arm.

He looked across the table at Winter, who was smiling tightly as she dialed the phone. "Aiden," she said in a soft tone, different than the one she used with Noah. He set his back teeth. "Sorry to bother you. How are you feeling? I'm hoping you can help me out with something." She paused. Laughed. "Absolutely. You're the best. I'll email you."

Women were absolute monsters, Noah decided. And he couldn't wait until this case was done so he could get out of whatever thing was going on here. Getting caught between two warring females was dangerous. He'd almost prefer a gunfight.

15

They'd done it.

They'd pulled it off.

Heidi felt an unaccustomed urge to grin as she watched the news coverage on CNN.

"Two suspects escaped a police pursuit after a robbery and multiple murders were committed at The Phoenix Hotel in New York City," the newscaster read in an alarmingly cheerful voice. "Law enforcement officials are being tight-lipped about the situation, but our sources say that the suspects got away in an Uber vehicle. The driver has been questioned, but all he could tell officers was that he dropped the two off at LaGuardia. They could be anywhere at this point."

A grainy photo popped up on the screen, taken from the lobby security camera footage. They'd never be identified by the photo, that was for sure.

And now they were safe at the place she'd picked out ahead of time. Vermont was beautiful around Christmas, she thought, feeling more than a little smug.

"How much did you get from the old lady?" she asked

Ryan. She'd had him going through the bags, taking inventory.

"She didn't have as much as I thought she would," he said, looking at the small pile of cash and jewelry in front of him. "It looks like about 400K in cash and six pieces of jewelry. A brooch, a diamond pin, three necklaces, one with a pretty nice-sized ruby, and an old wedding ring. Probably another two hundred thousand. I'm no jewelry expert, though. How about the prince?"

"Two million." She lifted her chin in satisfaction. "The suitcases were full of banded bills. Makes you wonder what he'd planned on doing with his time in the country."

"So?" Ryan said, looking at her carefully. "Are we done, then, love? You've pulled off an excellent, if a bit bloody, heist."

The satisfaction drained away, irritation taking its place. "I told you. You're in for three jobs," Heidi replied with a breeziness she didn't feel. "You've got two more to go."

His face fell even as his eyes narrowed into slits. "*One* more." He lifted a single finger as if to cement the point. "I did the bank with you, remember?"

"And that was a practice run," she pointed out. He was such a weak man. Pretty, but weak.

He was silent for a moment, and then seemed to rally. "Well, what's next then?"

"You'll find out when we get to it."

A muscle popped in his jaw. "Of course."

He stood up from where he'd been sprawled out on the floor, counting cash. If she were honest with herself, his weakness repelled her, but it was almost equal to the physical attraction she felt for him.

He really was good-looking. He had that long, lean frame with interesting, understated muscles. And with the "Oliver Brown" face washed away, the wig gone, and the contacts ditched, he was appealing. His blue eyes glittered, and the contrast was striking with his fair skin and dark hair.

He went to the window, looking out on the snow. On a ski hill, small dots in bright colors whizzed down the slopes like little bits of confetti in the distance.

"Do you ski?" he asked, keeping his back to her.

"No."

"You want to try and learn?" He shot her that quicksilver grin of his.

"We're not here on vacation, O'Connelly."

"How long are we here?" he asked. "Before the next gig?"

"Two days."

"And knowing you, love," he persisted, his voice lowering, growing more smoky, "you've got everything all planned out ahead of time. Seems we've probably got a bit of time on our hands."

He was throwing her off-balance. Uncomfortable, she looked back down at the suitcase she'd been repacking. To her annoyance, she felt a flush burning in her cheeks. "I'm not going skiing with you."

"Oh, that's fine. There are lots of things to do when you're cooped up in a little chalet."

Was he flirting with her? She was torn between wanting to put him in his place and wanting him to keep talking. To see what outrageous thing would come out of his mouth next.

"For instance," he said, his voice fading as he moved toward the kitchen. "I found something a previous tenant left behind in the fridge."

She snuck a look at the kitchen. He was bent over, looking in the open refrigerator. She looked back down. It was becoming obvious, what he was doing. Men were all after one thing. She wasn't exactly naive.

She frowned as a cork popped.

A moment later, Ryan came out of the kitchen grinning. He held two flutes of champagne, the sparkling bubbles zipping upward in zigzagging lines.

"You've had champagne before, haven't you?" he asked. His eyes had gone soft blue, and he was looking at her in a way that made her feel hot and cold at the same time. In a good way.

She fumbled one of the bundles of money, and it thumped softly to the carpet.

"Here," he said, holding out a glass. "To a job well done. We can drink to the brilliant genius who planned all of this."

Something flickered across his face, but it was there and gone so fast, she thought maybe she'd imagined it. "Well…"

"Come on," he said, that grin back in place, "I promise I won't corrupt you. One little celebratory glass of champagne."

She took the glass, still watching him. He clinked the flute against hers in a jaunty little movement, making a tinging sound. "Okay."

"To success," he said, the grin growing even wider.

"To success," she murmured back, taking a sip. The champagne was good. Light and fizzy. Sweet, with just a hint of tartness.

She took another sip, a longer one this time.

Normally, Heidi didn't drink. Her father had, and that was enough to keep her away from alcohol for life. But her dad never drank champagne. She liked the little tingle she felt when the champagne went down.

Ryan kicked back on a lounge chair with a view of the mountains. "This is a nice place. How far in advance did you have to rent it? I might come back here someday."

"I booked it a year and a half ago."

He shot her a glance, and she thought she read respect in

the blue depths. "Talk about foresight." He raised the glass to her. "You've been working on this that long?"

She flushed a little. Or maybe it was the champagne. "Yeah. The planning stages go back a lot longer than that."

"I guess I'm in the hands of an expert, then," Ryan said and drained his glass. "This is good. You want some more?"

She nodded and handed over her empty champagne flute.

He was back in a moment with a refill. "Your cheeks are pink," he said, his voice low, brushing her fingers with his as he handed her the flute. Her fingers felt like they'd been scalded when he moved his hand away. "The bubbles must've gone to your head."

"I'm fine," she countered, taking another sip. "It's just warm in here."

She knew what he was doing. She wasn't stupid, she reminded herself.

"Maybe a little," he replied, his eyes seeming to dance with good humor…and something else. "So, where are you really from? So far, I've been all over the country with you. I feel like North Dakota, where we met, wasn't where you'd call home."

Why not tell him? It didn't matter at this point. Or it wouldn't, for long.

"Northern Michigan," she answered.

"Really?" He sat back down on the chaise, this time facing her, his arms on his knees. He was either interested in hearing more or doing a good job of pretending. "Which part? I've been to Mackinaw Island before. I had a fun job there once, but no farther north than that. What is it they call you people up there? 'Yoopers?'"

"Yeah. I'm from Saint Ignace, just on the other side of the Mackinac Bridge."

He asked more questions, his blue eyes looking so sincere. When she talked, he seemed to absorb every word.

She found herself opening up a little bit, telling him small snippets about what life was like in Saint Ignace, just north of the bridge. None of the important things, of course. She'd never do that. But what it had been like, living in a big old house perched on top of the tallest hill in town.

Her family had done some renovation work on it. They'd converted an old coal room into usable space, among other things. An elderly neighbor had told her later, that one winter, in the early 1900s, dozens of people had died from an illness that went through the community. The ground was too frozen to bury anyone, so they'd ended up storing them in the "big house," as they called it, until spring, when the ground thawed. They'd stacked the bodies up like cordwood in what was now the Presley living room.

She'd never thought it was haunted, but her mom was a nervous, neurotic woman. Her erratic behavior had gotten worse in the house after that. Heidi didn't tell Ryan that piece of her history.

Ryan refilled their glasses—or maybe just hers, she wasn't sure. He told her about a hotel he'd stayed in in Europe one time. How at night, someone or something had yanked the covers off the top of his bed in the middle of the night. It had scared him so badly, he'd run straight down to the reception desk. The only problem was, he hadn't taken the time to put on clothes.

"I sleep in the nude," he admitted, his eyes twinkling in a wicked way.

It surprised a giggle out of her. She was *not* a giggler.

"I think you might have gotten me drunk," she said in surprise. Her head felt like it was wobbling a little on her neck, and she was warm. Deliciously warm.

"Maybe," he said, his tone mischievous. "That depends. Do you like it?"

"Maybe," she said back. She couldn't believe she was bantering. She was *not* a banterer.

"You want some more?"

She nodded. Ryan was right. They were celebrating. She'd pulled off the first two stages of her plan without a hitch. Or much of one anyway.

Ryan brought her glass back. His fingers lingered against hers longer this time.

"Are you flirting with me?" She needed to concentrate hard on pronouncing the words.

"Do you want me to be?"

Looking at him, carelessly handsome, with his black hair falling down over his forehead, barefoot in jeans with a plaid flannel shirt unbuttoned just a bit at the neck.

She drained the rest of the glass, feeling the warmth spread through her belly and elsewhere. "Maybe I do."

❄

THANK GOD, Ryan thought, looking down at Heidi. She was out cold. Her lips were parted a little, and as he watched, a soft snore escaped.

He eased off the bed, careful not to jostle her.

He'd sooner have sex with a praying mantis and had worried for a while there that he might have to follow through. He'd gotten her drunk enough, though, pouring his second glass into hers when he'd gone to the kitchen for refills, and giving her the rest of the bottle.

She shifted, and he stilled, but she just murmured something in her sleep. Her wig—brown again—had come a little askew, and beneath, he thought he could see a little blonde. It made sense, with her fair coloring.

But she could be as hot as the lingerie model he'd once

hoped for, and it wouldn't matter now. The bitch was stone-cold crazy. Not a turn on.

He could still see the face of the helpless security guard when he'd fallen backward. His mouth opened in shock as what looked like a harmless, wealthy, middle-aged woman, who shot him in the chest twice. All because he'd been trying to offer her a fucking tissue.

Between that and the way she'd been covered in blood when she came out of Covington's room had him on edge. And the cold expression on her face as she'd shot the prince's bodyguards. She was ruthless and scary as hell.

He moved across the carpet of the bedroom, heading toward her bags.

He'd admit it freely. He'd gotten Heidi drunk, and...he grimaced, tried to seduce her for the purpose of going through her things. The laptop would be useless, as he'd watched her log in to it before. The password was probably forty characters long, not all of them letters. Her phone was the same way. But he needed to find any kind of leverage he could. He wanted out.

He made no noise as he rustled through her belongings. That, at least, was his forte. It was like he'd told the spritely Miss Charlotte. He was a thief. Not a killer.

Heidi was paranoid, though, and it showed in her things. Or in the lack of them. No ID, no personal items. Nothing except as it related to the jobs they'd done so far.

And there was the big, black gun she seemed to favor, tucked in at the bottom of the duffel bag. He touched the metal, just grazing his fingers over it, where it glinted cold in the moonlight that poured through the window.

He could take it out. Shoot her while she slept.

He'd probably be saving dozens of lives, if not more. Including his own.

But he wasn't a killer. Besides, she'd already told him that she had a dead man's switch that would activate if anything happened to her. If that happened, the dossier of information she had accumulated on him would be broadcasted to who knew who.

So…he kept looking. Until, behind him, came a voice that wasn't the least bit sleepy.

"What are you doing, Ryan?"

He turned around, managing to have a sheepish smile already on his face, but Heidi was sitting up in the bed with a look that told him she wouldn't be buying any of the bullshit he had to sell.

"Well, love, I—"

"Did I tell you, by the way," she interrupted with a smile, the conversational beginning not easing his nerves, "that I did some recognizance on you when you were in Jamaica? I followed you around a bit. Just to get a feel for what you were like. It was one thing to hear stories about the legend, but it was another to see him in action."

She slipped from the bed to stand, almost eye to eye with him. He felt the hair on the back of his neck rise in response.

"I saw you flirt," she said. "With all kinds of women. But there was one in particular that I noticed you seemed to have a real fondness for. Ionie, I think her name was?"

Ionie. Dammit to hell, not Ionie. He tried to keep any reaction from his face. Tried and failed.

Then, knowing she had him, Heidi smiled.

16

Winter was grateful for the accommodations of The Phoenix. Under the circumstances, she wished she wasn't staying there at the expense of so many lives, but the FBI on-the-road accommodations didn't normally extend to the luxury that The Phoenix had to offer.

She felt better that morning, after having had a mocha and a scone, and a decent night's sleep on a mattress better than the one she had at home.

And because of the time difference, she'd been able to call and check in on Sheriff Marchwood in San Clemente late the previous evening. Winter had been told that Shannon was stable. She'd made it through the first critical twenty-four hours, and that was a good sign. She was resting, sedated, and would be undergoing skin grafts as soon as she was deemed strong enough to make it through the procedure.

It would be horrible and painful, but if Marchwood could survive an exploding house, she could live through skin grafts.

Winter breakfasted early, served by the hotel's skeleton staff, hoping to miss everyone else from the unit. Sun had reversed any goodwill they'd developed in California, and Winter seemed to have a target on her back. Poor Bull wasn't much better. He had thick skin, though, and let Sun's insults roll off his brawny shoulders.

Noah had become the teacher's pet. Sun stuck to his side, hung on every word, and had been throwing darts with her eyes at Winter every twelve seconds. It was partly annoying and partly gratifying. On the one hand, she was doing it in an attempt to get under Winter's skin. On the other, Noah was super uncomfortable, and after him blowing up at her in the bathroom the day before, it was nice to see him squirm.

Winter hoped he had taken her warning seriously. They'd become good friends, but the second he betrayed her trust, he was gone.

She wasn't the first in the conference room set aside for their use. Noah was already there. He nodded good morning, giving her a searching look before he relaxed a little. "You look like you're feeling better today."

"I'm fine. Thanks." She took a sip of her coffee. "How long have you been in here? You look beat."

He shrugged, still looking at his computer. "A couple hours. Believe it or not, I had a late date."

She couldn't help it. She pictured Noah and Sun together and fake-gagged.

"With Charlotte Edwards," he explained, grinning. "I got the summons last night after we all split up to go to our rooms. She claimed to need someone to play poker with. Like your Grandpa Jack, based on my Texan accent, she decided that I'd suit her just fine."

"Really?" Winter chuckled, not liking the fact that she was greatly relieved that he hadn't been hooking up with the senior agent. "I can picture that, actually. Did she tell you any more about the robbery?"

"Just the same stuff she'd told us the day before. To be

totally honest, I think she's got a little crush on Ryan O'Connelly," he added. "She seemed pretty taken with him. Told me he could come back and burgle her again anytime, and that it was the most fun she'd had in years."

They were both laughing when Sun sailed in, followed by Bull at a dragging walk.

She shot Winter a glare. "Where were you? I called your room an hour ago."

"You should have tried my cell," Winter answered, her tone chilled. "I was having breakfast. And in case you were concerned, they think Shannon Marchwood will be okay. She pulled through the first twenty-four hours. Detective Patterson is gone, though. They were able to identify his remains yesterday. The dishwasher was rigged with dynamite."

Sun's eyes widened. "The dishwasher. Of course. In the original job, the perpetrators completely cleaned up the townhouse they'd used as base but forgot to run the dishwasher. It was full of dishes and fingerprints. I should have figured that out sooner." Instead of focusing on the news about the police that had been involved, Sun went on, looking impressed. "By filling the dishwasher with dynamite, they managed to connect it even tighter to the original case. Remember, the gang used dynamite to get in through a hole in the bank roof? Genius."

"That wasn't my takeaway." Winter's tone was heavy with disgust. Sun had a one-track mind.

Instead of responding, Sun pulled out her laptop and sat down. The rebuke had flown right over her head.

"All right, everyone. I've got our next target. We need to go back to California. Los Angeles, this time. These guys are brilliant, but we're going to get ahead of them."

She turned around the computer screen and showed

them a story on another old robbery—the Dunbar armored car depot.

"How do you—"

Sun held up her hand, cutting Noah off. "This is the next likely target. It was widely regarded as one of the biggest heists in U.S. history. Allen Pace, a regional safety inspector, pulled it off. He knew the cameras and how to avoid them, got a gang together, and did the job on a Friday night when the vault was kept unlocked sometimes because of the heavy volume of deliveries coming in. They got away with close to twenty million."

It sounded plausible. Likely, even. But something didn't feel right. As Noah asked questions and Bull slumped in his chair, looking like he desperately wanted coffee and a couple more hours of sleep, Winter pulled up her own computer and grabbed her notebook. She'd spent some time the night before, thinking about her vision. Without any additional clues, she'd tried to focus in on the emblems on the uniforms.

She'd ended up with a sketch, not a very good one, but it didn't look like the Dunbar logo. Maybe they'd changed logos over the years. She needed to—

"Winter? Are you with us?" Sun snapped out, her voice impatient.

She didn't look up, just kept skimming through the Google images page she'd pulled up. "Yeah," she finally said, waiting just long enough to piss Sun off. "I think you're on it with the armored car depot thing, but I don't know if the location is right."

"What do you mean?" Sun demanded. "Why would you even think the location is wrong?" Sun scowled, tapping her pen on the table. "Los Angeles is where the depot was located. It's still there. The Phoenix robbery was done here, at The Phoenix Hotel. The only reason the bank robbery was done elsewhere was that there was an empty storefront where the United California Bank used to be in Laguna Niguel. The San Clemente bank was a substitute."

"I know."

Winter kept scrolling. Finally, a picture popped out at her. The logo looked similar to the one in her vision, and her heartbeat quickened. This was it. This was the one she'd seen. She was certain.

Excited now, she clicked through the image to an article: "ArmorGuard Security Buys out Dunbar Armored." The article was dated earlier in the year.

Her fingers flew over the keys, typing in another search term, wanting to know the locations.

Bingo.

"I think it's going to be here," Winter said, looking up to meet Sun's glare. "In New York."

Noah looked at her with interest. Even Bull perked up.

"Why's that?" the older agent asked. "I sure would rather not have to fly if I don't have to."

"Bear with me," she said to Sun, knowing she'd be the one to convince. "I think you're right with the Dunbar angle. It's the most logical choice for the next job, if there's going to be one. But I think that it's going to be here in New York. ArmorGuard Security bought out Dunbar earlier this year. There's an armored depot right in Brooklyn. If you were the suspects, even working with an advance plan, wouldn't it make sense to stick close to the site of your last job?"

"Then why fly all the way across the country in the first place?" Sun clearly wasn't buying it. Her face was set and tight.

"Maybe the first job was a warm up," Winter guessed. "I don't know. I just have a feeling that we're looking too far away. They would have likely figured out that we'd be on to the theme of this whole spectacle by now. Maybe they'd expect we'd go to the original site while they sit tight here and get ready to pull their next heist."

"You have a 'feeling?'" Sun mocked, practically sneering the word. "We're FBI. We don't put stock in feelings. We deal in facts."

"Then why have you been operating on hunches since we started this investigation?" Winter burst out.

Noah watched the two of them, appearing to be uncertain as to whether he should intervene. Bull just looked fascinated by the back and forth.

"What kind of solid evidence did you have that a random bank robbery in California would just happen to be the first in a string of historically based cases?"

For a second, Sun looked stymied. Her mouth opened but no excuse was forthcoming.

Understanding dawned.

"You knew." Winter said the words in a quiet voice, underlaid with menace.

"How could I have known?" Sun's retort sounded a little desperate.

"You knew," Winter repeated. "Was it an anonymous tip? Why didn't you tell anyone?"

"Shut the fuck up," Sun blustered, shoving to her feet. "I'm the case agent on this. You don't get to question me."

"I do when it relates to the case I'm assigned to," Winter said, standing too. "What else are you hiding?"

"Sit down." Noah's firm voice cut in. "Both of you, cut it out. Going at each other's throats will not bring this case to a close."

Bull had crossed his arms, a slight grin on his face, looking like he was watching a tennis match. "I don't know, Dalton," he said, the remark sly. "Don't stop 'em now. We might get to see a catfight."

"Shut up, Bull," Noah said mildly, his eyes still on Ming. "Sun, did you know about this?"

She'd subsided into her seat. Caught out. A minute passed. Two. When Noah opened his mouth to ask again, she held up a hand. "I got an email," Sun admitted. "I didn't think anything of it until I saw the headlines on the San Clemente job."

"Why wouldn't you tell anyone?" Winter couldn't believe it. This whole time, they'd had a lead right in front of them. Her face went hot with anger. "We could have handed the address over to IT or the computer forensics team. They could have tried to trace it."

"It doesn't matter." Noah still looked pissed, but he was shaking his head. "We know now. What did the email say?"

At first, Sun looked mutinous, like she wasn't going to tell them. "It said that I'd been chosen," she admitted, "as one of the FBI's best agents. They'd decided to give me an early clue about a series of robberies that were going to take place, and that I should watch the news out of California. That I'd know it was them when I saw it."

"Call Max." Noah tapped his knuckles on the table. "Now."

Sun looked like she was about to argue. She glanced around the table, but there was no sympathy or understanding there.

Even Bull, not the most sensitive of the lot, realized that what Sun had done had jeopardized the case from the beginning. He shook his head at her, looking grim. "You'll be lucky not to get fired. You know that, right?"

"No. I won't." She looked stubborn but determined. "Who else would have known about all the old cases? Who would have had an interest in them and put together the clues so quickly? I *am* the right person to lead this case, and they knew it."

"And how would a completely anonymous person have known?" Noah asked. "Are we looking at an inside job?"

Sun flushed. "No. I don't think so. I had an old blog about the biggest heists in history. I hadn't even thought about it in years, hadn't written on the site since like 2006. When blogging first started to be a thing, I would do posts on old cases. It didn't occur to me until a couple of days ago that that's how they could have tracked me down. It's still on my LinkedIn profile. I haven't updated that in a few years, either. Not since I started working in Richmond."

"Great. Okay. Well, Sun, you've got a phone call to make." Noah looked disgusted. "I don't envy you this one. Bull, you need coffee. You guys want to go get that while Sun makes her phone call?"

They each got up and left the room without speaking. Bull was shaking his head on the way out.

Winter glanced at Sun, who was staring daggers back at her. "It's not my fault," Winter pointed out, turning to face her nemesis head-on. "It was your decision not to tell anyone about that. How far are you willing to go to get in the spotlight you accused me of hogging?"

Sun didn't answer. She pulled out her phone as Winter left the room, her expression miserable.

17

"I can't believe she got away with it," Bull said mournfully. "We'll have to start calling her Teflon. That shit just slid right off of her."

It was true. They didn't know how she'd done it, but Sun had managed to not only *not* get fired, but she was still in charge of the case, and she and Noah were in the air, on their way to Los Angeles.

"Doesn't matter," Winter said. "She's got Noah with her, so that'll keep her out of trouble. I really don't think she's going to find what she's looking for in California, though. I think it was a false trail to keep us chasing our tails."

"I'm a good tail-chaser," Bull grinned. "Ask anybody."

Winter rolled her eyes. He was annoying but harmless.

They were on their way to the armored truck depot in Manhattan. Winter had been told to follow her lead while Sun did her thing. She had a feeling bets were being placed on whose would pan out. She didn't care. She did believe in gut feelings, and hers was telling her she was on the right track. They might finally pull out ahead of the suspects.

"That's the place," Bull muttered. "I can think of easier places to rob. Shit looks like Fort Knox, with all that fencing."

"Well, let's get in there and see what we can find out."

They were buzzed through the gate by a guard, and at the sight of his uniform, Winter was sure that these were the uniforms she'd seen. She shuddered, hoping that the vision could be changed. So far, they'd all ended up coming true, but why would she get them if she couldn't do anything about them?

They entered the offices, where a receptionist invited them to have a seat while she called out the manager, Mike Garofalo. He only kept them waiting a few moments.

"Welcome!" The word was said in a voice a shade too cheerful to be sincere. Mike was a short man, probably about five-four without the lifts that made him an inch or two taller. His thinning, dyed black hair was combed over to one side to hide a gleaming bald spot. It wasn't working.

She heard Bull snort. He'd obviously embraced his own baldness and had little respect for anyone else who didn't do the same.

She shook Mike's hand, finding it warm and damp. She wiped her palm on her pants, not liking the feeling the man had left behind.

"Come on back into my office. Becky, hold my calls, will you?"

The receptionist wrinkled her nose. "It's not like he gets any," she muttered as Winter walked by her.

Mike's office was untidy, piles of paperwork stacked around. He moved a couple of stacks from a chair. "Sorry, guys, I only have one extra," he said. "I don't get a lot of visitors."

"No problem," Bull replied, sitting down.

Winter wanted to laugh at his complete oblivion to basic manners. That was fine—he could sit. They'd decided to let him take the lead, anyway. She leaned forward and brushed an invisible piece of lint off the shoulder of Bull's jacket. That was their signal.

He gave her a surprised look and a subtle nod.

They'd planned on warning the manager that his facility was a possible target. It had been Winter's idea to come up with a second story, just in case it didn't feel right, or the manager started acting suspiciously.

Bull obviously hadn't noticed Mike's nervousness, but he started in with their cover story anyway. "We're here because we think one of your employees might be involved in a kidnapping case from a few weeks back."

Mike's eyes widened. "I hadn't heard about any kidnapping cases."

"No." Bull nodded, looking wise. He lowered his voice, as if imparting confidential information. "It's been kept strictly on the DL. We're thinking we might be on to a whole ring of kidnappers, and we're trying to bring down the kingpin. We need to swear you to secrecy on this."

Tone it down, Bull, Winter thought to herself, looking around the room. It sounded like he was reciting the plot of a TV episode. It was fortunate that Mike was eating it up. He looked relieved at the line of questioning. As Bull explained that they wanted to walk through the facility, take a look at who was working, she studied the stacks of papers. One stack, on top of Mike's desk, drew her eye.

There was just a faint reddish light toward the bottom of the stack, as if the papers were covering something.

Bull and Mike were winding down, with Mike offering to give them a tour of the facility.

Winter started coughing.

Bull looked at her first, his brows drawn together in confusion. She coughed harder, the initial fake coughs taking on a life of their own. Bull started looking concerned.

They hadn't talked about this, and she could tell he was teetering on the line between wanting to think this was a signal and wanting to leap up and pound his hand on her back.

"Water," she gasped out between hacks.

Finally, the lightbulb went on over Bull's head.

"Asthma attack?" he asked, getting to his feet.

Close enough. She nodded.

"Can you get her a glass of water?" he asked Mike. "She does this sometimes."

"Sure." Mike edged around the room, as if Winter's coughs could be contagious. "Uh, hang on. I'll be right back."

He left the door open behind him.

Winter kept coughing, just in case he could hear her from down the hallway and moved to the pile of papers. Lifting them, she nodded at Bull to pull a datebook out from beneath. It was the source of the red glow she'd seen. He grabbed it, and she set the papers down. He slipped it beneath his butt just as Mike came back with the water. Winter had gotten back to her original spot in the corner of the room.

She took the paper cup he held out and sipped at the tepid liquid. "Thanks. I hate it when that happens."

"I've choked on my own spit before," Bull put in helpfully. "Sounds just like that."

"Well, if you're sure you're okay." Mike eyed her in doubt.

"I'm fine." Winter smiled, handing him the paper cup back. "Lead the way."

He headed out into the hall, and Bull followed close behind, using his bulk to give her the cover she needed to grab the book and slip it into her bag. She tried to ignore the fact that it was warm from Bull's ass.

The depot itself wasn't impressive. It just looked like a very secure loading dock, with trucks backing up to be unloaded. But instead of skids of building materials or car parts, their delivery product was money.

"As you can see," Mike said, "we've got everyone on camera all the time." He pointed out the CCTV cameras posted every few feet. "This is a secure facility. Just like Fort Knox."

"Told you," Bull said, nudging Winter's arm. "Fort Knox."

"Everyone who works here goes through a rigorous background check." Mike preened with pride. "We don't let just anybody get a job here. That's why I'm so surprised that—" He stopped short as one of the employees walked by in uniform, pushing a dolly with lockboxes loaded on it. "That's why I'm surprised to hear why you're here," he continued in a stage whisper after the man had walked on.

"Well," Bull said, his tone equally secretive. "You never can tell with people. You should hear about this one case I had. This little old lady was…"

Bull was buying her time to look around. She tuned out the old lady story and studied the exits, the docks, the offices, trying to memorize the layout. They needed to have as much information as possible so they could try and plan out how a heist could be pulled off at this location. They kept moving, and Winter kept her eyes open for anything else that might stand out, either glowing red or just unusual.

She might have some weird form of enhanced intuition, but she didn't want to rely on anything that mysterious. She wanted to enhance her normal intuition too, just in case the enhanced version left as quickly as it had appeared.

Lagging behind Bull and the manager, Winter studied everything carefully.

The employees, too, all blended together. No one looked particularly sinister or nervous to see black-suited strangers —who were obviously law enforcement officials—in their workplace.

Mike wrapped up the tour, keeping things brief. "I've got some pressing work to take care of," he said, striving to sound important. "I'm going to head back to my office. You keep looking around as much as you want. Let me know if you find…you know. Anyone."

He walked away, his heels clicking a rapid beat on the concrete floor.

"Looked a little eager to get away from us all the sudden," Bull muttered.

"Almost like he wanted to go call someone?" Winter asked.

Bull scratched the back of his bald head. "Maybe."

❄

MIKE GAROFALO WAS SWEATING hard underneath the heat-trapping polyester suit jacket he wore. If he played his cards right, though, he wouldn't be wearing cheap polyester for long.

He passed Becky at the reception desk, ignoring her curious look. Closing his door to block out her nosy eavesdropping, he looked around. The agent's coughing fit had struck him as weird, but he couldn't see where anything was disturbed. Still. It seemed like too much of a coincidence.

He picked up his phone and dialed the number he'd been given. When he reached the voicemail, an automated message told him to state his business after the beep. He spoke quietly. "I have FBI agents here." He licked his dry lips. "They say they're looking for a kidnapping suspect, but something feels funny. Just giving you a heads-up."

Hanging up the phone, he looked around the office again. He still had an itchy feeling. One of his sticky notes had fallen to the floor. Those little yellow bastards were always getting everywhere.

He picked it up and put it back on top of the stack where it belonged.

Then he froze. His breath was coming out in rapid gasps as he picked up the stack of papers and moved it to one side.

"Son of a bitch," he whispered. Frantically, he moved other papers, dropping them to the floor in his hurry.

It was gone.

His fucking datebook was gone.

He sank down in his chair, feeling the sweat pooling in his armpits. Dampening the top of his head. He wiped at his upper lip, where nervous sweat had gathered.

Think, Mikey, he told himself. What had he written in the book? He'd never put down anything about the person that had come to see him a couple of months ago. It wasn't like he'd write that. He wasn't stupid.

After thinking through every possible scenario, he felt sure that there was nothing in there to tie him to what was about to go down. He relaxed a little. The only possible incriminating thing was written in code. There was no way anyone could link it to him.

And, he thought, brightening a little more, if the FBI agents really had taken the book, they'd see he had nothing to hide. And if they did find something, they'd taken the date book illegally. Even the dumbest attorney could have that illegal seizure tossed out in court by even the dumbest judge.

He was okay, either way.

He couldn't have anything to do with something that happened while he was out having dinner at his favorite restaurant. Everybody knew him there, and his cousin was the maître de. Plus, they were going to a friend's house for a party afterward. Very public things they were doing that night. Alibis in every direction.

He sat back in his chair.

Everything would be fine. While shit blew up around here, he'd be hanging out with his girlfriend.

He thought about calling the number back that he'd memorized, letting them know the Feds had his datebook too, but there was no point. It was in code. No one would be able to crack it. It wouldn't do to make anyone annoyed, and maybe blame him for the loss of the datebook. It wasn't his fault.

Besides, everything was going to be just fine.

After tomorrow night, anyway.

18

"So, you really think he had something to do with it?" Bull asked after they'd gotten back to the rental car.

"Just a feeling." Winter gave Bull a sideways glance. "You don't have a problem with that, do you?" she asked, referring back to Sun's outburst.

Bull laughed. "Hell no. I don't care what a guy's gotta do to solve a case. As long as it gets the job done, you can dance around naked for all I care." He paused, considering. "Hey, you don't want to dance around naked by chance, do ya?"

Winter snorted, putting the car in gear. No matter how far equal rights and sexual harassment had come to make the workplace a bit safer, she didn't think it would ever keep testosterone driven men from flirting, at least just a bit. She'd just have to keep verbally neutering them until shooting them was legalized. "Keep dreaming."

Still grinning, Bull shot her a glance. "Well, you went next level with that coughing shit. Good job. I thought you were going to keel over or honk up a lung, for a minute there."

She laughed as she pulled out of the parking lot. "Hopefully, I didn't just throw some guy's life organization system into chaos for no reason. But I have a feeling there's something in the datebook. We'll find out."

"You know you can't use that in court, right?"

Winter nodded. "I'm more interested in stopping the murder of innocents at the moment. I'll deal with prosecution later."

"Sounds about right." His stomach growled loudly, and he patted it with his hand. "You mind if we find out over a beer and some chicken wings? Or nachos. Nachos sound really good right now." There was hope in Bull's voice.

She grinned. "I'm used to working over food. Dalton is a bottomless pit that thinks better on a full stomach. Find me a restaurant around here that sounds good."

Bull pulled one up and set the GPS on his phone.

"Hey…" She could feel his eyes on her as he spoke, his tone curious. "You got a thing going with Noah? It's fine if you do, but everybody in the unit wants to know."

"Everybody in the unit should mind their own business."

Bull snorted. "You know if you say that, it just makes it sound like you're saying yes, right?"

"No. It doesn't make it sound that way at all." Winter grimaced, feeling his eyes still on her. She glanced in his direction, and sure enough, he was staring, a little grin playing on his mouth. Bull was still clearly waiting for an answer. "No, Bull," she huffed, enunciating the words. "Dalton and I don't have a thing going on."

Bull snapped his fingers. "Damn it. Miguel is going to take the pool. Me and…" he caught the glare she threw him, "ah, me and everybody else said yes."

At the restaurant, Winter flipped through the pages of Mike Garofalo's calendar. He wasn't Mister Popular, as far as she could tell.

She flipped to the weekly schedule layout. It still wasn't very interesting. Doctors' appointments. Cosmetic dentist visit for a capping consultation. Work meeting. And then there was tomorrow's date, written in what looked like a coded message.

"What do you think of this?" Winter asked Bull, who was shoving nachos down his throat like he was afraid someone was going to take them away from him.

"I think," he said after a moment, spraying a crumb onto the calendar, "that looks like a bunch of letters and numbers."

"A code," she prompted patiently. "Does it look like a code to you?"

Bull squinted, like that would change what the words looked like on the paper. "Maybe. Are there any more on any other dates?"

She shook her head and flicked the crumb back at him, where it stuck to his wrinkled white shirt. Turning the book around, she looked at it again. She tried a couple of different simple letter/number substitutions, like A for 1, B for 2 and so on, but nothing fit.

"Do we have somebody at the office who specializes in codes?" she asked Bull.

He nodded, taking a swig of PBR. "Bobby Goldsboro. Text it to him."

She did, using the number Bull rattled off.

"Even if we don't know what it means, it seems significant, doesn't it?"

Bull took another long drink. "Maybe it's the day they change the Wi-Fi password in the office. Doesn't mean somebody's going to rob the place on Tuesday."

Winter shrugged. "You could be right, but I don't know. Seems unusual to me."

"Eat your chicken fingers, Prognostico, and wait for Bobby to text back," Bull advised. "Unless you want to give those to me instead."

Yep. Working with Bull was just like working with the Neanderthal version of Noah.

Mike Garofalo wasn't very bright, or at least not very good at designing uncrackable codes. Bobby Goldsboro, Richmond's resident code specialist, called them before they'd even left the restaurant. He sounded disappointed that she hadn't sent him something more difficult.

"It says 'Molly, 7:00 p.m.'"

"That's it?" Winter was a little disappointed herself that it didn't just translate to "Armored truck depot robbery." That would be enough for her to go to the NYPD for police presence.

But Bull was right. It was too vague. The message could just mean he was cheating on his wife on that night, and he'd coded it in case she discovered his book. Garofalo seemed like the type.

"Yep. I hope it turns out to mean something helpful."

She thanked him and hung up.

Bull looked at her. "You want to go anyway?"

"Yeah."

"Let's do it, then."

She couldn't hide her surprise. "Just like that? On a hunch?"

He shrugged. "It's not like we have anything better to do. Besides, you smell nicer than the last guy I went on a stakeout with."

Winter looked at him for a moment. He had a smidge of nacho cheese stuck to his cheek.

"You're an interesting man, Bull."

19

H eidi listened to the message and grimaced.
They'd already figured out the location. The FBI agent she'd picked for her case was a little too good.

Oh, well. She was still a step ahead. They didn't know yet that she knew that *they* knew. Knowledge was power.

Ryan sat across from her, his face stony. He'd been significantly less charming since she'd threatened his Jamaican lover. In her opinion, he should be grateful that she hadn't capped his ass after the little seduction stunt he'd pulled.

"What is it?" he asked, but he sounded distinctly uninterested.

"It looks like the FBI are on to our next job already."

"Are we going to cancel it, then?"

She didn't miss the faint flicker of hope that chased across his face. She enjoyed squashing it.

"Sorry, *love*, but they only know where, not when. I think," she added with a thoughtful look, "that I hope our two agents show up tomorrow night. I'm going to be ready for them."

✳

WINTER'S CELL phone rang that evening as she was getting ready for bed. She checked the caller ID, expecting Gramma Beth. She and Grandpa Jack were spending some time in Florida before they all met up for Christmas.

At least, she hoped this thing would be wrapped in time for Christmas.

But the number was Aiden's.

She picked up fast.

"What's wrong?" she demanded as she tucked her wet toothbrush back into its case.

He laughed, a low chuckle. "Nothing. Does something have to be wrong for me to call you?"

"Yeah, pretty much." She turned off the bathroom light and sat down on the bed, pulling the covers over her legs. "We're not exactly phone buddies these days."

But back when she was fourteen and needed someone to talk to, she'd thought of him that way. He'd always answered when she called.

"Fine." He sighed, the sound drawn out and pitiful. "I'm bored. I may have given you a hard time, but it's quiet over here without you barging into my apartment, bringing food."

Winter relaxed a little and settled back against the pillows, muting her TV. "How are you feeling?" she asked. "Doing your PT like a good boy?"

"Yeah." The word was little more than a growl. "I'm getting there. The therapist is a sadist, though. I swear she enjoys my pain. She feeds off of it."

"She just wants you back on your feet, so you'll be out of her hair, and she won't have to deal with you anymore."

It was crazy, how easy they fell into the smooth back-and-forth that had characterized their early relationship, Winter thought. Aiden had been there for her more times than she could count. She'd been able to call him any time in the years following her parents' murder. She could talk to him about things that she hadn't felt comfortable bringing up with her grandparents, mostly related to the case.

But sometimes their conversations had ranged far. He was an interesting conversationalist, and she'd appreciated his distractions back then. The least she could do was distract him now.

"You're bored," she repeated. "What do you want me to do about it, all the way up here in my fancy hotel room?"

"I was thinking we could talk about work."

"You're sick, Aiden. Addicted. You need help."

He chuckled. "Maybe. I did some profile work on the suspects."

"Yeah? Anything you can tell us at this point would be helpful."

"You need to be careful," he warned. "Not that you wouldn't be anyway, but there's a good chance you're dealing with a very smart, very focused sociopath."

A smile played on her lips. "I know Sun is difficult, but I don't know that I'd go that far."

"Winter…"

"Right. A sociopath. Do you think we're on the right track with Ryan O'Connelly?"

"I do. I've read everything I could find about him, which hasn't been a lot, but what you guys have theorized appears to be consistent. He seems like a decent guy, despite being a felon multiple times over. It's the woman you have to worry about."

"Is this unusual? Having a woman mastermind something like this?"

He paused, and she could almost hear the gears moving in his head. "Women can be just as vicious as men, as I'm sure you're aware. But no, I don't think our suspect is a run-of-the-mill woman. Most of the actions she's taken have come off cold and calculated. Logical and mostly emotionless. The level of detail shows a lot of forethought. My guess is that she's young, maybe in her thirties. She works in a man's world—probably IT or dev, based on the type of work she's done with hacking the security systems and bank software. She's got a chip on her shoulder from being overlooked in favor of her male colleagues. In fact, she's got something on O'Connelly, some kind of hold or leverage, and is very much enjoying being in the power position. But I'd say, too, that there's something deeper with her."

"You're thinking about the Covington killing."

"I am," Aiden replied darkly. "I did some digging on Covington too. He was broke. Lost his money in some shady investments. I don't know how he was still managing to stay at The Phoenix long-term, like he was. It was just a matter of time until he was found out, couldn't pay, and got kicked to the curb. Unfortunately for him, it didn't happen soon enough."

"You think maybe suspect number two didn't know that? That she was angry when she found out that he was broke and took it out on him?"

"That's what I think. There was no cold calculation in the way he was slaughtered. And the blood everywhere...the footprints in the hall. She was out of control. Berserk."

That was how it had seemed to Winter too. She was glad to have her opinion backed up.

"What do you think about the location?" she asked. "I've got a solid feeling about it, and Bull is just going along with whatever I do, but do you think they'll hit in California or NYC next?"

She could hear the clink of ice in a glass over the line. "I'm not a fortune teller," Aiden answered after a moment. "It could go either way. Be careful, though."

"You be careful. Only one of those, you hear? Alcohol doesn't mix with your medication."

"What alcohol?"

"Don't bullshit me. That very nice, eighteen-year-old Glenlivet you're drinking right now. That's what alcohol."

"Yes, mom," Aiden said, amusement thick in his voice.

Winter decided against telling Aiden about their stakeout at the depot the following night. It was good to get his input, but she couldn't shake the feeling that he was wrestling with the need to interfere. The last thing she needed was for him to show up brandishing his cane, being his weirdly protective self.

Not that he would. He'd send someone. Still, it was unnecessary.

"Anything else you want to share?" It was almost like he could read her mind.

"Nope," she answered blithely. "I think you're caught up. Maybe I'll have more to update you on tomorrow."

"All right. How's it going with Sun?"

She snorted.

"That good?"

"If I tell you, *I'll* need to go find some whiskey."

20

Mike Garofalo was just patting a final coat of hair gel into place when the doorbell rang. He pulled back his top lip to make sure none of the spinach frittata he'd had for lunch still lingered in his teeth.

All clear. He spritzed on some cologne as the doorbell rang again.

Wouldn't do to keep Molly waiting, but he wasn't running to the door for the woman, either. She was early—unusual for her.

Normally, she spent a shit-ton of time on her makeup, and right now, it wasn't quite six. But he'd told her he had a surprise for her and warned her that it was so sparkly that the bling might hurt her eyes. He patted the box in his pocket that held a diamond tennis bracelet and smiled in satisfaction. She'd been thrilled. Promised in that husky voice to be on time for a change, and to bring sunglasses.

She must be impatient.

He opened the door, already grinning, but it wasn't Molly on the front steps.

"Hi," said a sweet-looking blonde with a killer rack. "Are you Mike Garofalo?"

"Yeah, honey. That's me." His tone was cocky. Life was good. He had a hot date tonight and planned to score with the voluptuous Molly St. Clair. Now, he was faced with another gorgeous woman. "What can I do for you?"

"Can I come in for a second?" she asked. "A mutual friend said that I might be able to help you with something."

Hell, maybe she and Molly could *both* help him with something. "Sure thing, honey. Come in where it's warm."

She was taller than he'd realized, he noticed as he moved back to let her in. "Thanks," she said. Her voice was soft and low. Suggestive, he thought. "It's cold out there."

Boy, it was. Deliberately, he let his eyes drop to her cleavage, where her nipples poked at the thin cotton shirt underneath her open jacket.

As he did, he missed the hard look that came into her eyes. She pulled out a pistol, fitted with a silencer.

"What the hell?" He took a stumbling step back. "Who are you?"

The sweet-looking blonde didn't bother to answer. She just squeezed the trigger with calm, steady hands, firing off two rounds to his chest at near point-blank range. The last thing he heard was a high, thin squeal of terror—Molly had arrived.

The two shots that came next, he didn't hear at all.

21

W inter might smell better than Bull's last stakeout partner, but he didn't smell better than hers. Grimacing, she rolled down her window a bit to let in a stream of frigid air when he let out another smothered belch.

"Sorry," he said, not sounding very sorry. He thumped his fist on his chest. "Heartburn."

"Not a problem," Winter replied, her tone wry as she stared at the empty parking lot through the windshield. It was 6:52, and Winter's body thrummed with nervous tension. If something was going to happen, it would be soon.

Bull seemed unconcerned as he played Angry Birds on his phone, whooping or cursing with each advance or set back.

The gate on the fence rattled as it slid open. "Incoming," Winter muttered.

Bull shut the phone off and sat up straighter, half-turning in his seat to watch a vehicle come in. And just like that, he went from buffoon to experienced agent in the blink of the eye.

"Armored truck. Imagine seeing one of those around here."

The truck pulled around and backed up to one of the loading docks. They watched as two people got out and went in. They were uniformed and didn't look out of the ordinary. No alarms sounded. Still, they watched.

A few minutes later, one of them came back out, pulled something out of the truck before disappearing back into the building. The man didn't appear to be in a hurry.

"Looks like one of those old-fashioned metal lunchboxes," Bull noted. "You see how he was carrying it, by the handle at the top. Probably on a break."

Five minutes went by with no more activity. Bull picked his phone back up and went back to his virtual flinging of colorful, pissed off avians. Winter stayed alert, her senses humming with a warning she didn't quite understand.

"Someone's coming out," she said after another few minutes had gone by.

A tall figure in a navy uniform was headed their way, hands in the pockets of his jacket, shoulders huddled against the cold winter air. He moved at a normal pace and went to the passenger window.

Winter tensed, her hand going for her weapon just as pain seared across her eyes, exploding in her head.

"I'm going to roll down the window," Bull said, drawing his own weapon. His voice was tight with barely suppressed unease. "Just a little, though."

"Don't..." Winter ground out, her entire body gripped in pain, her vision turning red. "It's—"

He ignored her, rolling down his window a good four inches as the person came up to the side of the car. The bill of the man's cap shaded his face in the brightly lit parking lot.

"Can I help you?" Bull called out.

"No, I'm just dropping something off." It was a woman, and Winter felt something warm spray from her nose. The result of The Preacher's touch still cursing her life. Revealing itself at the worst possible time.

Through the haze of red and pain, Winter could do nothing but watch the woman push a small object through the gap in the window.

Before Winter could react, Bull was yelling. "What the fu—?"

A small silver canister came to rest in his lap, some kind of gas or vapor already pouring out of it. He tried to pick it up, but as Winter watched, his hands move slowly. Too slowly. Bull's head lolled forward, and his hands fell to his lap, fingers spasming.

Winter tried to hold her breath, fumbled for the door handle, but her eyes were burning, and her hands didn't want to move the way they were supposed to.

In what felt like only a moment in time, her chest grew tight. It spread, and she started to choke. Whatever it was worked fast. Her movements felt sluggish, and she tried to fight it.

But it was too late. With one gasp of air, she went under.

❄

WINTER BECAME aware of a beeping sound first. It was too quiet to be an alarm clock, but it was just as persistent. Then, her stomach roiled and cramped.

She rolled over to her side, feeling like she was about to throw up. Gravity was working overtime. Her body felt like it was made out of lead. She cracked her eyes open, breathing in slow and deep to calm her stomach. The nausea subsided, but her head ached as if she'd been hit with a sledgehammer.

She pushed against the floor, trying to get herself up, but her arms were too weak to support her. The light in the room was dim, but it still hurt her eyes as she fought against her weighted lids to get them open.

Finally, she made her way to her hands and knees, her hair hanging in a loose curtain around her face. Her braid had come undone. Everything smelled weird. Metallic, almost. Sinking back on her knees as strength started to seep back into her limbs, she looked around. She was in an office with cinderblock walls. There were no windows, either in the walls or the door.

Computer monitors sat on a desk against one wall. The screens were split, divided into sections, but her eyes wouldn't focus. She couldn't make out what was on them.

Memory came back in a trickle. She had been at the armored car depot. In the parking lot. The woman. The canister. Bull.

He was lying a few feet away, completely still. The gas had apparently not worn off for him yet.

Painfully, she crawled toward him. Her stomach lurched in time with the pounding in her head. She tried to call out. Her voice was scratchy sounding, wavering in a way that sounded weak to her own ears.

"Bull."

He was on his side, facing the metal door like he'd been dropped there, just inside the room.

She grabbed hold of his shoulder and pulled with as much strength as she could. He flopped, more than rolled, onto his back.

His face was waxy-looking, his eyes half-open.

"Bull," she whispered, feeling for a pulse. There was none.

The effects of the gas started to dissipate faster as adrenaline pumped through her body, but she was still weak as she lifted his chin back and desperately listened for any hint of air, her fingers still on his non-existent pulse.

"No…"

For the second time in less than a week, she did CPR. This time, though, she already knew it wouldn't be successful.

She tried. She kept going until her arms trembled like overcooked pasta, and she just physically couldn't do chest compressions anymore. She kept trying to breathe for him, but his lips were cold against hers.

Her throat tightened. It wasn't any good. She had no idea how long she'd been out. He may have stopped breathing ten minutes before. It could have been an hour.

What she did know for certain was that his skin was cold to the touch.

He was gone.

22

W inter shoved back her grief and guilt and crawled to the desk. Grabbing it, she struggled to her feet.

She was in a security office. The computer monitors showed split screens, divided into camera views. The depot was still, with no movement. There were bodies scattered around, like discarded dolls. On one screen, she saw the scene from her vision. A pile of uniformed employees.

But they might not be dead. *She* was alive.

She couldn't be the only survivor.

She tried the doorknob first, but it was locked.

There was a phone on the desk with an intercom, but the line was out. The display read "server offline," and it was the source of the beeping. Movement on one screen caught her attention. It was two of the armored truck employees, or at least two people wearing their uniforms. As she watched, they pulled cases from a cart and loaded them into the back of a waiting truck.

Unlike normal employees, they wore gas masks.

Her phone was gone, so she couldn't call anyone. Her weapon was gone.

Bull was gone.

And as she watched, the loaded truck pulled away. The suspects were gone too.

She wanted to scream in frustration and grief. Curl up on the floor and give in to the nagging effects of the gas. Hit rewind to back up to the point where she'd suggested she and Bull do the stakeout.

Instead, she swallowed back tears and started digging through the desk, looking for something to get her out of the security office. She found it in the form of a screwdriver.

With hands that shook, she used it to remove the screws on the plate that covered the door handle mechanism. It felt like the task took hours, but in moments, she'd removed the doorknob itself. By wedging the screwdriver in, she was able to unlock it.

Thankfully, the suspects had left the overhead door open, and the gas had dissipated.

The first security guard she reached was breathing, but still out. She went through his pockets and found a phone. She sank down on the ground next to the unconscious man and dialed 911 with fingers that still felt numb.

❄

"THAT'S SURELY ENOUGH, isn't it?"

They'd made the transfer of the money, leaving the armored truck in an empty industrial warehouse and loading the money they'd gotten into a waiting SUV. Now, Heidi drove them to a new, unknown safe house where they'd prepare for the last scene in her game.

Ryan hoped they'd be pulled over for a traffic ticket. Arrest, and even the thought of prison, would be better than this.

She glanced at him and gave him an odd smile.

"Where's your enthusiasm, O'Connelly? You're a thief. We've just gotten away with millions. You should be in your element right now."

It had been a rush. He could admit that. Everything had gone off without a hitch, but the nerve gas in the little silver canisters would have worn off by now, leaving a bunch of confused—but alive—security employees and two baffled federal agents. He'd discreetly checked a couple of guards before he'd left. They were alive, just knocked out cold.

Plus, he'd gotten one up on Heidi, though she didn't know it yet.

The bitch was going down.

"Yeah. The money is nice, and it was better this time, given that we didn't have to kill anyone to get it. But you can't just call it good and end it here? What more could you want, love? You can't top what you did tonight."

Heidi didn't answer for a moment. When she did, her voice was different. Friendlier, somehow. It sent a shiver of fear and revulsion down his back. "You're right. You've done well. We'll have to tally everything up, but the armored depot take was even better than I'd expected. If you want out, I'll let you go."

Ryan didn't believe her. He'd seen her sadistic nature too many times before. Instead, he felt the hair on the back of his neck prickle at her words. Whatever she had planned for the next robbery, it involved him.

Her motives, her background, her thoughts…Heidi Presley was still an enigma. He knew her well enough by now, though, to know she didn't just abandon plans. She stuck with them until the end.

If she was playing nice now, that didn't bode well for him. She wasn't going to let him go that easily.

❄

No way was he getting out of this so easily, Heidi thought as she took the last turn to the safe house. Correction...there was no way he was getting out of this at all.

Everything had gone so perfectly, even better than expected.

No, that wasn't true. The agent she'd been expecting hadn't been there, and Heidi was bitterly disappointed that she hadn't been able to meet the ambitious Sun Ming in person. But Sun's replacement had been interesting, especially the way her nose had started to bleed as she'd approached the stakeout car. It was as if Heidi's own omnipotence had affected the young agent from even yards away.

It had been fascinating. Eerie, but fascinating, and Heidi hoped to meet the dark-haired agent again. Maybe she would. Next time.

The nerve gas had been perfect. It had been such a rush being so close to the FBI agents. Better yet, taking them down. One permanently, though that hadn't been exactly in the plan.

Oh, well.

All that did was intensify the suspense, and Heidi had always done better under pressure. She had no reason to believe this would prove to be any different.

Her only regret was needing to leave before Agent Black was awake. Heidi had very much wanted to talk to the agent, get to know her a bit better.

Maybe she'd still get that chance.

But now...first things first.

"Grab the bags," she ordered Ryan as she turned off the engine to the SUV.

His jaw tightened, but only for a moment before he turned his bright smile on her. "Sure thing."

While he did as he was told, Heidi opened the door to the

safe house, stepping back for Ryan to get everything inside. It took three trips, but she was patient.

She'd always been filled with patience. It was one of her greatest virtues.

"I think that's all," Ryan said as he dropped the last bag onto the pile.

Heidi slipped on the gas mask, enjoyed the surprised look on his handsome face as he turned to face her.

This was going to be fun.

23

Winter was released from the hospital and back in Richmond by the following afternoon.

She didn't want to go into the office. She was afraid to face her co-workers. Miguel, Brian, Bree...all people who, like Bull, she knew. But she didn't really know them. Would they look at her with pity? Accusation? She had no way to judge. No reference point, because she'd gone out of her way to keep from building any relationships.

With the exception of Noah, she hadn't tried to connect with anyone. That was on purpose. She was in the FBI for a reason, and making connections wasn't it. Connections could just get you hurt.

The only reason she had Noah for a friend was that he wouldn't have it any other way. His nice-guy act was a cover for a mulish, stubborn man. His good nature was a force to be reckoned with, chipping away at the walls she'd put up.

As far as the rest of the office went, she wouldn't be making any new friends now. Winter Black, still basically a newbie to the unit, was the reason that Bull was dead.

When she'd spoken to Max on the phone from the hospital, he'd been stricken. He'd known Bull for a long time. They'd started their jobs within a couple of weeks of each other. He hadn't sounded like he blamed her, though. His raspy voice had been filled with concern, and he'd asked if she wanted him to contact anyone for her.

She hadn't wanted to scare her grandparents. They were old, and her Grandpa Jack hadn't been in the best health since a rough flu bug had knocked him back a few months before.

She thought about Aiden. But he was at home in his chair, drinking whiskey and probably cursing his bad leg. Another mark in her responsibility column.

Noah was with Sun. They'd have been summoned back to HQ, she was sure. But she wasn't about to take anyone away from the case now.

In the end, she'd just signed herself out of the hospital and flown back on her own, despite the doctor's insistence that she stay until they could be sure there were no aftereffects from the unknown gas.

The office was quiet when she went in. She could hear keyboards clacking. There was no chatter, though. No talk about sports. No case discussions held over cubicle walls. There was a pall over the office that was palpable.

Max must have been waiting for her. He opened his office door before she could get to her own cubicle. "Agent Black," he called out in a low voice. "Come on in here."

She stiffened. Braced for what, she didn't know.

But the awkward hug she received from the SAC took her off guard. She almost lost it then.

"You can take some time," he offered, letting her go. His eyes were red-rimmed and bloodshot, as if he hadn't slept at all the night before.

She shook her head and cleared her throat. "No thank you, sir. I want to catch them."

He nodded, as if expecting that. "Noah and Sun are back. They're in the small conference room."

"Listen," she began, her voice sounding like a hand was wrapped around her throat. "I'm sorry—"

"No." In an instant, blustery Max was back. His face reddened. "Don't even fucking say that. I know where the blame lies, and it's not with you," he barked. "Now, get back to work."

She left his office, feeling a little bit better.

"Winter."

Noah shot to his feet and crossed the room in three quick strides as soon as she entered. He wrapped his arms around her and hugged her so tight that her face was pressed into his shirt. He smelled like peppermint and fabric softener. She relaxed a little bit into his embrace. He didn't say anything. He didn't have to. He just comforted her.

❄

SUN COULDN'T STAND IT.

She'd been wrong. She was so convinced that the next hit would go down in California, at the site of the original robbery. There had been no reason to think it wouldn't. It fit the pattern.

Instead, she ended up looking like an ass, flying across the country in the opposite direction of where all the action would go down.

Leaving Winter to get it right.

And now, Winter was being heralded as some kind of hero and victim, all at the same time. Noah, so big and hot, hadn't given Sun a second glance when she'd thrown some pretty heavy hints in his direction over dinner the night before. But he'd jumped up like a trained spaniel as soon as the damn rookie had come into the room. She'd looked all pale and wan and fragile, like the tragic heroine in a novel.

Milking it, Sun decided in disgust.

Now, he was cradling her in his arms like she would break.

Until Sun cleared her throat. The noise was loud in the silent room. "That's enough." Her voice was cold. "We have work to do."

Noah shot her a loaded look, but she refused to cower, staring him down. They still had a case to solve. He let Winter go.

She waited until Noah and Winter were seated to begin.

"The armored truck was found this morning at a warehouse two miles from the depot. It had been emptied. A double homicide reported two hours before the robbery turned out to be the depot manager and a woman named Molly St. Claire. His girlfriend, according to neighbors. No witnesses. At the depot, we lost one of ours," she looked toward Winter, who visibly flinched, "and two guards were unable to be revived at the scene."

She knew she was coming off as unfeeling, and she *did* regret Bull's death, but she was more frustrated by her own lack of foresight. She'd been chosen to catch these suspects. So far, she was doing a shit job. Winter was only doing marginally better, but she was still coming out smelling like roses. Sun's competitive streak wouldn't—couldn't—let that slide.

"The depot robbery wasn't a total bust," Sun added, making an attempt to shake off her black mood. "NYPD managed to lift a full fingerprint off one of the gas canisters. It was not a match for Ryan O'Connelly."

Noah's eyes went sharp. "Whose was it?"

"A woman named Heidi Presley." She looked down at her laptop, drawing out the suspense on purpose. "I believe she's suspect number two. She's an IT employee and works remotely from a location in northern Michigan. No criminal priors. She's apparently single, lives alone in the house she grew up in. She inherited it after her mother's death in a local assisted living facility a year and a half ago. Father is deceased. Died of cancer in the early nineties."

Noah leaned forward. "She sounds low-key. How do we have her on file?"

"Government contract work. About a decade ago, she was put through a full security clearance. She didn't raise any red flags then, but it put her in the system." Again, she glanced up at Winter. "I've spoken with Aiden Parrish this morning. He's in agreement that she could fit the profile, but we need to know more about her. We've got a search warrant for her house. You two leave tonight."

She was being petty. She didn't care.

Winter didn't react, just sat there like a lump.

Milking it.

Noah's eyes narrowed. "Is that wise at this point? Wouldn't it make sense to just do this remotely? Or have the locals search her place? If the suspects stick to the pattern, they'll be hitting again in less than forty-eight hours."

"Case agent," she reminded him, pointing at herself. "My decision."

Sure, she'd be down two team members out of the three they were left with at this point, but she didn't need them. This was her last chance to break the case on her own. She had time. She'd gotten another email, this one giving her a date. They'd extended the deadline, giving her three days this time until the final act.

"I've got a tech team split between working on the emails

and digging into Heidi Presley's background. I'll hold things down here and figure out where the next hit will be. You two are going to Michigan."

The only person you could really count on was yourself, anyway.

24

They pulled up in front of a large, burgundy house. The early morning sunshine was just cresting the top of the roof, glimmering over the tall, Victorian peaks.

"Nice place," Noah murmured. "If you like horror movies."

The place was empty, no lights showing from any of the windows on any of the three floors.

Snow lay thick on the ground, and the front walk hadn't been shoveled. The mailbox had been removed, indicating the owner didn't plan on coming back right away.

Noah glanced at Winter. She'd been quiet on the flight, sleeping most of the time. She'd also been tight-lipped on the drive from the Traverse City Airport, once their plane landed in Michigan. Of course, he'd been quiet too, trying to navigate the rental through what felt like a blizzard. They'd gone their separate ways at the hotel.

Noah was still pissed off at the way Sun had acted. She was in full-on bitch mode, not focusing on anything but moving the case forward. Which was fine. But she'd showed no feeling at all and had treated Bull's death with complete dismissal. Then, she'd pulled Winter aside and said something to her before they left. Winter refused to talk about it, but whatever it was had left her face chalky white.

He'd find out.

"Let's get in there and see what we can find out about Heidi," he said. "Hopefully she's written out a convenient manifesto."

Winter didn't respond, just stared toward the darkened house.

"First, though," Noah began, "you need to snap out of it."

This was going to be painful, but it had to be done. He left the car running, the air vents blasting to combat the fifteen-degree temperature outside. She looked at him, surprised by his harsh tone.

"You're kicking your own ass here over Bull, and you've let Sun get to you. All your bad guys are winning right now."

"That's not true," she countered, stirring in her seat a little. "I'm fine. You're the one wasting time right now."

"You're a shell." Noah's words were blunt. "You're not going to do anyone any good like this. What did Sun say to you before we left?"

Her eyes seemed to darken a shade. "Nothing that wasn't true."

"Out with it."

Without emotion, she stared out at the snow. At first, he thought she wouldn't answer, but she finally sighed, exhaling a long breath. "She told me that this was what came of a rookie trying to get on the fast-track. Letting ambition blind me, insisting I knew better than more experienced agents, and putting my co-workers in the line of fire. That it wasn't the first time and it wouldn't be the last."

"And you bought that?" He snorted. "Why'd you believe that load of crap was true, and not that you were the office slut?"

"Because this time, what she said *is* true!"

She finally got some color in her cheeks, even if it was the angry kind. He was just glad to get a reaction. She'd been eerily quiet.

"How can you say I didn't get Bull killed? It was my idea to do the stakeout. It was my idea to focus on the Brooklyn facility. If I'd been wrong, we'd still be in the same position. A robbery committed, prints on the canisters...but Bull wouldn't be dead. Technically, I was right. I guessed the location correctly. But my actions after that didn't change anything, except for the worse."

"Sun is jealous. You know that, right?"

It was Winter's turn to snort. "Why would she be? You all do nothing but sing her praises. She's smart, focused, intense...exactly what an agent should be like."

"She's missing the compassion," he pointed out, still trying to be reasonable.

"Compassion doesn't catch killers."

It was time to change tactics, and this one would be a doozy. He went with it anyway. "Look, you're being self-indulgent right now," he barked, raising his voice at her for the first time. "Stop."

Her face went crimson. "I'm—"

"It's true." He was treading in dangerous waters. "Bull is gone. It wasn't your fault. You didn't gas him. Did you somehow know that the suspects planned on using some kind of weapons-grade nerve gas?"

He'd gotten an email full of preliminary reports and read it on the plane. He knew she hadn't known that.

She shook her head in the negative, mute, though her interest was finally engaged.

"That's right. One of the suspects managed to score a chemical weapon. They're still working on finding out how. You can't just pick up that stuff at Walmart, you know. And tell me, you spent time with Bull. Would you say he was in good physical health?"

"He was strong—"

"His heart wasn't," Noah interrupted. "What'd he eat when you guys had your meals?"

"Nachos." She laughed a little. It sounded more like a sob. "I think. He ate them so fast, it was hard to tell."

"The initial autopsy showed he had a couple of almost complete arterial blockages. His heart was already working overtime, which could have been why the gas proved fatal for him. The other two people who died in the attack were also out of shape. According to their medical records, one had diabetes. The other was carrying an extra hundred pounds. They were susceptible."

He let that sink in for a second before he drove the point home.

"You're letting the people who did get away with it *win* by wallowing around in your own self-pity. We have clues. We have leads. We just need to follow them. The FBI, the NYPD, they're all throwing everything they have at this right now. We have people digging into Presley and O'Connelly's backgrounds. Their digital histories. They're tracking the encrypted emails, the phone records of the manager who was murdered. Now, we need to do our part."

He indicated the creepy old house.

"We might find information in there that will help us figure out where the next, and according to Sun, last hit will take place. Get your shit together now, or I'll go in there and do it myself."

Winter stared him down, frustrated. Finally, the tension on her face eased.

"Thanks." With that, she got out of the car.

Noah breathed a sigh of relief and shut off the engine, following her through the snow. He hadn't been sure he could pull that off. In her way, Winter could be just as scary as Sun.

※

NOAH WAS RIGHT. She had to get her shit together. Grab on to her anger and channel it into something productive.

The floorboards creaked on the front porch as Winter climbed the steps, stomping loose snow off her boots. Winter was thankful she'd been with it enough to grab them in her dull attempt to pack the day before.

She grabbed hold of the doorknob, icy beneath her hand. It was locked.

"I'll take care of it," Noah offered, search warrant stuffed securely in his pocket. One solid kick sent the door swinging inward with a crash.

"Be careful," she warned, though she didn't sense any immediate danger. "Heidi likes booby traps. She's probably not expecting that we'll have found her place, but you never know."

They stepped through the front door, Winter's senses on full alert. The kitchen area was tidy, the table clean. There were no dirty dishes in the sink. No sign anyone had cooked in the farmhouse-style kitchen for a while. She opened one of the cupboards. Empty of food.

To the right, a short set of stairs led down to a sunken living room that looked to be an addition or a remodel of an existing structure. There was a TV, a couch, and a couple of end tables. The furniture was old but clean.

To the left, a doorway led to a formal dining area with china cabinets. The dishes were antique. Not great quality, but not junk, either. A formal parlor was on the other side of that, with bookshelves and higher-quality furniture. Everything in the house seemed to be a testament to someone's preference for scrupulous cleanliness and order.

That fit with Aiden's profile of Heidi.

A finished jigsaw puzzle sat on a card table. The slight coating of dust on the picture of two cats in Santa Claus hats made her think that no one had started a new puzzle in a long time. Or that the clean freak who kept the place so spotless hadn't been home in a while to do chores.

"Interesting reading material," Noah commented from across the room, studying the books on the shelves. "True crime, mostly. Circumstantial, but it establishes an interest, anyway."

A bathroom and a staircase sat at the other end of the room.

"Shall we go up?" he asked.

The heat in the house hovered at a low temperature, just warm enough to keep the pipes from freezing. Upstairs, it got colder.

There were three good-sized bedrooms. One was used for storage, with neatly packed bins of what looked like clothes and more books. Another, the master bedroom, looked like it was unused.

A high bed was covered with a crocheted throw, lightly yellowed with age. The dark headboard matched the end tables and the dresser, with the mirror mounted above. Antiques. Maybe family heirlooms.

There was a wedding photo on the dresser. A small, blonde woman and a tall, dark-haired man were dressed in what passed for wedding finery in the seventies. The woman wore a hesitant smile. The man, older than his bride, scowled. Deep lines in his cheeks indicated that it was a normal expression for him.

The room smelled like mothballs. A look in the dresser drawers showed the source. Men and women's clothes were folded and tucked inside, looking ready to wear. It was creepy, since the owners of the clothing were dead.

In the hallway, a quick look through another doorway showed a bathroom. Old-fashioned pansy wallpaper surrounded an antique, claw-footed bathtub, and the toilet was one of the impossibly old ones with a water tank perched on pipes three-quarters of the way up the wall. A chain hung down, presumably for flushing.

The doorway at the end of the hall stood open too. This was Heidi's place, Winter knew instinctively. They had to step down into the room. It had been built at a different level as the rest of the upstairs. The roofline was a sharp slope on both sides, and the floors were creaky, dark wood. There was a simple brass bedstead, and the twin mattress was covered with a neat patchwork quilt. There was nothing else in the room, not even a rug beside the bed.

No pictures. No mementos. No stray books. Things you would find in a normal person's house.

"Spartan accommodations." Noah's voice echoed in the silent upstairs. "Maybe Heidi is a Stoic. Should we check the basement? Attic?"

"I feel like she'd have some kind of office or something," Winter said, her words sounding loud in the empty room. "A computer somewhere. She works from home."

"Attic, it is," Noah replied.

The narrow staircase extended another flight up. In front of her, she watched Noah try to angle his big feet on the narrow stair treads just to climb it.

This was where Heidi's bat cave was located.

The room ran the length of the house and was even colder than the previous two floors. However, there were space heaters that probably kept the temperature tolerable when the room was in use. Cheap throw rugs were scattered here and there in an attempt to try and hold in some of the heat. Three dormer windows looked out over the snowy street below. One had a desk tucked into its alcove.

The desk was empty, except for a mouse and a keyboard. Noah moved to start checking the drawers while Winter studied the area. It was too clean. Heidi had to have a hiding place.

She found it at the far end of the room.

A red light shone weakly through the spaces between the old, scarred pine floors. "You have anything over there?" Winter asked Noah, who was still working on the desk. Knowing he wouldn't, but she wanted to keep up appearances.

He closed the last drawer. "Nothing but office supplies. What have you got?"

"Stash spot." She indicated a small hole in the floor. "That could be a missing knot from a pine board, but I think it's how she opens it."

Noah crouched down, fitted his finger into the opening. He pulled up, and after a small jerk, a small section of the floor came up too.

Winter tensed, sudden unease flooding her system as he made an approving noise.

"Good catch. There's a burner phone and a laptop."

A second later, Winter noticed a broken strand of wire hanging from one side of the section of floor he'd pulled up.

"Grab them fast," she said, sudden urgency pounding at her. "I think it's rigged."

His eyes flew to hers for a second before he grabbed the laptop and shoved the phone in his pocket. "What—"

"Let's go. Now."

They'd made it down two flights and as far as the parlor, when a blast seemed to rock the foundation of the big house. Her ears rang from the shock of the explosion, throwing off her equilibrium.

Noah grabbed her arm with his free hand and pulled hard. His mouth was moving, but she couldn't hear his words over the shrilling in her head. Smoke detectors went off, shrieking on the second floor. Those, she could hear.

By the time they stumbled out the still-open front door, neighbors had come out of their houses to see what was going on. The entire top of the house was in flames, and fire raged, probably helped along by some kind of accelerant.

The ringing in her ears subsided to a loud, continuous hum that left them feeling numb.

"Good job," she saw Noah say more than she heard. His words were muffled, and she could barely make them out. "You saved our asses again."

25

Ryan regained consciousness in fits and starts. His brain felt fuzzy and confused. His head throbbed. When he tried to lift a hand to his aching forehead, he was only able to raise it a short distance before it was yanked back.

Opening his eyes, he blinked a few times. He was in a windowless room, the walls white-painted cinderblocks. Bright light reflected off of them, and he squinted against it, turning his head at an awkward angle to identify the source of the light. A work lamp, one of the super-bright halogens contractors used at construction sites, beamed hot beside the bed he was on. It was probably there to function as heat for the dank room, as well as light.

He moved his hands again, pulling upward. Again, he only had less than twelve inches of mobility. Bracelets bit into his wrists as he pulled harder. Metal clanked on metal. He was handcuffed to a bed frame.

He had a vague memory of a movie with Kathy Bates in it. She'd been a psychopath, obsessed with Steven King. No, the movie was based on a book *by* Steven King.

The mist in his brain cleared a little, and he raised his head. His feet, luckily, weren't tethered to the other end of the bed. Both of them appeared to be intact.

Understanding rushed over him in a sickening wave. Heidi was his psychopath.

As if the thought had conjured her, a metal door on the other side of the room screeched open on rusty-sounding hinges. She slipped through the gap, studied him with dispassion.

"Good. I didn't kill you."

"Did you try?" His voice was little more than a rusty croak, and he realized how thirsty he was.

"No. Not yet."

She had a glass in her hand, he saw. If he hadn't had such a bad case of cottonmouth, he would have drooled. She set it on a small table next to his bed. He was so thirsty, he thought he could smell it. She pulled a metal folding chair from one corner closer to him and sat down, studying him like he was a bug on a dissection board.

Had she been watching him off and on since he'd been out? The thought made his skin creep.

"Care to let me know what's going on, love?" He tried for a light tone. Failed.

"Nothing. Yet." She continued to watch him. Her eyes, a pale, almost colorless blue today, were cold. "I'm afraid I lied to you about cutting you loose," she told him in a matter-of-fact way. As if he hadn't already guessed. "We do still have to finish the last act. I couldn't do it without you. You're going to be the star of the show."

His chest tightened. He'd never felt the kind of fear he was experiencing right now, but something told him it was just the beginning. It would get worse.

"I figured as much." He rattled the handcuff at his wrist. "Is that water for me, love? I'm a bit thirsty after my nap."

"It is for you. But you can't have it yet."

He tried to remember what had happened after they'd arrived back at Heidi's safe house in Vermont, but there was a blank where his memory should be. Maybe they weren't even *in* Vermont. He couldn't remember shit.

No. That wasn't true. As his memory cleared a bit, he remembered bringing in the bags. Remembered turning around to find her wearing a damn gas mask.

Then…nothing.

He licked his lips again. Damn, he was thirsty.

He had to stop obsessing over his thirst and focus.

He licked his dry lips with his equally dry tongue. "Are we just going to chat then?"

"Yeah. I think I'd like that." Heidi gave him a small, tight smile and leaned back in the chair. She was dressed in casual clothes. Jeans, tennis shoes, and a Michigan State sweatshirt. Her hair was straight and blonde. Her eyes were that faded-looking blue. Maybe he was seeing her actual appearance for a change? Real-life Heidi?

That, also, didn't bode well for his life expectancy.

"We could kill some time," he replied. Poor choice of words, he thought, smothering a wince. "What do you want to talk about? Politics? Movies? Pop culture?"

"I told you a little bit about my life story," she mused. "I could tell you some more."

"If you want."

Ryan didn't want. It would be too much like the mono-logue a villain always gave before he tried to kill the hero.

Not that he was any kind of hero, he thought to himself in disgust.

"My dad molested me from the time I was seven."

He winced for real this time. This definitely had all of the earmarks of a confession and villain backstory scene.

"I'm sorry to hear that," he said, knowing the words were

inadequate. Maybe that's why she was so bloody crazy. He knew a bit about grabby hands messing with you when you were too little to stop them.

"My mom knew about it, but she didn't care enough to stop him," Heidi went on. "I killed him when I was twelve." She delivered that pronouncement like it was of no more importance than a football score.

"Did you now? It sounds like he deserved it."

"He did. And I got away with the murder, I might add. Put rat poison in his food and watched him die a slow, lingering death. I thought sure they'd find the cause of death in his autopsy and throw my mom in prison, but it turned out he had cancer too. He'd have croaked in a couple of months anyway."

"That's lovely. Very fitting."

Tone down the sarcasm, Ryan, he told himself. He didn't want to piss off a psychopath who had him chained to a bed. She was going to kill him, but he wasn't dead yet, and hope sprang eternal. He didn't need to goad her into deciding to end his existence now while he lay there like a trussed-up turkey.

"It *was* lovely." She smiled a little wider, reminiscing. "I did my research at the library. In actual books, of course. Things on the internet don't stay private." She gave him a significant look.

"Right," was the only thing he could think to say in response.

"Did you know that rat poison contains the kind of blood thinner used in stroke and heart attack patients? It causes all kinds of things when given in the right dose. Say, in your father's morning oatmeal. Nosebleeds, bleeding gums, blood in your pee."

"Fun stuff."

"I thought about having my mom implicated in the crime

anyway, but she was so weak. She wouldn't have lasted in prison. I got around to her later."

She confessed to matricide in the same tone anyone else would use to announce they were going to the grocery store to buy hot dog buns. The disassociation was chilling to hear.

"I could have just let her go, but she wouldn't die fast enough. She was in assisted living," Heidi explained. "Had a stroke and lingered for years. I finally pulled the plug on her for the insurance money, just so I could get this plan moving. She could have lasted another five years, and I wasn't prepared to wait."

"So, you've been working at this for a while, then?"

"Years. At least six. No one else has put as much time as I have into a project like this," she added proudly. "I knew it would work from the beginning."

"So far, so good, I guess," Ryan replied. "Congratulations."

Good for Heidi, anyway. For him? Not so much.

"I watched all sorts of crime shows. *Dateline*. Old episodes of *Unsolved Mysteries*. Documentaries. I researched crimes with the same methods I'd searched out information on rat poison. What the librarians must've thought about me. I read hundreds of books. Did research. Picked several different potential crimes and then ran scenarios on how I'd do them. Even the crimes where the masterminds got away," she gave a disgusted snort, "most of them still made idiotic mistakes and got nailed for them later on. I'm smarter than that."

"You've certainly managed to outsmart me."

And they'd moved on to the revealing of her master plan phase. He was doomed.

She waved a hand, dismissing his backward compliment. "That's simple. You're easy to manipulate. All I had to do was appeal to your pride. Once I hooked you, keeping you on the line wasn't a problem. You're essentially self-centered and respond well to threats to your own well-being."

It took everything inside him to keep his face carefully blank and not try to work up a wad of saliva to spit in her face. He had never felt so impotent in his life.

Heidi yawned, a big, exaggerated opening of her mouth. "I was surprised to find out that threats against other people were an even better motivator. Ionie was pure inspiration on my part. I never actually went to Jamaica and couldn't have cared less if you were fucking some local bimbo there. But I checked your emails, and your exotic lover has been trying to reach you, begging you to come back, and declaring her love. You'll be happy to know she's not a target."

That did relieve his mind, but not much. Heidi's word couldn't be trusted, as he well knew.

Ionie was a sweet woman, and he didn't want anything to happen to her. As long as Heidi knew her name and even her general location, she wouldn't be safe. God help them if she discovered Ionie had a child. Something told him that this insane woman wouldn't balk at murdering children.

"That's nice of you. Ionie was just a vacation distraction," he lied. "It's too bad she had a stronger attachment than I did. She doesn't deserve to die for it."

It was a nice try. But if the story wasn't about Heidi, Heidi wasn't listening.

"I can't wait for you to see the last part of my plan. Would you like some water now?"

"Sure." That was an understatement. Whatever she'd given to him had the aftereffect of making his tongue shrivel up like an old sponge.

Heidi's hands were almost gentle as she held his head up and moved the cup to his lips. He drank fast, afraid she'd take it away. Even though it tasted like straight sulphur from a bad well, he gulped it down so that water trickled down his chin.

"Good boy," she murmured as he finished off the glass. "Time for your nap now, *love*."

"It was drugged, wasn't it?" It didn't surprise him. He would have drunk hellbroth from the Devil himself to quench that awful thirst.

"It was drugged," she confirmed, looking into the glass. "I hope you don't mind, but I have a lot of work to do, and I don't want you whining or banging around in here and distracting me."

Maybe it was just his imagination, but his limbs already felt heavy. His head felt woozy.

He could get lucky. She could overdose him by accident, and he'd mess up her final scene.

"Sleep well, and I'll see you later."

She went to the door, pulling it open. Beyond her was darkness. He assumed he was in a basement, but it could be a bomb shelter in Winnipeg, Canada, for all he knew. After she walked out, he realized he had to take a piss.

Drifting off, though, it didn't seem to matter that much. He'd rather wet himself in his sleep like a toddler than ask her to help him use the bathroom.

❄

HEIDI CLIMBED the short staircase that led to the main floor and locked the door behind her. The key went in her pocket.

She was pleased.

With few exceptions, everything had gone exactly the way she'd wanted it to. Three jobs down, and only the final—and probably the easiest and most satisfying—left to go.

Ryan would be surprised, of course. She'd thought about letting him off the hook, but that was before he'd tried to seduce her and go through her things. She'd softened toward him, but he had shown her the mistake in that. With that one mistake, he'd signed his own death warrant.

She didn't forgive easily. As a matter of fact, she didn't forgive at all.

In fact, she was planning on tracking down Ionie afterward and killing her, just for fun. Jamaica could be just one stop on her victory tour after this last phase was complete. Ryan's weak attempts at diversion had been pathetic. He'd be beyond caring if his woman was dead, but she'd have the satisfaction of revenge to look forward to.

Jamaica wasn't a bad idea. She wouldn't be going back to Saint Ignace, that was for sure. The house there could rot like her parents for all she cared. Maybe, eventually, the FBI would identify her despite her precautions. Maybe they'd find the house. It wouldn't matter. Let them waste their time. It wouldn't affect her in the slightest.

Thinking about the house, she grabbed a can of Pepsi out of the refrigerator of the rental she'd booked for this last, most epic event.

The chance of the FBI agent she'd picked identifying her was slim. Even if Sun Ming *was* the best FBI agent since J. Edgar Hoover, according to her own overinflated bio.

Heidi's disguises were perfect. She'd covered all of her tracks. No one would be able to hack her emails with all the walls she'd put into place. Not within the short timeline she'd given them, anyway.

But if, by chance, Special Agent Ming had managed to find out who she was, she'd probably found the house that Heidi had made no effort to hide. And if she'd found the house *and* the hiding place under the floorboards, she was already dead.

That would be a little disappointing. She'd planned a front row seat for Sun during the final festivities.

She opened her laptop and went to the program that ran her security cameras.

They were blank.

She was surprised, but not put out about it.

Her cameras were all rigged to a backup generator, in case of a winter storm or a power outage. The only way the screens should be blank was if the trap had blown. Interesting.

She skimmed through the different camera files until she found the one that showed the driveway view and skimmed back through the footage. She wished she had some popcorn to go with her soda. Watching this would be better than anything cable TV had to offer.

She found the moment a car pulled up in the driveway. A white SUV with two people inside. They sat talking for a while and then got out, slogging through the snow to the front porch. They looked like law enforcement, but neither one was a petite Asian American woman.

Sun had sent her minions. Even better.

Heidi got a good look at both their faces. The man was tall and broad, built like a football player. She disliked him on sight. He was good-looking, like Ryan, and moved in a confident way that said he knew it. The woman was more interesting, and Heidi recognized her right away. Winter Black. She had a way of looking at things that made you think she saw everything. She was intense.

Heidi related to intensity. Was drawn to it.

It was like watching the buildup to a movie that you knew the ending to but still liked. She switched cameras as they moved through the house, tracking their movements until they got to the attic floor. She'd set the camera up there just above where she kept her things, so she'd be able to get a good last look at anyone who was smart enough to find where she'd hidden them.

To her fascination, the male agent started poking around the obvious places. The female agent, though, just looked around the room. As if she had x-ray vision or something, her eyes locked on the floor, and she walked directly to the right spot. The room wasn't wired for sound, so she couldn't hear what they were saying to each other, and she regretted that oversight.

Heidi almost clapped her hands in excitement when the cocky guy was the one to crouch down and remove the lid. She could no longer see him since he was below the view of the camera, but she still had a good view of the other agent. She wondered how much of their deaths she'd see before the blast destroyed the camera. A few seconds, maybe? It would be worth it.

And then, as if she'd known about the trip wire, the female's face changed. Her mouth moved, and the two ran for the exit. The room was empty, and less than fifteen seconds later, there was a bright flash of light, and the camera went dark.

Surprised, Heidi switched to the upstairs hallway view.

The agents were disappearing down the stairs.

Main floor. They got almost all the way through the parlor before the explosion happened. She couldn't believe it. She should have given the detonator a shorter timer, but then again, no one should have been able to tell that a trip wire had been triggered.

Heidi switched again to the outside shot. The big guy had his arm around the woman, who was dialing a number on her phone. He had Heidi's laptop under his other arm, and he was grinning like an idiot that hadn't realized how close he'd just come to being blown to pieces.

Let him think he'd gotten away with a prize, Heidi thought, unconcerned. The second the idiot tried to log on, he would erase the entire hard drive in the process.

The woman, though, was staring up at the house, her face intent. Agent Black. She remembered her from the armored depot takedown.

As Heidi studied the agent's pale face, she shivered…in dread and anticipation. This must be the agent who'd located her childhood home, Heidi thought with a certainty she couldn't explain.

Sitting back in her chair, Heidi was starting to think she'd chosen the wrong FBI agent.

She hated to be wrong.

26

"On the one hand, it's good we came here ourselves," Noah said. "Otherwise, we might have more bodies to add to the count. Not everyone's as fortunate as I am to have a built-in bomb detector for a partner. On the other hand, I wish Heidi Presley lived in a more metropolitan area. The next flight to New York doesn't leave for another five hours. Traverse City doesn't exactly have a bustling airport."

"No problem," Winter replied. "That'll give us a chance to go to Heidi's mom's assisted living complex before we have to make the drive back down to the airport. Might as well get as complete a picture as we can."

Shady Oaks was a small facility on the edge of the small town, tidy and well-kept. Inside, it didn't carry the odor of depression and urine, like a lot of places that catered to older adults. The lobby was neat and attractive, with small seating areas and vases of fresh flowers.

A pretty receptionist in her mid-twenties smiled up at them from behind the counter. "Can I help you folks?"

Noah turned on his mega-watt smile. "Maybe," he said.

"You don't look old enough to have worked here long enough, though."

She giggled, focusing all her attention on charismatic Noah. Winter had seen the power of that smile in action dozens of times, and it never failed to amaze her how effective it continued to be. "I've been here four years now," she offered.

"Oh, wow. I stand corrected. Maybe you can help me. Do you remember a woman who was a resident here? Her name was Monica Presley? Oh, and it's okay to tell us," he added, showing her his badge. "We're with the FBI. We're looking for any information on Monica's daughter, Heidi."

The receptionist, Katie, according to her nametag, furrowed her brow in thought. "It rings a bell. I remember Monica, but not her daughter. Let me ask around and see if any of the nurses remember her."

Within moments, one nurse came around to corner them at the desk.

"Is this the kind of turnaround time the FBI has? Over a year?" she demanded. The woman was short and generously rounded, with tightly permed brown hair. She looked like she was in her late forties or early fifties. "It's about time you answered my calls."

"Your calls?" Winter asked. "When was this? And what about?"

"Well over a year ago! Almost a year and a half," she replied indignantly. "About that poor Monica."

"Monica Presley? What about her?" Winter blinked, trying to keep up with this unexpected development. Stopping at the nursing home had been more of a time killer than anything. She hadn't expected one of the nurses to have already contacted a field office.

The woman's face was still tight with anger. "We're supposed to report any elder abuse or anything to do with patient disability rights, and no one would listen to me. Neither the Saint Ignace police department or the state cops. As a matter of fact, Dennis Hodgson, the administrator here, threatened to fire me if I didn't let the issue go." She sneered. "He's good buddies with the police chief. Probably didn't want any scandal and covered the whole thing up."

"What kind of abuse?" Noah asked.

"Neglect. And I'd call murder a kind of abuse, wouldn't you? Monica Presley, that poor woman, wasn't dying. She'd had a stroke, yes, but you could just tell that daughter was itching to knock her off, tired of waiting around for some money that might never come."

"Money?" Winter asked the question. This might solve the question of why money from the first robbery was donated to the church in California.

"Yep," said the woman. She lowered her voice. "I don't want to get in trouble for violating any HIPAA laws by telling you this, but hell, I guess if you can't tell the feds, you can't tell anyone."

She gave a hard look at the receptionist, who raised her hands in an innocent *I'm not going to say anything* gesture.

"Monica Presley had a life insurance policy on her worth millions."

Winter glanced at Noah. They were both thinking the same thing. An IT contractor didn't get paid enough to have access to the kind of resources it would take to travel all over, bribing people, buying weapons-grade knockout gas, sourcing materials off the dark web.

"Did Heidi visit her mother a lot?" Noah asked. "What did she act like when you saw her?"

"Cold," said the nurse. "She came in like clockwork, twice a week. But she'd just sit by her momma's bed, tapping on that laptop of hers she always carried with her. Monica was bad off, but she could still hear. Most patients in her condition can respond, if not verbally, at least with hand gestures or facial expressions. That daughter of hers didn't even try to engage with her. She'd just sit there next to the bed. She could have been at a coffee shop for all the attention she paid her mom."

"What about the day Monica died?" Winter asked. "Did Heidi visit that day?"

"She sure did. That poor lady passed on not a half-hour after she left. I don't know how she did it, but Monica's daughter killed her. I'm certain of it. She never even came back to pick up her momma's belongings after. There wasn't even a service. Just a cremation." The nurse's eyes filled with tears, and she blinked rapidly to keep them at bay. "I always go to my patient's services if they pass on my watch. Monica's was the only one I ever missed."

A man walked in then, wearing a suit and an official-looking expression that marked him as administration. Dennis Hodgson. The nurse clammed up, and the receptionist ducked her head.

"Linda," he said, his voice flat with an extra-nasal Midwest tone. "We need you in room twelve."

"Yes, sir." The nurse ducked her head deferentially and gave Noah and Winter a pleading look behind her boss's back as she headed back to work.

"Can I help you?" the man asked. He smiled, but it felt forced to Winter. She already knew what he was thinking. He didn't want them in his facility, asking questions. What would it look like to their visitors? Which meant that they'd already gotten all the information here that they were going to get.

Noah was clearly thinking on the same track. He shook his head and smiled at the man. "No, thank you. We were looking for a patient who was said to be at this facility, but I'm afraid we have the wrong location."

They headed out to the car.

"Want to look into Administrator Hodges?" Noah asked. "I gotta say, I didn't care for the guy on sight. Plus, a cover-up like that is super illegal."

Winter shook her head. "I don't think we'll find anything to tie him to Heidi. There's a chance that he's aware that Heidi killed her mother, but I think he was just a run-of-the-mill jerk. Heidi doesn't leave witnesses. If he'd received a payoff from her in exchange for not asking any questions, he'd already be dead."

Noah still looked troubled. "It still doesn't seem right. That nurse went to a lot of trouble to blow the whistle, and no one listened. I'm going to send out some inquiries when this is all over. Covering up what might have been the murder of someone vulnerable should be punished."

Winter looked at him for a long moment. "You're quite the softie for a big bad FBI agent. Might want to watch that reputation of yours."

He shrugged, and to her amusement, she saw that she'd embarrassed him.

"Let's head to the airport," he said, rubbing the back of his neck. "We can grab something to eat and go through the numbers on the burner phone while we wait for the flight."

They decided to leave the laptop to the experts since Heidi was so fond of kill switches. Her laptop was probably full of them. But it was a simple process to match up the numbers on the burner phone Noah had grabbed, with people they belonged to. Cheap technology like that didn't include much in the way of security.

While they sat in the Cherry Country Café inside the airport, waiting for their flight, Winter divided the phone numbers between the two of them. One by one, they looked up the owners of each number.

The calls spanned about the last twelve months and

ranged in area codes. One of them matched Mike Garofalo's phone number. He was the manager who'd been killed with his girlfriend.

Another belonged to a guy named Romeo Martinez, out of New York. His Facebook page confirmed that he worked in housekeeping at The Phoenix Hotel. Winter made a call to one of their case contacts at the NYPD and asked them to do a well-check on Martinez. A couple of the messages left on his page were from people who'd been trying to get ahold of him in the last several days. There was a pretty good chance he'd already been eliminated.

"See if you can find anything on this," Winter said, pointing out a number on the list. "I haven't had any luck with it."

"Sure. I've got a couple tricks I can try for finding unlisted phone number owners." Noah wiggled his eyebrows. "I'll do it on the condition that I get the French fries you didn't eat."

"Fine." She pushed the plate over. She wasn't hungry anymore anyway. His answer reminded her of Bull. She'd managed to push back the thoughts of him, and of Sun's behavior, but it was hard. She had to keep her focus.

Her phone rang, and she frowned when she didn't recognize the number. "Hello?"

A voice, harsh and low-pitched, was on the other end. "Agent Black?"

Goose bumps prickled on her arms.

"Yes? Who's speaking?"

"Shannon...Marchwood."

"Oh my god," Winter breathed, everything else forgotten for the moment. "How are you? Should you be talking? Your voice sounds horrible." She winced. Like the sheriff needed to be reminded of that.

There was a choked laugh on the other end of the line that broke into a painful-sounding cough. After a long pause, she came back. "No. Shouldn't be talking. Had to thank you."

Winter pictured the last time she'd seen the woman. She'd been so close to death, and now she was on the other end of the phone. Sounding horrible, yeah, but also very much alive.

"You don't need to thank me," Winter said, trying to keep the emotion out of her voice. "You're the one doing all the work. Go. Get better and call me back when you can talk again."

There was a rustle, and another woman's voice came on the line.

"Special Agent Black?"

"Winter. Yes." Winter swallowed back the emotion that was threatening to overwhelm her.

"This is Jodi Marchwood, Shannon's wife. She insisted on speaking with you personally, but I wanted to talk to you too."

"I'm so glad she's doing better."

Don't cry, don't cry, Winter cautioned herself.

Jodi heaved a sigh that was part relief and part exasperation. "She's got a long road to recovery ahead of her, but she'll get there. If, of course, I don't kill her first. Shannon's not the best patient. I won't keep you since I understand you're still working hard. But I wanted to thank you too."

Noah was watching her, a half-smile playing about his lips. She looked away. "Thanks, Jodi, but honestly, it wasn't—"

"Oh, but it was." The interruption was polite but firm. "There was a traffic accident that happened around the same time as the house explosion. It took extra time for the ambulances to get there, because of the backup in both lanes of the highway. The paramedics told me that if you hadn't been on the scene when it happened, hadn't kept up the CPR... seconds counted. Shannon wouldn't be alive right now if it weren't for you. I almost lost her. You saved me that day too."

When Winter was finally able to hang up, after giving Jodi her email address and making her promise to keep her updated on Shannon's progress, Noah was still watching her.

Her emotions felt raw. Scraped and exposed.

"Don't say anything, all right?" She didn't care if she was pleading.

"Me?" His voice was innocent, his green eyes lit with humor and understanding. "I'd never."

The moment expanded, growing too thick for her comfort. She busied herself by looking back down at her own list. "Have you matched up any more of those phone numbers? Like the unlisted one?"

"No. I think it might be Ryan, though. None of the others appear to be."

"One way to find out for sure." She picked up her own phone.

"You should use the burner," Noah cautioned. "No need to freak anyone out on the other end if we don't have to. I've already sent the number back to Sun. She'll get a warrant to trace it."

"I'm betting there were cameras everywhere in Heidi's house." Winter chewed thoughtfully on her lower lip, trying to think everything through. "Chances are she already knows we were there. And this could be a way to establish contact. We've already decided that the crimes don't fit Ryan's usual M.O., and it's one theory that he's participating in this whole thing against his will. Maybe we'll get lucky, and he'll call back, or answer."

The phone, though, just went straight to voicemail. The message was an automated one, instructing the caller to leave a message after the beep.

"No luck," she told Noah. She tried one more time, but

the phone didn't even ring before going again to voicemail. This time, she left a message. "Ryan, I'd like to talk to you. Give me a call back when you get a chance." She rattled off her own number but didn't leave her name.

"Who knows," Noah shrugged, gathering up his gear as their boarding announcement was called overhead. "Maybe he'll call back and give us detailed instructions on where we can find them, and there won't *be* a last hit. Weirder things have happened."

27

Ryan blinked, groggy, staring up at the ceiling. A fat spider was spinning a web between two rafters. It looked like a shiny black blob. He was pretty sure it was a spider. He couldn't make out any legs on the critter.

After what could have been hours or minutes, the spider came into focus. It was wrapping a bug in its web, getting ready for a snack.

Heidi.

Bloody hell, she'd drugged him again. It all came back in a nauseating wave.

He was in a shitload of trouble.

He glanced around the room, his gut twisting in fear, but nothing had changed in the time he'd been out. Thankfully, he hadn't pissed himself, either, though it looked like it might be a near thing.

He gave a couple of test tugs at the wrist restraints that still held him shackled to the bed. The right one was a bit looser than the left, maybe by a notch. Good. Something in his favor, finally.

He braced himself and pulled, squeezing his thumb into

the center of his palm as much as he could. He felt his pinkie pop out of joint and bit back a roar of pain as his hand slipped free.

It was a trick he'd used once before. It hurt like hell, but it was effective.

His hand would swell and be all but bloody useless for a while, but those were the breaks.

He now had one arm free. It would remain to be seen if he could get the other loose. He scanned everything within arm's reach. A bobby pin would be ideal, but there weren't any convenient hairpins lying around. He rolled over on his side and focused on the cuff. Single locking, which was another stroke of luck. Double locking cuffs were far more difficult.

He looked at the bed frame itself. It was metal, and old. Not very sturdy.

He could get a screw loose from it, but it would take time and wasn't guaranteed to work. He needed something pliable. A nail thin enough to bend. A small piece of metal to use as a shim. He didn't know when Heidi would be back.

When his palms started to sweat, Ryan cautioned himself to calm down. It wouldn't help anything to go chickenshit now.

What if the rattling of the bed brought Heidi down from upstairs to investigate? Would she get pissed off enough to take it out on Ionie? For all he knew, she could call up a hit in Jamaica with the ease some would have in ordering a pizza. If Heidi had known how credible her threat was, she wouldn't hesitate.

Ionie had a child. Christopher. The sweetest little four-year-old, with dusky skin and soft brown curls just like his mother's. A smile that stretched from ear to ear every time Ryan had visited, bringing him a little toy or some candy before Ionie sent him over to a neighbor's house to play.

If Ryan were completely honest with himself, he'd started bringing Christopher little treats and gifts because he wanted to butter up the boy's mother. But after a few visits, when Christopher would come running to the door to see him, his pudgy hands outstretched, his dark eyes lit in avaricious glee and natural good humor...something about the kid reminded him of himself. Greedy, sure, for whatever he could get. But good-natured and charming about it. Not that he'd ever been that young.

Heidi hadn't mentioned knowing about the child, but he couldn't take any chances. He didn't want that vicious bitch anywhere near either one of them.

Cursing, he went back to work.

He hit the jackpot with a loose slat in the headboard. With some wrenching, he was able to rock the bed enough to pull the narrow metal tube loose. At one end, a small metal notch, slightly rusted, stuck off about an inch long. It was just thin enough that it might work as a shim.

Working with the finesse that he'd become notorious for, he eased the notch at the end into the space where the teeth on the cuffs entered the bracelet. He had to push the cuff inward, tightening it for this to work, and if it didn't, the cuff would be tighter than before, and he'd still be stuck.

That would suck.

Holding his breath, ignoring the pounding pain in the side of his hand, he eased the shim into the bracelet and started to pray.

❄

HEIDI PULLED up in front of the house in Erie that she'd rented several months ago. It was dingy and old, with flaking white paint and bedraggled bushes in the front yard, but they wouldn't be there long. Her heartbeat sped up. This was it. The final scene in her well-orchestrated play.

She wondered how her leading man was doing. Hopefully, she hadn't given him too much of the sedative she'd added to his water.

She grabbed her laptop bag from the back seat of the rental car, along with the bags of McDonald's takeout she'd picked up. She was too revved up to eat, but her captive was probably hungry. Not that she cared. The food was an excuse. The real reason for her trip to the drive-thru was to get an in-person look at the first target that Ryan would find on his list.

Google Maps was good for planning purposes but seeing things in person was much more satisfying.

The door creaked as it swung inward, and she wrinkled her nose at the mildew smell of the stained beige carpeting. She dropped her laptop on the sagging brown sofa that had come with the place. Just another couple of days, she reminded herself. Then, she'd be off for greener pastures.

The floor creaked under her feet as she moved through the dim house. The basement door was shut and locked, just as she'd left it. Heidi tucked the bag of food under her arm and pulled out the key ring that held the key to the lock she'd installed as soon as they'd arrived in Pennsylvania, Ryan still passed out like a drunk from the first dose of sedatives.

On the landing, she locked the door behind her. Couldn't be too careful.

The mildew smell was stronger in the basement and it mixed with the greasy smell of cooling French fries. She juggled the bag again, unlocking the basement storage room where she'd stashed her "partner."

The door scraped along the cement floor, and she moved in with caution. Ryan was still out, she saw, sprawled on his back and snoring softly, his mouth opened just a bit. She relaxed, but not completely. Never completely.

Since he'd been a good boy, she'd unlock one of his cuffs and leave the bag next to his bed. He could eat when he came to. She set the fast food bag on the small, rickety table beside his bed and shuffled through her key ring for the key to the handcuffs.

Leaning down, she reached for his wrist. A second too late, she realized that the cuff wasn't fastened.

Before she could react, his fist hit the side of her head in a crushing blow that knocked her off-balance. She smashed into the halogen light on the floor, knocking it over. The bulb shattered against the cement, and the room was plunged into darkness.

Heidi tried to scramble to her feet but got tangled in the cord of the work light. She heard heavy breathing and a thump, and then the metal door screeching open. Enough light leaked in from the main room outside for her to get her bearings. She grabbed for her gun, tucked in its underarm holster. She could hear more thudding outside, along with muffled curses, and her lips parted in a grim smile.

Silent, gritting her teeth against a surge of lightheadedness, she made her way to her feet and moved for the door. Ryan had gotten across the room and was at the top of the basement stairs, throwing his weight against the heavy wooden door that she'd locked behind her.

She took careful aim, just like her dad had taught her when he'd taken her deer hunting years ago. As soon as he stopped moving for the briefest moment, she fired.

The blast echoed off the cinder block walls, muffling Ryan's grunt as he stumbled against the railing. The old wood splintered with a loud cracking noise and gave out under his weight. He went backward, falling the eight feet or so to land heavily on his back on the dirty floor.

Heidi went to his motionless body.

He wasn't dead, but the wind had been knocked out of him. She kicked him hard in the ribs as he struggled to pull in a breath. He hardly reacted. Just opened his eyes and stared up at her, his blue eyes dull and defeated, clouding with pain. Blood seeped from the bullet wound high on his arm, soaking his shirt through his clutching fingers.

"Get on with it then, you sadistic whore," he wheezed in a low, flattened voice, as soon as he'd sucked enough air into his lungs. "Fucking end it, will you?"

"Get up."

At first, she didn't think he'd move. But, with slow, painful movements, he pushed to his feet. Shuffling like an old man, he made his way back to the storage room.

She stood at the open door of the darkened room, still aiming the Ruger at his dim outline, center mass. "The next time you try anything, I will blow out one of your kneecaps."

The words were just for dramatic effect, she admitted to herself. She knew defeat when she saw it. Ryan's shoulders slumped, his body trembled in pain, and his face. Oh, his face was the best. She wished she could see it better. Hopelessness and resignation and pain blended together in one dreary mix.

Piling on a little more wouldn't hurt.

"Just so you know, I'm not going to punish you for this little attempt. But Ionie? She is so dead. And I'm going to make it very, very painful for her. You try another escape, and I'll look forward to putting some of my knowledge of torture methods to good use."

Without another word, she slammed the door and locked him in. There was no more need for handcuffs. She was pretty sure Ryan had gotten the point this time. He wasn't going anywhere.

28

"Any luck yet on the trace?" Winter asked Doug Jepson, the IT guy that Noah insisted had a crush on her.

He blushed, which looked strange and kind of endearing on a guy his size. Doug didn't look like your stereotypical tech. He was muscular, broad-shouldered, and hard-faced, and could probably stunt double for the actor Terry Cruz. He had hands like sledgehammers but tapped at his keyboard with the delicacy of a brain surgeon...if the brain surgeon was a mafia enforcer in his spare time.

"Nothing yet," he replied in a deep, slow baritone. "We're not picking up any signal from it. The carrier company hasn't shown a ping from the phone since almost three days ago in New York, at The Phoenix. Usually, even if the battery is dead, we can detect a signal."

"Thanks, Doug." She hadn't really expected anything, but it was still disappointing. "Let me know if you get anything else."

He nodded in agreement and went back to his multiple-screen desk setup.

Winter was at loose ends. Sun had cut her out of the investigation almost completely since they'd gotten back from Michigan. She'd been closeted in a conference room with Noah for hours, having given Winter curt instructions to work on her own angles, since she was "good at flying solo." The woman was driving her nuts. It was unfair, but she didn't want to go to Max and seem petty.

Things around the office were still quiet and subdued. Bree, one of the other members of their unit, was the only person who had tried to make a tentative approach.

Winter, though, didn't feel like talking to anyone. She appreciated the show of support but shut the other woman's attempts at conversation down with as much politeness and gratitude as she could. Bree hadn't taken offense. She just gave Winter a commiserating nod and a sympathetic look and left her alone.

After three more hours, there was still no progress with the phone. The computer forensics team was working on Heidi's laptop but hadn't cracked it yet. As they'd figured, the entire system was locked up tight, with kill switches in place to wipe the hard drive if anyone trying to hack it made one wrong move. The mood in their department was intense, and she caught dirty looks every time she tried to pop in for a progress update.

Knowing she wasn't doing any good at the office, Winter gathered up her things and left.

She made a phone call from her car in the parking lot, and Aiden agreed to help her out with the profiling issue. She headed for his apartment, hoping he'd have some insights. In her head, it felt like there was a clock ticking down to explosion time. She'd even been hoping for a vision. She'd gladly deal with the pain and brief incapacitation for a chance to stop whatever Heidi planned to do next.

Aiden looked better when she got to his place. Despite her not being around for a while to bring him food, he'd gained a little weight. The hollows in his cheeks were filling out, and he looked like he was moving around more easily on his bad leg.

His face creased in a wry smile when she walked through the door, clutching a bag of donuts she'd stopped and grabbed on the way.

"Still trying to feed me?"

"Still scrawny and half-dead?"

"Not quite that bad. I've been doing my PT."

"Nurse Ratched hasn't driven you crazy yet?"

"It's been close." He sneered, but there was no heat in it. "I think she's starting to like me. I wasn't in nearly as much pain after a session with her yesterday. Come on in."

She dropped the donuts on Aiden's coffee table, within easy reach, but he made no move to take one.

"Catch me up," he instructed instead, as she sank down into the chair across from him.

"There's not much you don't know," Winter began, letting her head fall back against the soft upholstered back. "We found her house, and she blew it up. We've got phones to trace and a laptop that would probably break everything wide open if we could get into it, but so far, no luck."

"Why aren't you with Ming and Dalton?"

"She cut me off." Winter opened her eyes. She knew they glittered, hard and bright with anger. "That brilliant, knowledgeable, professional agent you all rave about? She's not only a bitch, but she doesn't like anyone who's a threat to her. Did you hear that she had inside info and didn't come to anyone with it? The suspects, or at least Heidi, had been emailing her directly. She deliberately kept it quiet. We should be looking into her computer."

Aiden looked thoughtful. "I heard about that. I know she's ambitious, but I didn't think she'd pull something like this."

"She's Teflon. That's what Bull said." The words were tinged with guilt. "How'd she slide out of it?"

Aiden just looked at her, raising one eyebrow. "That's between Sun and Osbourne."

She felt chastised, and it irritated her. "Still, it's not right."

"No," he agreed. "She should have known better. But you'd better bet she's on thin ice now. You okay? I've lost a colleague before. It's not easy, even if you didn't know them well."

"No, it's not easy. I feel like it's my fault." She held up a hand to stave off his automatic argument. "Save it," she advised. "You can't say anything I haven't heard or somehow make me feel better about the whole thing. I'm dealing with it."

He nodded. Sometimes she really appreciated his no-nonsense, emotionless attitude, and this was one of them. She didn't want anyone's sympathy, and he wasn't offering it.

"Just be sure to talk to someone about it if you need to."

"I will. What about you? Has that super-intelligent brain of yours come up with anything we can use?"

Aiden's face went thoughtful. He reached for the bag of donuts and fished out a plain one.

"Plain?" She grimaced at his choice. "Why am I not surprised."

"Shut up," he responded mildly, taking a bite. "I've been thinking about this, doing some research. I might have an idea of Heidi's last hit, but it's just a guess."

Winter leaned forward. "Tell me."

"Don't take this and run with it without bouncing it off the rest of your team first," he warned her.

She shook her head and gave him an impatient look. "You're stalling."

"I think she's going to finish off with the Collar Bomb."

Winter immediately knew what case Aiden was referring to. It had baffled investigators when it happened. It also made a sick kind of sense when you put all the previous cases together.

A pizza man had shown up at a National Bank Group bank in 2003, demanding that the tellers give him two hundred and fifty thousand in cash. They didn't have it on hand. He instead got away with just under nine thousand, seeming nonchalant as he grabbed a sucker from a container on the counter on his way out the door.

The police caught him not far from the crime scene. He'd been fitted with a bomb around his neck. He told them a fishy-sounding story about some people putting it on him and giving him a list of instructions to follow. If he didn't do as they told him, they'd detonate the bomb.

The bomb had indeed detonated a short time after, moments before the bomb squad arrived to dismantle it. It had blown a fist-sized hole in the man's chest, killing him on the spot. The motives and suspects in the case ended up being confusing and muddled, but it had been a highly sensationalized heist. The man was killed on camera, and videos still floated around the internet of his death.

"Why do you think she'd choose that one?" Winter asked, unconsciously assigning Heidi the responsibility for the theoretical crime. "To get rid of Ryan O'Connelly?"

Aiden nodded. "So far, she's chosen high-profile cases. I think she's planned these out to gain notoriety. To thumb her nose at everyone, us included, and prove that she's smarter than any previous criminal that's come along, *and* the cops that are investigating her. So far," he admitted, "she's done a decent job of it."

"So, you think she only brought Ryan in for his name and reputation. In the end, she'll blow him up, proving that she was smarter than he was too. When the press puts it all together, she'll be infamous."

"I think that's the plan."

"You think she'll do it at the original location?"

"That part, I'm not sure of." Aiden took another bite of his donut. "She changed up the location of the last hit. Maybe because she thought it made sense in a convoluted way, with the ArmorGuard Security and Dunbar acquisition. Maybe because it would keep us off track. Or she just figured it would have been too much of a pain in the ass to get across the country. The NBG bank where the Collar Bomb heist began is in Erie, Pennsylvania. It's only a six- or seven-hour drive from New York."

"But how is she getting O'Connelly to go along with all of this?"

Aiden shrugged, frustration evident in the movement. "You'd have to ask him."

"Hopefully, we'll get the chance." The theory was a long shot, admittedly. But it was more than they'd had before.

"I need to get back to the office. Try and get Sun to listen to me. Maybe Noah can help."

"Try to spin it in a way that she'll see the benefit for herself," Aiden advised. "Have her call me if you think that will help."

Winter pushed to her feet. Yeah, it was a long shot, but it felt right, judging by the new urgency that pulsed through her body. They were running out of time, she knew. Playing against a clock they couldn't see. "I'm going to get back. Thanks."

"Don't thank me yet." Aiden grinned. "If I'm right, be sure to give credit where it's due. If I'm not, keep it to yourself."

She headed for the door, new motivation running strong. "I'll check in with you. Let you know what's going on."

"Do that," he called after her. "Keep me posted."

She shut the door behind her, her steps quick to the elevator. Pulling out her phone, she texted Noah: *Got an idea. Prep Sun and get her as receptive as possible. Tell her Parrish has some insight for us and I'm on my way.*

By the time the elevator got to the main floor, he'd texted back: *Will do. See u in a bit.*

She'd try Ryan's phone in the car one more time. It couldn't hurt.

❄

AFTER SHE'D GONE, Aiden's mood dipped.

It had been like that lately. Winter would burst in, full of angst and energy. When she left, it was like she sucked all of that vibrancy out of the room with her, leaving him more acutely aware of his self-imposed solitude when she was gone.

It disturbed him. His control, his discipline, his detachment…every time he was around her, he could feel his grasp slipping. Uncomfortable, he thought about the package that had come in the mail the day before. It was sitting in his office on the desk.

The gift had seemed like a good idea at the time, but now it just felt maudlin. Sentimental. He'd still give it to her. He seldom second-guessed his own decisions. But after that…he had to move her aside. Tuck her back into the safe compartment she'd been in before his injury.

Eying the clock, he wondered how early was really too early for a drink.

Fuck it. He was an adult.

He pushed to his feet and headed toward the carved teak liquor cabinet tucked into a corner of the room. He hoped he was right about Heidi Presley's next step. He didn't want to see that fiery light of hope—and hell, hero worship—in Winter's eyes diminished.

It would be, eventually, he thought with some regret. No need to hurry the process along.

29

I t was as dark as a pit. The kind of darkness where you couldn't tell if your eyes were open or closed.

Ryan moved painfully toward the bed, the throbbing in his arm competing with the knot that was rising on the back of his head, where he'd slammed it against the floor when he fell. He barely registered the cobwebs that brushed against his face, or the knee he knocked hard into the corner of the metal bed frame.

Once he'd located the bed, he collapsed heavily on the mattress. There were no sheets or anything to tear to make a bandage. He struggled out of his shirt, wanting to yell with every movement that jarred his injured arm or his swollen hand. Carefully, he pressed the wadded-up shirt against his arm and hissed at the starburst of pain the contact caused.

He was in bad shape. But not as bad as he could have been.

Ryan hadn't come back into the room empty-handed. He'd spotted a small gray packet on his way out the door, the only item sitting on a shelf just outside of the storage room. Heidi had insisted he keep his cell phone in it. He figured the little nylon bag must be some kind of Faraday cage, blocking any signal the phone might give off that would allow it to be tracked.

Ryan smiled in the darkness as he slipped his phone out. His spirits lifted a little as he felt the smooth, familiar shape of his iPhone in his hand. He pushed the volume down to vibrate and switched on the power save mode to conserve the eight percent battery charge that was left.

He was still in trouble, but he wasn't out of options yet. He touched his chest without thinking, where his Saint Dismas medal usually hung. It only served to remind him that he'd been shit out of luck since this whole thing began.

Then, his phone rang.

He stared at it for a second as it glowed and vibrated in his hand. He didn't recognize the number. Upstairs, he thought he heard a floorboard creak. It could have been the normal noise of a building settling, but he couldn't be sure.

He hit the button to answer the call.

"Hello?" he answered, keeping his voice just above a whisper.

✳

HOLY SHIT, she'd gotten him. Ryan O'Connelly.

Winter's fingers tightened on her steering wheel.

"Ryan? This is Special Agent Black with the FBI. You're in danger. You need to tell me where you're at."

There was a short laugh, quickly muffled. "You're bloody right I'm in danger. She just fucking shot me. I don't think it'll kill me, but I'm with this crazy wo—"

"Heidi Presley," Winter confirmed. "Tell me where you are."

"I don't know. She knocked me out. I'm in a room in a

basement, but I couldn't fucking tell you where if my life depended on it. Which I guess it does."

Winter wanted to growl in frustration. He could be playing her, laying a trap, but his voice rang with sincerity, and more convincingly, fear. "I'm going to try to help you, but I need you to stay on the phone with me as long as you can."

She put the car in drive and pulled out of the parking spot, her nerves jumping.

"My phone battery is running low," he warned. "And I don't know when she's coming back."

"I'm hurrying."

She didn't want to hang up, now that she had him, but she had to get back to the office and have the techs try and locate the phone again. It had to be pinging now.

"Where are you shot? What happened?"

"I tried to get away," Ryan admitted, chagrin in his voice. "It wasn't well thought out."

Winter glanced either way at the next red light and sped through. "What happened?"

"I got out of some handcuffs. I hit her, took her by surprise. Hoped I knocked her out. She got me, though. Upper arm. Threatened to do my knees next. I think she wants me alive, but I don't know why. She sure as hell looked like she wanted to shoot me in the head."

Keep talking, she urged him silently. She was two minutes out.

"Do you know what she has planned next? Do you think you could be in Pennsylvania?"

"I don't know why we would be. I thought we were in Vermont. That's where we were at between the Parrish job and the armored depot thing. Listen, I'm sorry—"

"No time for that right now," she interrupted. "Tell me all about it later. Where in Vermont were you?"

He named a town she didn't recognize, and she committed it to memory as she made the last turn, practically on two wheels.

"We're going to find you," she promised.

Exactly how, she wasn't sure.

She parked and took off for the building at a dead run, glad she'd chosen comfortable flats that morning. She caught a few curious glances on the way through the lobby but ignored them. Luck was with her. The elevator had just reached the ground floor, with two people getting out. She pushed past them and hit the button. The door slid shut with agonizing slowness.

"Listen," Ryan said. "I need a favor."

"Gutsy of you, but I'm listening." The numbers ticked by on the display above the elevator doors. One...two...she hoped she didn't lose service.

But Ryan's voice came through clear, as did the urgency that underlaid his words. "There's a woman in Jamaica. She has a little boy. I want them protected. Heidi's been using her as a threat. I can face whatever I have to...just please, make sure she's protected."

"What's her name and where does she live?"

"Ionie Clarke. She lives in Ocho Rios. Works in housekeeping at Jamaica Inn."

"I'll see what we can arrange."

The doors finally opened, and she headed straight for Doug's office. He gave her a shy smile that shifted to concern once he got a look at her face.

"Track it now. The cell phone," she whispered, holding a hand over the receiver.

Once he started typing, she put the phone down on the desk and hit the speaker button.

"Thanks," Ryan said, his voice sounding a little bit lighter. "Now, if you could just—"

Whatever else he'd been getting ready to request, it was cut off in a loud, screeching sound, and his sharp, indrawn breath.

"You got your phone, didn't you," came a woman's voice. "How enterprising of you. I didn't even think about it until just now. Hand it over." There was a metallic click, then the rustling sounds of a struggle, and a grunt of pain.

"Who is this?" Heidi Presley's voice contained nothing but a detached curiosity.

Winter wasn't sure how to answer. She looked at Doug. He stared back at her, motioning for her to talk while he typed with one hand. Around them, other agents gathered closely.

"Winter Black," she answered, matching Heidi's tone. Cool and detached.

"Well, Winter," Heidi replied. "What are you? Local police? FBI?"

Winter narrowed her eyes. The woman was playing with her, she could tell. Heidi Presley knew exactly who she was. Winter played along anyway. "FBI."

"I was hoping for Sun." There was another loud screech and a slam. She must've locked Ryan back in. "Although, she's really been a disappointment so far."

Winter reached for a piece of paper and scribbled *Get Ming and Dalton*, handing it to the nearest agent. She took off at a run.

"She'd be sorry to hear you say that," Winter replied. "She was pretty flattered that you chose her to work your case."

There was a brief pause, and Winter thought the call had been disconnected. But she heard the sound of another door close and a lock clicking into place.

"You're the agent who found my house, aren't you?"

"One of them. Yes." *Stroke her ego,* she thought to herself. *Keep her talking.* "You've been quite a challenge."

"You're the girl. The one with the long, dark hair. How'd you know where my cubby was? At the house in Saint Ignace?"

Winter felt eyes on her. Everyone knew the story by now. Apparently, more people than just Heidi had been wondering the same thing. She deflected, a little uncomfortably.

"You saw us, huh? I'm not surprised. It'd be a shame to set a clever trap like that, and then miss the fireworks when it went off. What kind of accelerant did you use on that explosion? I've been curious about how you got the fire to burn so hot so fast and eat up so much fuel."

Heidi let out a little chuckle. It sounded rusty and awkward. Not a noise that she was comfortable making.

"Maybe we'll sit down when this is all over. Have a chat," Heidi offered. "I'd love to share all of my little details with someone who will appreciate them."

"How about tomorrow morning? I'm sure there's a coffee place somewhere near the NBG bank in Erie," Winter replied, going with instinct.

Behind her, the door opened, and Sun and Noah burst in. Sun pushed her way through the small, gathering crowd, her face furious.

Winter ignored her, addressing Heidi. "I'd be happy to sit down with you today, but I'm afraid it'll take me some time to get to Pennsylvania from Richmond."

"Oh, I did pick the wrong agent, didn't I?" Heidi's voice sounded almost admiring. "You're the one I should have been talking to all along. This will be so much more fun, knowing you're right behind me."

"Just you," Winter confirmed. "Not O'Connelly. I can tell he's just a cog in the machine. Not an organizer." It felt like she was laying it on a little thick, and Winter winced. *Dial it back.*

Doug pushed a piece of paper over to her. Before Winter

could grab it, Sun did. She'd seen what it said, though. *Erie, PA.* The cellphone had pinged off of a tower in Erie. Aiden was right.

Sun's face was mottled red, her eyes snapping in furious anger. She opened her mouth to speak, but Noah put a restraining hand on her shoulder, shaking his head.

"No, of course O'Connelly didn't have anything to do with this," Heidi went on, coldly casual. "He's just a convenient accomplice whose use is almost at an end. I'm pretty sure even he's figured that out by now, as dumb as he is otherwise."

"How convenient has he really been, though? He hasn't appreciated the finer points of your plan."

"You're so right. He's squeamish." Disgust rang in Heidi's voice. "I'd researched him carefully beforehand, but it didn't take long to figure out that I'd have had better results out of a hired thug."

"He pulled off the Charlotte Edwards killing. He'll fry for that alone."

Heidi snorted. "He said he shot her in the head while she slept. I don't believe that."

Winter tensed. Did she know the elderly heiress had survived? Had she done follow-up, checking her "partner's" work?

"No, he didn't shoot her in the head," Winter replied, trying for a confiding tone. "The autopsy showed she died of heart failure. He scared her to death."

Again, Heidi laughed. There was a harsh edge of madness to it.

"I knew he'd lied to me. Fucking coward."

"Why even use him? You didn't need him. You were capable of pulling everything off on your own."

"Well, everything but this last heist," Heidi pointed out. "I could have picked something else, but the ending wouldn't have been as much fun. Now, as much as I'd like to keep talking, I've got lots of things to do before tomorrow morning. I'm sure I've given you plenty of time to confirm your hunch. We're in Pennsylvania. You're welcome to come find us, but Ryan won't be available until nine o'clock tomorrow morning. Try to see him before that, and I'll just kill him early. See you soon, Agent Black."

Heidi disconnected, and it seemed like everyone in the room took a collective breath.

"Agent Black," Sun clipped out, her tone sheathed in ice. "I need to see you privately. Now."

For the moment, at her own peril, she knew, Winter ignored the other agent. She locked eyes with Doug.

"We need that laptop. Please."

He nodded, not speaking, still stunned at the conversation he'd just overheard. He lumbered to his feet and gathered his team with a gesture.

"Winter," Sun barked.

She could feel Noah's eyes on her, but she followed Sun.

30

"Save it," Winter advised, taking a seat in the conference room.

Sun looked furious. "You—"

"We need to make plane reservations now. We don't have any time to waste on petty, power-struggle bullshit."

"You would say that, wouldn't you," Sun accused in bitter rage. "You're swooping in and saving the day again. Going lone cowboy and bringing the bad guy down all by yourself."

"Seriously?" Winter folded her arms and leaned back against the chair. "You want to hash this all out now? At least one life hangs in the balance here."

"I don't give a fuck about Ryan O'Connelly."

"And, apparently, you give zero fucks about a bank manager in California who was taken from her husband of decades? Or a security guard in New York who won't be going home to kiss his grandkids again? Bull Durham? Our teammate? The only fuck you give is about yourself. How can this be all about me when you *knew* you had inside information. You're the lone cowboy here."

Sun paled but stood firm. "I care about the fact that you're a loose cannon. You're a new agent. You can't just go around directing everyone like lackeys, basing all of your work on hunches. Putting everyone else at risk. Impulsively contacting suspects on your own with no plan in place. No backup."

"Really, Sun? You think I'm a loose cannon? You don't think if you'd turned over your information as soon as you found it that you could have lowered some risks?"

It was a direct hit, finally.

Sun seemed to crumble, without moving. Her face stayed hard, but her voice was low. "Fine. You win. You're better."

"Oh, grow up." Winter, impatient with the delay and having to face someone else's emotional angst, was brusque. "Now you're just feeling sorry for yourself. If it's important to you, I didn't come up with this latest theory, a reenactment of the Collar Bomb heist, by the way, taking place tomorrow at nine a.m. in Erie, Pennsylvania. It was Parrish. I went to get his take on things this morning when you cut me out and refused to let me work with you and Noah on the case. If this is a competition, *he* wins. *He's* better."

Sun pulled out a chair and sat down. Her face was a study in misery. She didn't let any tears fall, but her eyes were rimmed in red. She took a heavy breath.

"I'm sorry. I'm not going to say it again, and this never leaves the room, but I'm sorry. It's all my fault, from the beginning. I handled this all wrong. It was supposed to be my moment. Heidi Presley sent that email to me. I was going to take her down. Make my career."

"And instead of working on it solo, you got stuck with me."

Sun nodded. "I got stuck with you. How am I supposed to shine, when every time I turn around, you're saving someone's life or coming up with another lead or being in just the right place at the right time?"

"You think I'm doing all of that to make you look bad?" Winter snorted but gentled her voice as much as she could, under the circumstances. "I can only tell you, I'm here to do a job. I couldn't care less about advancement, and I am not out to be your rival. But slogging this out now? We can't. We can only go forward and try to end this the right way. We need to make some plane reservations, now."

"You're right. I'm sorry," Sun repeated. Picking up the phone in the conference room, she made a call. "We need the next flight out of Richmond for Erie. There won't be a non-stop, but we need to be there yesterday. Better yet, charter something and call me back as soon as you have it."

"Do you have a new personal assistant I don't know about?"

"That was Dalton." Sun narrowed her eyes at Winter. "He, at least, lets me boss him around."

"He's easy like that. So, what's the plan, case agent?"

It was a concession, and Sun took it as one. She acknowledged Winter's effort with a small smile.

"We go to Erie, coordinate with the local LEOs and hope we find O'Connelly before she blows him or anyone else up. Other than that, there is no plan." She hesitated, but only briefly. "Do you have any ideas?"

"Not yet. I might if Doug Jepson comes through with anything for us from Heidi's computer. In the meantime, I think we just need to stay flexible and have each other's backs."

Sun raised an eyebrow. "*Do* we have each other's backs?"

"We better."

The conference room phone rang again, and Sun picked it up. She listened for a moment and made an approving sound. "Thanks, Dalton. We're on our way."

❄

THIS WAS IT. Heidi prided herself on keeping a tight rein on her emotions. But right now, she felt like giggling.

Six years of planning. Longer than that, really, when she thought about the dark days with her father. The long, irritating hours she'd spent by her ailing mother's bedside. The decade and a half she'd spent working in IT contracting, constantly being hit on, overlooked for promotions, and used as the general dumping ground for crap jobs and problems no one else wanted to take the time to work out.

It had all led up to today.

The small house she'd rented for the final act was just outside of Erie, chosen for its secluded but nearby location. The property was wooded. The driveway alone was a quarter-mile long, and she had every point of it covered with cameras. No one would be sneaking up on her. And, in the meantime, she had the only window to the world she needed, right in the palm of her hands.

She sat back on the couch, crossing her legs beneath her and pulling her computer up onto her lap. She panned through her surveillance feeds. All of them were working, but the pictures weren't as clear as they should have been. Heidi almost panicked, before she glanced out the living room window and realized it was snowing. Large flakes fell lazily outside the windows, already coating the ground. She relaxed again.

On the split screen in front of her, to the right, she had Ryan O'Connelly.

She clucked her tongue in disapproval. He was looking far worse for the wear than he had been when she'd first seen him in person at the airport in Bismarck. Now, his shining black hair looked lank and limp. His eyes, such a pretty shade of blue, were clouded, the skin around them scored with fine lines of stress and pain. He had a sore near his mouth, probably from stress. His shoulders were hunched inward, as if he could escape the contraption rigged around his neck if he just collapsed far enough in on himself.

She chuckled. "Sorry, Ryan," Heidi said out loud. "That thing's not coming off. They're going to have to bury you in it."

He twitched at her words.

"Oops. I forgot about the microphone. Sorry about that."

He was wearing a wireless headset. He had a written list of instructions, too, clutched in one hand, but she'd decided to rig him for sound as well. It would be nice to give him directions on the fly if any good ideas occurred to her. Keep everyone guessing.

On the other half of the screen, she had a view of the outside of the shabby little rental house.

There were at least a dozen police cars, parked at what they probably thought was a safe distance, in case of an explosion. A gray SUV held the FBI team. The tall, good-looking man, and the two women. The man, she wasn't interested in. It was the dynamic of the two female agents she was keeping an eye on.

Sun Ming, she'd picked because she'd bought into the woman's own hype. Winter Black, it looked like, was the better agent. Could she play them off each other somehow? The unflappable Special Agent Black, and the ego-tripping Special Agent Ming? It would be interesting to find out.

She checked her watch. Three minutes to nine.

It had been easier than she'd expected to get Ryan into the collar bomb. She'd built it based on the specs for the original that she'd found online, with just a few modifications. The original caused only minimum damage, limited to the man who wore it. This one, though, would take out Ryan and anyone unfortunate enough to be close to him. A specially added shrapnel case would add additional pain and suffering to bystanders.

She'd taken the original design, built like a large handcuff with attached explosives, and improved upon it.

The only dicey moment had been when she'd brought it into the room she'd kept Ryan in. She had to somehow get him to sit still long enough for her to put it on him while making sure he felt threatened enough to cooperate. That had been accomplished with the help of the remote—not yet activated, though he didn't know that—and the fact that he'd been weak and woozy from the loss of blood from his arm.

It was a good thing that Ryan was proving to be such a wuss. He had no way of knowing that he'd already blown his best chance of escape. She wished she'd taken the time to tell him that when she'd seen him for the last time.

During the last few days, she'd discovered that she liked to see desperation and fear in a person. It was more fun than viewing those emotions filtered through a camera.

He'd been such a good boy when he'd been fitted for his necklace, she'd even let him use the bathroom. A minor detail she'd forgotten. Oops.

Now, she could see him stand up. Cautiously start to pace. She smiled. He knew she held his life in her hands. He also knew she was going to destroy it. The rest of his life could very well be counted in minutes at this point.

He never should have pretended to seduce her. The fact that she'd fallen for his moves, letting him get her drunk like that…she flushed at the memory. He deserved every second of pain and fear he was going to experience. She'd drag it out forever, if she could.

At nine o'clock exactly, Agent Ming got out of the car and took out a bullhorn.

"Ryan O'Connelly," she could hear through Ryan's headset. "This is the FBI and the Erie police. Come out of the house slowly, with your hands in the air."

Ryan started to move, but hesitated.

"Go ahead," Heidi encouraged, speaking directly to him through the headset. "Let's get this show on the road."

He went to the front door, and she could see his hands shaking as he reached for the doorknob. Good. She wanted him terrified. Completely compliant.

"There's no hope for you, Ryan. Better just get it all over with," she crooned in his ear.

She switched cameras, so that she had the outdoor view pulled up, and the surveillance camera on the road outside of her current location. There was no way they could have tracked her, and she'd be long gone before they could, but it paid to be safe.

Ryan was on the front porch now.

"Go ahead," she ordered. "Tell them what the first item on your honey-do list is."

She adjusted the volume of her own headset when his voice boomed out. "I'm supposed to rob a NBG bank."

"I see you, Ryan," Heidi laughed. "Knock that off."

He'd mouthed the words "help me" to the officers. Not very subtlety, either.

"You have a headset on," Agent Black called out. "Can Heidi Presley hear us right now?"

"Tell them 'yes, I can.' And they'd better not try to stall this out, or I'm going to get impatient. My button pushing finger gets twitchy when I'm impatient."

He repeated her message to the group.

Then, Heidi had an idea. "Tell them I want Agent Black to drive you to the NBG."

She watched the reactions of the agents intently. Agent Ming looked angry. The big, dumb guy started shaking his head right away and took a protective step toward Agent Black. Interesting.

Time to stoke the embers a bit. "Tell them this isn't negotiable. Agent Ming is incompetent and useless. She's compromised the investigation from the beginning, with-holding information, by the way. Agent Black is the one I want."

Ryan relayed the information, word for word.

It was gratifying to watch Agent Ming turn pale and then practically vibrate in fury. Her scowl was immediate, and though the man tried to intervene, she got up into the other agent's face, hissing something at her. Agent Black shoved her back, and Heidi wished she could hear what they were saying.

It was like watching a soap opera, she thought. Regular people and their petty dramas were so predictable. Next step, catfight.

But the two got themselves under control. Agent Black was saying something to her team in an undertone, and neither of her co-workers looked happy about it.

"We're taking my car, Heidi," she called out. "O'Connelly, let's go."

The local officers gave Ryan a wide berth when he slowly, carefully walked down the stairs. He acted like any wrong move would turn him into a human fireball. He wasn't far off.

Heidi watched, delighted, as Agent Black held the door of a black sedan open for him, looking like a chauffeur. He slid into the seat, and she walked around the front of the car. Before she got in, she looked back at the house. Directly into the camera Heidi had mounted above the front door, which should have been damned near invisible.

Agent Black gave a small wave and smiled. It was like she could see through the camera. Just like in the house in Saint Ignace, with the hiding spot under the floorboards. She'd known immediately that the stash was there, and that it had been rigged to explode.

Heidi's good mood faltered at the reminder.

She stroked the button on the remote she held. She could push it now. End it.

It wouldn't be the big finale she'd hoped for, though.

No, she decided. Carry it through. Stick with the original plan. But when she did push the button, she'd make sure that Agent Black was nearby.

The freaky bitch.

Noah was furious.

He was pissed off at Winter, who should know better than to put herself in direct danger like she had. Again. Pissed off at Sun for letting her. And pissed off at himself for not putting a stop to it.

He'd also seen her little wave. Of course, the house would be rigged with cameras so Heidi could watch Ryan's last performance. She was deliberately goading a killer, while simultaneously loading the next victim into her car. The car that she would get into and drive.

If she lived, he might well decide to kill her himself.

"That was bullshit," he said, his voice hoarse with stifled anger. "Some 'case agent.' I can't believe you let things go down like that."

Sun looked away from the road for a moment. They were first in line in the convoy, following the rental car to NBG bank. "I'm not any happier about it than you are, being called out like that in front of the local cops."

"You are so self-centered," Noah burst out. "I was talking about letting Winter climb into that car with a suspect, wired to blow at the touch of a psychopath's button!"

"I knew what you meant." Sun sighed. "But, as much as it pains me to say it, Winter's *hunch* was right. Heidi is trying to play us off each other for her own entertainment. We need to let her think it's working. Keep her distracted from everything else that will be happening."

"Everything else." He snorted. "That's another thing. There are so many variables in this plan we cooked up that it'll be a miracle if it doesn't go south before we even get started. Too much shit could go wrong."

Sun's dark eyes were sympathetic, and a little sad, when she gave him a sidelong look. "You really like her, huh?"

"We're friends."

"That's not what everyone was saying after you guys went to Harrisonburg together."

"Not important right now, Sun."

He stared out the window at the outlines of the passengers in the car in front of them. Winter Black, FBI agent, and Ryan O'Connelly, acclaimed international art and jewelry thief. Off to rob a bank together. They looked so normal. Like two people carpooling on the way to work or going out to breakfast together. Except, of course, for the way the bomb he wore around his neck threw off his silhouette.

And it was starting to snow. Big, fat flakes that stuck wetly to every surface. Lake effect snow, off of Lake Erie. The local news channel was calling for over a foot of it to fall today. That could help or hurt their operation. Which one, remained to be seen.

Too many variables.

Like now, for example. What if the car hit an icy spot? Went off the road? Would the bomb explode on impact like that? Unconsciously, Noah pulled his worn deck of cards from the pocket of his shirt and began shuffling. The whisper and fluttering sound of the cards failed to soothe his nerves like they usually did.

He was glad that Sun was driving. He'd never be able to focus on keeping the vehicle on the road.

"She'll be okay, Dalton." The words were quiet and certain.

There was another thing that was pissing him off. Sun was so fucking calm about the whole thing. Winter, too. He was the only one whose guts were in a tangle right now.

"You'd better hope so, darlin,'" Noah replied grimly.

It wasn't a word of caution. It was a threat.

❄

RYAN COULD SMELL the acrid scent of his own fear. It was cold, the temperature hovering around the twenties outside, but his armpits were drenched with sweat.

He tried to control his harsh breathing. It echoed in the silent car, and he knew Heidi could hear him. Was feeding off of his fear.

The woman driving looked over at him and smiled.

She hadn't said a word since they'd gotten in the car, but every once in a while, she'd glance at him and give him one of those calm, soothing smiles. He tried to grin back, flirt a little, like the old Ryan O'Connelly would have, but it fell flat. His face felt like it was contorting into more of a grimace than anything.

The metal contraption on his neck was heavy. The wires —blue, red, green, black—he could see out of his peripheral vision. The weight, he imagined, was tightly packed explosive material, ready to end his life. With every heartbeat, he was afraid something he was going to do—or a whim of Heidi's—would set it off.

The past week or so had been a revelation to him. He was

a coward. He didn't want to die, but death didn't care. It was coming for him.

Would he do something heroic in his last moments? Or would he piss himself in fear? He was afraid it would be the latter.

More than his own death, though, he was afraid for Ionie and Christopher. He'd treated his relationship with Ionie no different than his casual encounters with any other woman. He had a knack for attracting beautiful women, but Ionie reminded him uncomfortably of his own past. She also had him thinking thoughts of the future, which was even more terrifying.

He didn't blame her. She had a sweet, giving, undemanding nature. He could still hear a melodic accent, whispering in his ear at night when they made love. He couldn't blame Christopher, either. The child was endearing and cute as hell, but that wasn't what had scared him. It was that he could picture them together, raising Christopher and living in the island paradise until they were old. Giving up his "career," such as it was. Supporting Ionie so she didn't have to work her fingers to the bone every day, picking up after careless tourists and sending her son to daycare.

It was that fear of settling down that had driven him to drink so much. To keep talking to the mystery woman who called him, instead of ignoring the seductive allure of the unknown.

The headset crackled in his ear, startling him.

"Why is it so quiet in there, Ryan? You're not plotting anything, are you?"

By the look the FBI agent gave him, she heard Heidi's voice as well as he did.

He cleared his throat. "No. Just enjoying the snow. It's a pretty drive."

"Sarcasm is misplaced at this point, wouldn't you think?"

A stab of fear shot through him.

"No. You're right. I'm sorry."

"You have your instructions for the NBG robbery?"

He did. The ink on the paper had all but bled away from being clutched in his damp palm, but he'd memorized it. "Go in. Tell the teller I need $250K."

The headset crackled again.

"What?" he asked, a panicky feeling in his chest. What if she was giving him instructions and he couldn't hear them?

"I said...getting interfere...the weather...will have...on camera...follow list."

Over his pounding heart, the agent said, "Sounds like the storm is interfering with the wireless signal." Her voice was so cool and conversational, as if they were strangers beside each other on a public bus.

"I think she said she'll have me on camera. Just to follow the written directions if I can't hear her."

"I'm Winter," the agent said, hitting the turn signal.

"Ryan."

"I know." She gave him a lopsided smile. "I've been following your recent career."

He winced.

She held a finger to her lips as the headset gave out another staticky burst.

There were no words forthcoming, though.

"We're just going to stay calm and do what Heidi tells us," Winter said. She switched on the windshield wipers to a faster speed. The snow was accumulating almost as fast as the blades could swish it away. "Everything will be okay."

"No, it won't." Heidi's voice and giggle came through crystal clear before the static took over again.

Winter rolled her eyes. *Yes, it will,* she mouthed.

Ryan tried not to hope. But she was so casual about the

whole thing. Did they have a plan in place? Would he get out of this after all?

He tried not to hope, but something dangerously like it unfurled in his chest anyway.

❄

WINTER COULD FEEL O'Connelly's fear. It was contagious.

For his sake, though, she kept her serene and professional mask in place.

"Just a few more minutes," she said, knowing Heidi could probably hear her. "As long as this snow doesn't slow us down. The NBG is about a mile out."

Ryan didn't say anything. Not that she expected him to. He was staring out the window at the thick curtain of white.

The snow was picking up, and so was the wind. She had to hope that was a good thing.

So many things hung in the balance.

Her life, for one.

She could still see Noah's face when she'd agreed to drive Ryan. If she got out of this alive, he was going to kill her. Hopefully, he'd understand. She knew he'd have done the same if he'd been in her position.

Ahead of them, a minivan fishtailed without warning, and Winter tapped the brakes lightly, clenching her teeth. The driver of the van overcompensated, swinging wildly to the right, and then the opposite direction.

Her knuckles turned white on the steering wheel. They did *not* want to get into an accident right now.

Luckily, she managed to avoid the same patch of ice that had taken out the minivan. She maneuvered around the other vehicle, which had gone mostly off the road. Its nose was in a ditch, the back end sticking partially out into her lane.

"That was close," she breathed out once they'd cleared it.

"No shit," Ryan agreed. It sounded like he was choking on the words.

"These roads are something else."

The interior of the car went silent again. Small talk seemed out of place in their current situation.

She wanted to say something reassuring. Tell Ryan that it was okay. They had a plan. But, conscious of their listening audience, she just drove in silence, her concentration on the messy slush of the road ahead of her.

32

Heidi was riding high on exultation.

She'd fitted the collar bomb with a front-facing camera and had a good view of the dashboard. If Ryan had been sitting up a little farther, she'd be able to see out the window, but for now, she had to settle for the dashboard view.

Every time the camera shuddered with one of Ryan's fearful trembles, she wanted to grin.

She didn't even mind that the connection wasn't clear on the wireless headsets. The body cam would let her know if they tried anything.

It was amazing how calm Agent Black was staying. It was admirable, really. She had to know that Heidi held her life in her hands right now. The woman was absolutely fascinating.

She caught another snippet of conversation.

Something about the bad roads.

It was a good thing the agent was driving. Ryan would have crashed into a telephone pole by now.

A sudden idea came to her. It would only add to the fun. "Take Agent Black into the bank with you."

"Agent Black," came Ryan's garbled response. "She wants you to go into the bank with me."

"Tell her I want her to hold the money bag," Heidi added. Why shouldn't she manipulate the situation for her own amusement? It couldn't hurt anything.

"I hear her," came the agent's response. "I'll go..." The rest of whatever she said dissolved in snaps and crackles. Then, the headset went out.

She watched Ryan's camera carefully, but he hadn't moved. The distance and the weather had been too much for the signal. Oh, well. That had been fun while it lasted. She switched off her own headset and pulled it off, tossing it on the couch next to her. They would be at the bank soon. Her fingers flew over the keyboard as she accessed the NBG bank security cameras she'd pulled up earlier.

Time to watch the pigeon fly into the nest.

❄

"Don't move," Winter ordered.

Reaching over, she plucked the headset off Ryan's head.

"There we go," Winter said in satisfaction, after tossing it out into the snow. She watched in the rearview as the car behind them, with Noah driving and Sun riding shotgun, ran it over. "Now we can talk freely. How are you doing?"

"I'm bloody fucking scared," Ryan admitted. "Are you sure she can't hear us?"

"I'm sure. You have a body cam, though, so be careful where you point it."

"How do you know? She didn't say anything about it." Ryan looked down, searching his chest.

"I know lots of things. I can't tell you to relax yet, or not to worry, but hang in there."

"That's about all I can do right now."

"Your arm doing okay? You're holding it pretty stiffly."

"It hurts," he admitted. "But I've got bigger things on my mind right now."

"No more time for conversation," Winter said, glancing over at Ryan again, assessing his state of mind. Scared witless, bordering on shut-down panic. "The NBG is just ahead. Try to roll with the punches, okay?"

He gave her a weak smile. "Do I have a choice?"

"Nope."

"Were you able to do what I asked when I talked to you? Not that I deserve any favors at this point, but it wasn't for my sake—"

"The woman and her son are in protective custody until this is all over."

"Thank you." He let out a slow breath, and some of the tension went out of his shoulders. "I guess I'm ready for whatever, then."

Winter slowed the car, turning left. "Good. It's time to rob a bank."

The parking lot was mostly empty, and Ryan's hands were clenching and unclenching in his lap. "The bad weather is keeping people at home, at least."

Winter snorted. "Lucky, aren't we?" Winter parked the car. "I mean it, O'Connelly," she cautioned. "I need you to stay flexible here and trust me. Got it?"

"Sure. It's not like I have anything to lose."

"All right. Let's go."

She opened her car door and stepped out. He followed her lead.

The snow was like nothing he'd seen in years. He spent his downtime in temperate climates. The wind from Lake Erie cut through his long-sleeved shirt, blowing snow in his face. He hoped melting snow wouldn't cause his collar to short out. It hung heavily against the back of his neck, the metal a freezing, clunky weight.

He wanted to shield it from the snow somehow. Cross his arms and cover it, just in case. But he didn't want to touch it.

By the time they reached the front doors of the bank, Ryan was wearing a quarter inch of snow on top of his head and on his shoulders.

"You look like a yeti," Winter commented, holding the door open for him.

"You're not much better." She had snowflakes stuck in her long, black lashes. She grinned at him, and he appreciated the effort she was making to keep him calm. "Let's get this over with."

The lobby was empty, except for two tellers behind the counter.

"Hi," Ryan said. That was lame, but he hadn't really had time to give thought to this part. Best to be straight-out with it, he figured. He cleared his throat. "This is a robbery. I have a bomb attached to me, and I can promise you it *will* go off if you don't follow my orders exactly. I need you both to fill a bag with two hundred and fifty thousand dollars, or my...associate...will detonate this nasty little invention currently hanging around my neck, and then we're all screwed."

"Yes, sir."

The female teller closest to him went to a back room, surprisingly calm. The male stayed where he was. He looked tense but didn't say anything.

"Good job," Winter said, her voice light and still a little cheerful. "It's like you've done this before."

"Hope to never do it again."

"You probably won't get the opportunity, even if we make it through this."

"That's fine. I've lost my taste for larceny, I think."

"Make sure you look around," she ordered. "Give Heidi a good view, so she doesn't think anything hinky is going on."

Ryan obediently turned in a slow circle.

"Get your kicks, bitch," he muttered, his tone bitter.

In what felt like moments, the female teller returned with a bulging bag full of cash. She came around the counter and set it down a good distance away from Ryan, and then quickly retreated behind her desk again.

His nerves were strung tight, but no police came bursting through the door. No alarms rang. No inconvenient-timed customers with aspirations of heroism disturbed them.

He made sure to open the bag, show the money in front of the camera on his chest, so Heidi could see it. He didn't like her breathing in his ear. Listening to his every word. But he liked even less that he didn't know where she was or what she was doing. She was a snake, coiled to strike at any moment.

"I'll carry that," Winter said. "Don't forget to grab your sucker."

He looked at her in surprise, the hair on his arms rising in goose bumps. Was she in on it? Did Heidi have a third "partner?" "How did you know about the sucker?"

She didn't look at him, just shouldered the heavy load. "Like I said, I know a lot of things."

Ryan shoved back his paranoia and did as he was told, going to the nearest teller's booth. The man behind it shrank back, like he'd been confronted with a loaded gun. Close enough, Ryan figured.

He chose a cherry sucker from the canister at the counter. The thought of anything food-like made his stomach twist with nausea, but he pulled the wrapper off and popped the candy in his mouth. Sickly sweet fake cherry flavor flooded his tongue, and his salivary glands went into overdrive. He hoped he wouldn't throw up and embarrass himself.

"Ready?" Winter was waiting for him at the door. "What's next on your list?"

"We need to drive over to the McDonald's next door. It's a short walk, but she wants us on camera, and doesn't trust me to get there on my own bloody feet without supervision."

"Okey-doke." Winter clapped her hands together. "To McDonald's we go."

❄

HEIDI WATCHED THE SCREEN, tapping her fingers on the sofa beside her impatiently.

Ryan's time was running out, she thought. Just a couple more minutes.

So far, so good on the plan. The body cam, except for a brief, blurry moment when Ryan had gotten out of the car and faced into the wind, covering it with blowing, sticking snow, was picking everything up.

She watched as the two of them went into the bank, the view marred only by water droplets on the camera lens. The tellers didn't panic and did what they were told. A few minutes later, one of them came back out with the requested money.

"Good job," she murmured. She appreciated efficiency.

Ryan and Agent Black left the building and started for the car, the FBI agent carrying the heavy load. Ryan appeared to slip in the unplowed lot, and Heidi tensed. He did *not* want to fall down right now. It was too soon for him to blow.

But Agent Black grabbed his arm, steadying him. Good agent. Heidi couldn't quite believe the woman was a rookie. Who was she then? That question haunted her as she continued to stare at the screen.

Here was another tricky part. The camera range didn't quite extend to the part of the lot they'd parked the black rental car in. And the body cam was getting covered with snow again. Soon, the screen was blank. It would melt when he got in the warm car, but for now, Heidi had no eyes but the NBG security cameras.

She didn't like it, but she couldn't fret about that right then.

Her hand hovered over the remote as she watched them move out of view.

It would be fine, she assured herself. Better than fine.

It was brilliant.

She'd give them only a few moments to get to the McDonald's parking lot, where she could pick them up again.

In her head, a countdown timer started.

❄

WINTER'S HANDS shook with cold and nerves as she took Ryan's arm. His face was pale, as if he realized how close he'd come to falling and what might have happened if he had.

"Steady," she murmured.

He nodded stiffly but his dry mouth couldn't say a damn word.

An unmarked white van was parked in the road, on the other side of the landscaped berm that separated the parking lot from the street. Police had barricaded the street on either side, so no traffic could get through.

"I need you to move fast, but walk carefully," Winter said as she dropped the bag next to the car they'd arrived in.

The door immediately opened, and a dark-haired man with a bulky metal object around his neck reached down to grab it. Beside the man, Ryan saw a woman who looked just like Winter. If the agent wasn't still holding on to his arm, he would have thought it was her.

"What's going on?" Ryan asked, fear making his voice rasp.

"Change in Heidi's plans," Winter said, hurrying him along.

She helped him up over the berm, where a few inches of snow had already accumulated. The back doors of the van opened up, and she led him to them. Inside were two sober-looking bomb squad techs. One reached out immediately, putting white adhesive tape over the snow-covered camera lens.

"Let's defuse you," he said, "before the tape falls off."

In just a few seconds, after clipping several wires, both techs' expressions eased a considerable amount. The other tech nodded. "He's good."

Winter grinned at Ryan. "Congratulations. You're no longer a walking time bomb."

Ryan sagged to the floor of the van in disbelief, stress still written clearly on his face. "Are you sure?"

"I'm sure. These guys will take you to the hospital to get you checked over. By the way, you're now in official custody. You'll have your rights read to you on the way there."

One of the techs worked with swift, sure hands to unfasten the collar and lift it off Ryan's neck.

He shuddered as the weight was literally taken off his shoulders.

Behind them, the black rental car with two dark-haired officers in it, the man and woman he'd seen only moments before, pulled out of the parking spot with exaggerated care.

Their doubles.

For the first time, he really believed he was safe. The agents had done it.

"I never thought I'd be so glad to get arrested," Ryan said, a ghost of his old grin lighting his features. "Thanks."

"No problem." Winter smiled back. "You did good during

that last part. See you soon. We've got some things to take care of before we can officially interview you."

Another car pulled up beside the van and Winter climbed in, leaving O'Connelly in the care of the bomb squad and the Erie PD.

"Nice work, Black," Sun said. "Good job not fucking it up."

"Thanks. Nice to see you again, too, Ming. Noah?"

He was driving and barely spared her a glance in the rearview. His face was drawn in a scowl that promised retribution and lectures later, but Winter was too glad to be alive to care. She reached over the seat and squeezed his shoulder. The muscles beneath her hand were like rock.

"Drive carefully," she advised. "The roads are shit right now."

He drove carefully, but Winter could still feel his barely contained fury. Their last stop was only four miles away, but the roads *were* shit and time was of the essence. Houses flew by in a blur, and the car engine roared as they flew down State Street, heading for the outskirts of Erie.

They had safeguards in place, but only a few.

Heidi would be on to them soon.

33

"Come on, come on," Heidi muttered in impatience. Three minutes ticked by, and then four. Five. What the hell was taking them so long?

She glanced at the views of the property, the driveway that led down to the road. Empty. No tire tracks, no police, not even a stray deer.

Back to the NBG view. The car the agent had driven still hadn't appeared from the parking lot. Her fingers itched to set off the detonator, but she wanted to *see* it happen. Agent Black and Ryan were moving slower than frozen molasses.

She let out a breath as the car came into view. It backed out of the parking spot, and slowly, aggravatingly slowly, drove forward, toward the adjoining McDonald's.

"Trying to put off the inevitable," she muttered. "It won't work."

She switched to the security cameras there and saw the nose of the car come into view first. The camera quality was grainier, not as clear, but she could make out two figures inside. The passenger was obviously Ryan. His silhouette was bulkier. Winter was in the driver's seat.

Ryan's body cam was still obscured by snow. She wished she had the headset capabilities still, so she could tell him to wipe it off.

There was no way they could get out of this, so she shouldn't be worrying about it.

Still. Something was bothering her.

She watched the McDonald's cam as they pulled into a parking spot. Then, as the second set of instructions ordered, the two of them got out of the car. Agent Black stayed where she was, her dark hair whipping around her face in the snowy wind. Ryan, stoop shouldered and defeated, got out of the car. He grabbed the bag from the back seat and lifted it.

She frowned at his body cam footage. It would seem like the snow would have been dislodged or melted by now. It was still blurry, though. She couldn't see a thing from his vantage point, which was disappointing.

She'd hoped for a front and center view of the explosion. Literally.

He carried the bag, walking with exaggerated care on the slippery blacktop, over to the spot she'd designated. Right next to the glowing arrow that pointed the way to the golden-arched drive-through.

Heidi squinted at the screen and cursed the weather.

She'd been hoping for a minivan full of kids nearby. Maybe a basketball team on a bus, parking next to Ryan. Going to cram their faces full of greasy food and getting blasted with broken glass and nails instead.

Oh, well. She could control a lot of things—and had—but the weather wasn't one of them.

"Move closer, Agent Black," Heidi murmured. "Just a little closer."

As if she'd heard Heidi's words, Heidi watched the FBI agent pull a coat out of the back seat of the car. She walked over to Ryan, who was hunched in fear and misery on the ground and put the coat over his head.

"So sweet. Protect him from the snow."

She picked up the remote from the sofa beside her, eyes lit with glee.

"Say goodbye, my friends."

The door to Heidi's cabin flew open, slamming against the wall with a loud bang. It let in a gust of frigid air, a thick swirl of snowflakes, and a flash-bang grenade.

A concussive blast rent the air, along with a blinding, disorienting light. The officers in SWAT gear that stormed in after it had to dodge pieces of falling drywall from the ceiling.

"Police! Put your hands in the air!"

At least that was what she thought she saw and heard. Her ears were ringing, heartbeat thudding in her head. She could barely see, think, or hear, but she fought through it. With all the strength she could muster, Heidi lifted the remote for them to see.

"Come any closer, and I'll blow up your agent!" she screamed. At least that was what she thought she'd said. Her voice sounded muffled and tinny in her own ears.

Her vision was starting to come back, save for the dots still blurring everything she looked at. She blinked rapidly, trying to force them to clear.

She pushed the button, laughing, but none of the officers moved. Just stood there with guns pointed at her head.

She laughed louder, and it sounded maniacal to her own ears, and pushed the button again. "You killed them. You killed an agent. Your fault. Your fault." She barely understood what she was saying. Barely felt her thumb hitting the button over and over. Barely heard the click click click.

Why weren't they reacting?

The crowd of officers parted, allowing three more people

through the narrow doorway. Heidi blinked again. It was Agent Black and Agent Ming, both clad in bulletproof vests, followed by their big, dumb partner.

Agent Black locked eyes with Heidi and smiled.

❄

HEIDI SMILED BACK AT THEM. The look on her face sent an instinctive chill through Sun. It was a victorious grin. Not the expression you wanted to see on the face of a suspect you were about to apprehend.

Still smiling, Heidi lifted one finger and pressed a second button on the detonator.

The house seemed to jump on its foundation. A hole blasted through the floor in the northwest corner of the living room, throwing shards of wood and metal everywhere. Sun felt something hit her cheek, leaving a burning sting behind. Instantly, there was chaos.

"Everybody back!" Noah bellowed as the room rapidly filled with smoke.

Heidi was still motionless where she stood. There was a shard of metal at least three inches long sticking out of her left arm. She didn't appear to have noticed it at all.

She was too busy being smug about the fact that she'd turned the flash-bang concept back on them with a distraction of her own.

One officer, blood dripping from the side of his face, just past where the goggles he'd worn would have covered, jostled Sun hard on his way out the door. Nearby, a female officer was laid out on the cream-colored carpeting, moaning quietly. Noah crouched beside her, shielding her with his body.

Something in the basement of the house fell with an echoing clang. Her ears rang from the noise.

In the confusion, Sun almost missed Winter darting forward into the thickening smoke.

Heidi was no longer in the room. Winter had disappeared too.

Sun darted after them, into the haze.

34

W inter drew her service weapon. She squinted her eyes against the smoky sting and tried to hold her breath. The smoke was choking. Heidi must've added something to it to create such a dense screen so quickly.

So far, she hadn't missed a trick. They thought they'd caught up to her, but she was still a half-step ahead.

"Heidi, stop!" she yelled, her hands in front of her. She'd tried to memorize the layout of the room, but the rest of the house was a mystery. Bumping into a wall was a distinct possibility.

Ahead of her, she caught sight of a red glow through the fog of smoke.

She moved forward, a little more confident.

A shot rang out, and she was yanked backward simultaneously by the back of her vest.

"What the hell are you trying to do, cowboy?" Sun hissed angrily. "Get your head blown off?" The words sounded muffled. Winter could hardly hear her, but the look on her face made the tone clear.

Sun nodded her head toward the plaster wall to one side of them. A two-inch hole marred the smooth surface.

Winter acknowledged the save with a short nod. "She's moved to the back of the house. She's likely got an escape planned."

They crept forward, cautious inches at a time.

"Couldn't she be out already?" Sun asked in a low voice. "It's not like she'd waste time here. She's probably got a vehicle and a go-bag outside."

"No," Winter replied. She could still see a glow ahead of them and hoped she wasn't leading them both into a trap. "She's back here."

They passed an open door. Sun swept the room, but it was empty.

"How do you know?"

"I just know. Keep your head low."

"You're one to talk."

They passed a bathroom on the other side of the hall. It was getting harder to see, as smoke from the hole in the living room floor filled up the rest of the house.

The hallway opened up into a kitchen area. Before they could step out, two shots rang out, along with a high-pitched giggle. Winter returned fire, aiming for the reddish-colored light that she assumed was coming from Heidi's gun. She pulled Sun down to the floor with her.

"Enough, Heidi," Sun yelled. "It's over."

"Not yet," Heidi sang out in reply.

In the relative cover of the hallway, Sun came up into a crouch, training her weapon in the direction the voice had come from.

Another shot, this one taking out a chunk of plaster in the ceiling.

Sun fired back and was rewarded with a grunt as she found her target.

There were four more shots in rapid succession.

"You got her somewhere. She's firing wild," Winter told Sun through gritted teeth as plaster rained down on them.

There was the sound of a door opening, and cold light flooded the kitchen.

"Wait," Winter cautioned as Sun started forward. "They'll have the back of the house covered. She's not stupid. She knows that."

Sure enough, there was one more shot in their direction, and the red light went on the move.

Winter aimed, drew a breath to steady her hands, and fired.

This time, the red light went down with a shriek.

Heidi was on her back, behind the kitchen island she'd been using for cover. One of their shots had caught her in the right side.

"Last bullet," Heidi told them, and coughed wetly, spraying blood. She smiled up at them triumphantly. Her teeth were stained dark red. Her pale blue eyes glittered madly. "I saved it, just in case." She bent her arm and put her Ruger to her temple. "How long do you think it will take them to make a movie about me?"

Before Winter could respond, Heidi pulled the trigger.

❄

NOAH WAS WAITING FOR THEM, arms folded, when they exited the back of the house. Sun and Winter, arms slung across each other's shoulders like veterans of their own little war.

He looked them both over. Sun had a cut, high on her cheekbone, but neither had taken any hits. He, though, felt like thirty years had been shaved off his life, hearing the gunshots ringing out inside that smoky house.

"You two look satisfied."

"Game over," Sun said simply.

Winter nodded, shoving her hands into her pockets. "Heidi forfeited."

"Next time teams are picked, I don't want to be on either one of yours," Noah shot back. "You two are fucking crazy."

He turned on his heel and headed for the car, ignoring the snow that was finding its way into his shoes. Fury vibrated in every line of his body. He wanted to punch something. Break something. So when he felt a hand on his arm and swung around fiercely, it was no surprise that Winter stumbled back at the snarl on his face.

"Leave me alone." He enunciated every word in a low growl, so she'd be sure not to misunderstand him.

Part of her hair had come loose from the severe bun she'd tucked it back in, and long black strands powdered with plaster dust curved along her cheek. Fat snowflakes still fell, landing on the dusty shoulders of her jacket. Her blue eyes were almost laser-bright with the aftereffects of adrenaline.

He didn't think it through. Just grabbed her by the waist and pulled her in, fitting his mouth to hers in a bruising, punishing kiss.

Her lips were cold at first but heated fast. She was still for just a moment in his arms in hesitation. Not resisting, but not participating. Then, he jumped back with a yelp when she bit his bottom lip, hard.

He let her go and stumbled back.

"What the fuck was that for, Dalton?" Her pale face was flushed, and she was breathing heavily. Her lips were dark red.

He had to shove his hands in his pockets to keep from grabbing her again.

"The fuck if I know," he spat back. "You drive me crazy."

"Well, don't do that again." She watched him, wary, like he was going to jump her. Hell, maybe she wasn't wrong.

"Don't go flinging yourself in front of bullets anymore."

"Don't be so overprotective."

"Don't get into cars with strange men who have bombs strapped to them, just because a serial killer tells you to."

"Do you have plans for Christmas?"

He hesitated for only a moment, his eyes still narrowed. "No."

Hers were still narrowed too. "I just remembered. Gramma wanted me to invite you. Grampa is missing his poker buddy."

Noah stared her down. He'd never understand her.

"Will there be meatloaf?"

"Maybe."

She hauled off then and swung on him, punching him in the arm. He narrowed his eyes and resisted the urge to rub the spot where she'd hit. It hurt.

"What was that for?"

"You assaulted me. I assaulted you. Just evening things out. Friends again?"

He stared at her for a long moment.

"Sure. Friends."

He watched her walk away. Sun, nearby, snorted. He flushed. He'd forgotten she was there.

"Sorry you had to witness that," he told her.

"That's okay. Just so you know, though, I flung myself in front of a bullet."

"Yeah?" He was only half paying attention.

"And would have gotten in the car with O'Connelly if Heidi told me to."

That caught his attention. He truly looked at her this time and scowled. "That'd be dumb."

Her face split in a brilliant grin. "You want to punish me?"

He finally got it. "You're trying to make me uncomfortable on purpose. That's mean."

"I know. Sorry." The sparkle in her dark eyes negated the apology. "Oh, and Dalton?" She gestured toward her mouth. "Your bottom lip is bleeding."

35

I flipped through the television stations, restless, anticipation humming through me. There wasn't much on this late at night. Christmas movies, sappy and predictable on the Hallmark Channel. I sneered. Cartoons that were highly inappropriate for young 'uns. Night show hosts who thought they were funny. I almost gave in and turned the TV off, when I happened upon a 24-hour news channel.

I froze, the remote in my hand, still pointing it at the TV.

Would you look at that. I sat up straighter. It was my girlie.

They were replaying a press conference. The bank robbery in California, the hotel and armored truck depot in New York…it had all been the same lady who masterminded the whole thing. Who'd have thought? She almost got away with it, too, but she killed herself when the FBI caught up with her.

Women were weak.

The little Asian girl at the podium talked about how they did it, but I didn't pay any attention. I was watching Winter in the background. When the Asian girl tried to turn over the mike to Winter so she could speak about it, my girlie just refused with a little smile.

Good girlie.

"I do not permit a woman to teach or to have authority over a man; she must be silent."

1 Timothy, 2:12.

One of my favorites.

I chuckled, feeling an odd glow of pride and a strong sense of irony for what was about to happen next. My sweet little girlie wasn't an attention-hogger, that was for sure. I was really feeling like I was starting to get to know her. I wanted to spend some time with her. Get to know her better.

I watched the press conference until the end, enjoying the chance to look at her. It was so enjoyable, in fact, that I almost forgot where I was, until a car pulled up in the driveway and headlights cut a path across the ceiling.

Feeling regret and irritation that I didn't get to see the whole thing, I blew my girlie a little kiss.

"See you soon," I murmured, shutting the TV off so that I sat in the darkness.

I was ready.

The front door opened, and a man and a woman came in. He was laughing at something she'd said, and they stopped in the foyer to kiss under the heavy chandelier that hung overhead. I tried to wait them out. It was a long kiss, though, and growing inpatient, I cleared my throat loud.

The woman, dressed for a night out—probably a company Christmas party—jumped back with a squeak. The man turned the overhead light on in the living room, and I was glad, because I got to see the woman better. She was a cute little thing. Petite and curvy in all the right spots, with glossy, dark hair that hung to the middle of the back of her pretty red dress.

She was even prettier in real life than she was on TV, where she spouted scripture to a whole church filled with heathens, acting like preachin' to them was her place.

It wasn't her place.

Why wouldn't people listen to me?

"Who are you?" the man demanded, reaching into his pocket to pull out a cell phone.

The woman, not so preachy now, ducked behind him.

She screamed when I stood up from their comfortable leather couch. I hadn't even done nothing to make her scream yet, and that made me chuckle. I smiled and shushed her as I raised my pistol and shot the man in the forehead.

Easier than killing a possum.

The man crumpled to the floor with barely a sound, and the woman screamed again, a high, shrill noise that grated against my eardrums.

"Hush that noise," I ordered her in my sharpest tone.

She didn't listen.

Winter wouldn't scream like that, I thought. She'd fight me tooth and nail, for sure. The thought cheered me up a little bit.

"Stop it now," I said, pointing the gun at her. "Unless you want to end up on the floor next to your man there."

She finally quit her hollering, but her gray eyes were big and glassy with tears, and her mouth hung open a little like she might start up again any time.

"That's better," I said in approval. "You got no reason to be scared. I just need to teach you a little lesson, is all."

❄

A CHILL SKITTERED down the back of Winter's neck as she raised her hand to knock on Aiden's door. It was strong enough to make her pause. And the unsettled feeling that came with it left her feeling shaky.

She lowered her hand, almost ready to turn around and leave, but before she could, the door opened.

Aiden stood inside, giving her that enigmatic little half-smile. He'd shaved, his hair was damp, and he smelled like shower gel. He was also upright, without the use of a cane.

"Were you going to stand there all night?"

She shook free of the odd feeling that had gripped her. "Are you psychic or something?"

"No. The front desk security always gives me a heads-up when I have a visitor. Come in." He still wasn't moving easily, but his gait was much better.

"Are you supposed to be running around like that without your cane?" she asked him, suspicious.

He tossed her a mischievous look over his shoulder before sitting down in his chair. Sometimes, in the time she'd been gone, he'd lost a little of that dark edginess that had characterized his recovery. In comparison, this Aiden was almost cheerful. It was strange but welcome.

"You sound like Nurse Ratched. She says I've still got a month with it, and another two weeks before I go back to work. I'm trying to negotiate her down to one."

"You sound like you're starting to like her. What's she like?" Winter grinned, picturing an old battle ax with beefy arms.

Aiden smiled and held one hand up over his head. Sitting down as he was, his hand indicated five and a half feet. "About this tall." He moved his hands in an exaggerated hourglass shape. "And about this big."

She rolled her eyes and dropped down in the chair across from him, setting her purse on the floor beside her. "Men. You're all the same. I think Noah has decided to make a go for Bree. I haven't decided yet if I should tell him Bree doesn't swing that way."

Aiden chuckled and nodded. "Let him figure it out. Bree will let him down gently. Do you want to get us a glass of wine? I noticed you're not bringing food tonight."

"You make more money than me, even out on workman's comp. It's your turn to buy next time. But I'll take a drink as a down payment."

She took her time in his modern, streamlined kitchen. She wasn't much of a cook, but it looked a lot nicer than the one at her beige townhouse. Everything was stainless steel and brushed nickel.

"I'm waiting," Aiden reminded her. "I want to hear the story of your takedown."

She brought him a glass of Riesling and a dark, craft brew beer for herself.

He raised his eyebrows, his eyes sharp on her face. "Not in a wine mood after all?"

She sighed. "I don't know what kind of mood I'm in. A bottle of craft brew seemed more prudent than drinking all of your whiskey."

"Tell me."

Those two words and the easy silence that followed were more of a balm to her emotions than anything else could have been. She took a deep breath.

"It wasn't my takedown." She tucked a stray hair behind her ear. "It was just as much yours as it was Doug's or Sun's or Noah's or anyone else. You were right, about the collar bomb being the finale. That was our first big break. The rest of it, though, we owe to Doug and his computer forensics team."

"Doug." Aiden looked thoughtful. "Big guy? Terry Cruz lookalike?"

"That's him. He managed to work everything out while

we were on our way to Erie. He hacked into Heidi's computer and found her encrypted files. Said he never wanted to do anything that complicated ever again, by the way."

Aiden nodded. "But he was successful, clearly."

Winter took a long drink of her beer. "Yes. He managed to unencrypt them, using whatever magic that involves. By two in the morning, he provided us with detailed plans: the scavenger hunt list, the contact she used at each location and killed afterward, even how she'd managed to hurry her mother's death along. Fortunately, she also included instructions for defusing Ryan O'Connelly's collar bomb. By four in the morning, he'd hacked into every security camera we'd need to see what Heidi saw and manipulated them to our advantage."

"Give that man a raise."

"He needs one. He even thought to use her trick of looping footage, like outside of the cabin she'd holed up in, to cover the SWAT team's approach. I've already told Max to talk to Doug's SSA. There's probably some kind of commendation in the works."

"Good." Aiden gave her a narrow look. "Always give credit where it's due. It'll serve you well in the long run."

"I told Max to also pass along to ADD Ramirez that you helped."

"Also good." Aiden lifted his glass in a silent toast. "Thanks for remembering."

He shifted in his chair and took a sip of his wine. Obviously, showing off his recently regained walking abilities had bothered his bad leg, but Winter decided not to mention it.

"Did Heidi list her supplier for the nerve gas?" he asked.

"She did. Neatly ordered in a spreadsheet, with the costs and names and companies she'd used for everything. The gas was a fentanyl derivative, like we'd guessed. It has a fifteen percent fatality rate."

"And what about the stolen items?"

"Blown up in the final scene. The money is toast." Winter's smile was wry. "Charlotte Edwards will get her jewelry back, though, along with the ability to let everyone know she's alive. Thanks to Heidi's meticulous accounting, we could see that she didn't need the money. Even with the expense outlays she'd accumulated over the years, she still had millions scattered over several accounts. Her parents were apparently life insurance enthusiasts...or Heidi was."

Aiden shook his head, obviously fascinated. "So, in the end, she won."

"I've been thinking about that," Winter admitted. "She did. She never was in it for the money. Only the notoriety. And she most definitely got that. We can close the books on this one, or mostly, anyway, but in the end, she really did win. It's an unsettling feeling."

Aiden leaned forward, his elbows on his knees. "*Mostly* close the books? What didn't get wrapped up?"

She couldn't hide her surprise. "Ryan. He's gone. I'm surprised your sources didn't tell you that."

Aiden scowled. "I've been out of the office too long. They're starting to fear me less."

"That's the other thing that's bothering me. He escaped from the hospital. How does a guy get out of the hospital while he's handcuffed to a bed and under guard?"

"He has help?"

"I don't know." She shrugged, smiled a little. "And no one else seems to know anything, either. Don't get me wrong, I liked him. It was hard not to. Sun is working on tracking him, seeing it as a black eye on her watch, but I honestly don't care if he gets away."

Aiden shook his head, a grin teasing the corners of his lips. "I doubt that's a view shared by many in our profession."

Winter shrugged. "He's learned his lesson. A thief reformed."

"Shades of gray."

Winter took a last sip of her beer and stood. "I've got to head out. I'm going to spend Christmas with the grandparents." For a moment, she almost winced. She wasn't sure that Aiden had anyone to spend Christmas with, and she was taking Noah home with her. The dynamic would be too weird if she also invited Aiden, though. Even without Noah. Aiden wasn't the family celebration type. He was too much of a loner.

But he set her mind at ease.

"Have fun." His smile was wicked. "I'm going to schedule some extra physical therapy."

"Well, if Nurse Ratched doesn't keep you busy enough, there's this."

She picked up her purse. It had been a back and forth struggle with herself, whether she wanted to give it to him, but she trusted him. She might as well let him know that.

"Merry Christmas," she said dryly, handing him a manila envelope.

He looked at her for a moment. Opening the clasp, he slid out a photocopied picture and drew in a sharp breath. "This is him."

"The Preacher," Winter confirmed, unsurprised that he knew exactly who the drawing resembled. "Don't ask how, copy this, or show it to anyone else without my permission? Got it?"

"I wouldn't." Aiden ignored her bossy words and studied the drawing. The round face. Cheery smile. White hair and beard. The black, fathomless eyes.

"I thought maybe you'd want to help. There are some notes in there too. Ideas I've been kicking around."

Aiden looked up at her, his expression unreadable. "I do. I've just been waiting for you to ask." He stood up, a little stiff, and set the envelope down on the table beside his wine. "I actually have something for you too."

"I was joking," Winter protested as he headed back farther into the apartment. "That wasn't a real Christmas present." He ignored her and came out with a small box, wrapped with silver paper. "You didn't go out shopping, did you?"

"Amazon. They even gift wrap. You can open it in the car."

"Oh, no." Winter grinned, accepting the gift. "If you're going to make things awkward by giving me a gift, the least I can do is keep things awkward by opening it in front of you."

To her amusement, his cheeks reddened slightly.

The great SSA Aiden Parrish, got embarrassed like everyone else. The next thing she knew, he'd be telling her he put his pants on one leg at a time, just like other mortals. Used the bathroom, just like the hoi polloi.

Laughing at the thought, she ripped open the paper and opened the box inside. It was a tacky, but somehow adorable, stuffed cat. It was wearing a police officer's uniform.

To her horror, her eyes filled with tears.

"They didn't have any FBI agents."

She cleared her throat, but her voice still sounded choked. "You didn't have to do this."

"I wasn't trying to make you sad."

She dropped the box on the coffee table but tucked the cat under one arm. Closing the distance between them, she slid her arms around Aiden in a tight, impulsive hug. After a second of surprise, he hugged her back. The way his arms closed around her was brief, but tight.

"I'm sorry," Winter apologized, stepping away, avoiding

his eyes. "I know you're not a hugger. This just reminded me of the goofy gifts you used to send me around the holidays. I haven't gotten one in years, and I didn't realize how much I missed them."

Aiden cleared his throat. Leaned down and picked up the box, taking it to the kitchen recycling bin. "It's all right. I'm not sure what made me think to get it. You're not a kid anymore."

"I'm going to head out."

She grabbed her purse and moved for the door. This was excruciating.

"Drive carefully. Tell your grandparents hello for me."

"Will do. Merry Christmas, and I'll call you when I'm back in town."

Winter couldn't leave Aiden's apartment fast enough.

❄

WELL, that had been smooth.

Aiden grimaced as he moved back to his chair. His leg was killing him. He could lie straight-out to anyone else with no problem, but he had a hell of a time lying to Winter. She'd known him for too long. Since he was a younger, less cynical man. Before the biggest failure in his career had hardened him, and ambition had gotten its hooks into him.

"Nurse Ratched" was a fifty-eight-year-old grandmother of two. She'd slap him twice for the way he'd talked about her today. But he'd felt himself starting to get weak. To look forward to Winter's almost-nightly visits. He'd decided while she was gone that it was time to put some distance between them before he did something they'd both regret.

As long as she saw him as some poor, lonely charity case, a wounded animal, she'd keep coming around. Keep feeding him. Entertaining him. Cheering him up. It was torture.

He picked up the file she'd left him and pulled out the picture of The Preacher. It was as well-drawn as any police artist sketch. If he had a lineup of men in front of him, he could easily pick out the one she'd drawn.

Winter had talent, but she had something else. She had the key to catching The Preacher locked in that head of hers. And, judging by the folder in his hand, she trusted him.

He thought, not for the first time, about what skills like Winter's would do for his department. The behavioral analysis unit could use her. *He* could use her. Her insights, or hunches, or whatever they were would send apprehension rates through the roof. The accuracy of the profiles she could create...

He'd tried to get her transferred there at the beginning, when she'd been hired on, but she wasn't malleable or easily manipulated. He both admired and hated that.

Maybe he'd be in a better bargaining position now.

He just needed to distance himself, first.

36

"I'm glad Noah decided to join us." Gramma Beth sipped her coffee. She and Winter had just finished picking up the scraps of wrapping paper left over from their Christmas morning present unwrapping.

"It was nice of you to invite him." Winter took a small drink of her own coffee. Gramma had added Baileys in honor of the holiday. She tucked her feet under her and pulled an afghan off the back of the couch. "He said he was going to save all of his last paycheck, since he knew he'd be getting cleared out in Texas hold 'em."

As if on cue, there was a burst of male laughter from Grandpa's den at the back of the house. Followed by a loud groan from Noah.

"Sounds like he was right." Beth's reply was placid, a soft smile playing about her lips. "That grandpa of yours is a shark."

"Speaking of Grandpa Jack…" Winter began, biting her lower lip. "He—"

Beth held up a hand. "I know. You have enough worries in your life with that crazy job of yours. Your grandpa is fine."

"He's not looking good."

"Don't let him hear you say that. He's better in Florida, I think. He gets out more and loves the warmer weather."

With the tree lights glowing softly and the quiet crackle of logs in the fireplace, it was easy to pretend everything was all right.

"Has he been to the doctor?"

Beth snorted, which was more like a delicate sniff. "Getting him to go is harder than driving a team of mules."

"I can talk to him."

The grandpa who'd raised Winter had been a big, strapping man's man, full of ribald jokes and smelling like English Leather cologne. The grandpa who had greeted her when she'd come home for Christmas had seemed smaller, more shrunken. Old. Still good-natured and funny, but quieter. More hesitant.

Winter's grandmother, her face creased with soft lines, but still lovely, just smiled. It was both sad and reassuring at the same time.

"You can try, but he's almost eighty-seven. None of us live forever, sweetheart."

They fell quiet, watching the flames lick at the logs in the grate.

"I'm still going to talk to him. How are *you* doing?"

Beth gave her a sweet smile. "You know I plan to keep going until I'm a hundred. I have too much to do."

"Your bridge club. The volunteering. Making meatloaf for the bottomless pit you invited as a houseguest."

Beth chuckled. "It's nice to have my kitchen artistry appreciated."

Her grandmother was a mixture of June Cleaver and Betty Crocker. Grown men had been known to weep at the taste of her fudge brownies, and her grandpa still liked to say she had the best gams on any woman he'd ever seen.

Winter had never asked what gams were. She didn't want to know.

Beth stood up, shaking out the creases in her long, A-line shirt dress. She'd belted it at her trim waist with a green sash, and little jingle bell earrings peeped out from her white curls, tinkling when she walked. She'd given in to the informality of the occasion by wearing cheery red flats, instead of her usual heels.

"I know it's not even noon, but I'm going to pull out that peanut butter fudge we made. Do you need anything from the kitchen?"

"No, I'm good." Winter snuggled deeper into the afghan. "Perfect, actually."

But Beth had barely left the room before Winter's cell phone rang.

"Ignore it," she said out loud to herself. "You've cursed yourself by saying everything was perfect."

Being home for Christmas was heaven. They were having her grandmother's honey-glazed ham for dinner. Dammit, she wasn't ready for the outside world to intrude.

But she looked at the caller ID. It was Aiden.

"Please tell me you're just calling to wish me a Merry Christmas and have absolutely no work-related news to impart?"

"I'm sorry." Aiden's voice was tight. "I wouldn't have called you if it weren't important."

She pushed the afghan off of her and sat up. His tone gave her an instant chill, and her brain struggled to shift gears from laid-back Christmas relaxation into FBI-mode.

"What is it?"

"I think he's back. I think he's started again."

Noah had apparently picked up her mood from all the way across the house. He stepped through the hallway door. "What is it?" he hissed.

She shook her head at him and held up a hand. The last thing she needed was her grandparents coming to investigate. She didn't want to bring any of this stress to them.

"How do you know it's The Preacher?" She kept her voice hushed. Just above a whisper. Gramma Beth and Grampa Jack could *not* overhear this.

"I know it's him. I'm very familiar with his work." The reply was dark. "A man and a woman were found this morning by a neighbor who noticed their door standing open. He'd been killed with a single shot to the head. She was brutalized. Her throat slit. No witnesses. We're reopening his file. Not that it was ever really closed."

Winter closed her eyes. "Crosses?"

"Of course."

"What was the Bible verse?"

"First Timothy, chapter two, verse twelve."

Winter had tried to read the Bible after learning the media had dubbed her parents' killer as The Preacher. She wanted to understand the man's mind, even at a young age.

But she couldn't remember what that verse said, so she asked, "What's it mean?"

"I do not permit a woman to teach or to have authority over a man; she must be silent," Aiden quoted, and she had no doubt that he already knew it by heart.

"So, the woman wasn't silent?"

"No. She was actually a preacher on a highly popular televised show."

Winter pressed her fingertips to her temples. She didn't know if she'd ever be able to fully understand The Preacher or how he targeted women.

This one was, at least, pretty clear. The Preacher targeted a female preacher, believing women should be silent and shouldn't hold any authority over a man.

But why had he targeted Winter's mother?

She needed to understand that question as much as she needed to capture the bastard.

"Where at?" she asked, gathering what information she could.

"Chattanooga."

"All right. We'll head back."

"We?"

"Noah's here."

There was a brief pause, and Winter winced.

"All right," Aiden went on, his voice brusque. "Let me know when you're in town. I'm coming into the office."

"Are you sure you're up for that?"

"I'll get a driver. It's fine. See you later." He hung up, leaving no room for argument.

She dropped the phone on the couch.

Sheer hatred overwhelmed her for a moment, and she had to drop her head into her hands to get herself under control.

"I fucking hate him," she whispered. She felt the cushions sag as Noah sat down beside her. He pulled her into his side, but even his warm bulk couldn't penetrate the ice that had encased her at Aiden's news.

"Parrish?" he asked hopefully. There was no love lost between the two of them, but his question was facetious, and she knew it.

"No."

"I'll get my things packed up," Noah said. "I can be ready to roll in ten minutes." He didn't move. She was grateful for his solid presence at her side.

"I don't want to go." The words sounded petulant, but it was a visceral feeling. With every fiber of her being, she did not want to leave this house, her family, her safe zone. Even Noah, with his friendship, was part of this charmed circle.

If she left now, she had the feeling she'd be putting everything at risk.

"I don't blame you. I don't want to leave, either."

"He took my parents, my brother. Now he's stealing time from me and my grandparents."

"Then go get him. Bring it all to a close."

Gramma Beth's sharp voice had Winter's head flying up. She held a small plate of fudge in her hands. Her blue eyes were clear and steady on Winter's, and Grampa Jack stood behind her, his hand on her shoulder. They were such a team, Winter thought. But Grampa, usually the stronger of the two, had abdicated his strength to Beth. She was the one whose face was hard in determination.

"I'll make you both plates to go." Despite her fierce expression, Beth's voice was even and serene. "I did most of my cooking yesterday, just in case something like this might happen."

"I'm sorry." The words felt weak and inadequate, and tears clogged Winter's throat.

"Don't be." Gramma Beth was firm. "This is your path. We've come to terms with it. You need to go and finish this."

"You're a badass FBI agent," Grampa Jack growled. "Don't forget it. We'll be here waiting for you when you're finished."

Noah squeezed her shoulder in a comforting gesture, his grip strong and bracing.

This was it, Winter vowed. The Preacher had taken enough from them.

She was going to bring him down.

The End

To be continued...

Want to Read More About Winter?

Will Winter finally get The Preacher before he gets her? Find out in Book Three, *Winter's Redemption*. Now available! Find it on Amazon Now!

ACKNOWLEDGMENTS

How does one properly thank everyone involved in taking a dream and making it a reality? Let me try.

In addition to my family, whose unending support provided the foundation for me to find the time and energy to put these thoughts on paper, I want to thank the editors who polished my words and made them shine.

Many thanks to my publisher for risking taking on a newbie and giving me the confidence to become a bona fide author.

More than anyone, I want to thank you, my reader, for clicking on a nobody and sharing your most important asset, your time, with this book. I hope with all my heart I made it worthwhile.

Much love,
Mary

ABOUT THE AUTHOR

Mary Stone lives among the majestic Blue Ridge Mountains of East Tennessee with her two dogs, four cats, a couple of energetic boys, and a very patient husband.

As a young girl, she would go to bed every night, wondering what type of creature might be lurking underneath. It wasn't until she was older that she learned that the creatures she needed to most fear were human.

Today, she creates vivid stories with courageous, strong heroines and dastardly villains. She invites you to enter her world of serial killers, FBI agents but never damsels in distress. Her female characters can handle themselves, going toe-to-toe with any male character, protagonist or antagonist.

Discover more about Mary Stone on her website.
www.authormarystone.com

facebook.com/authormarystone

instagram.com/marystone_author

goodreads.com/AuthorMaryStone

bookbub.com/profile/3378576590

pinterest.com/MaryStoneAuthor

instead giving us practical tools and encouragement to unlock the power and potential of prayer in our lives. I love Debbie and her genuine heart for God and people, and it is therefore my great honor to recommend this spiritual game-changing book to every girl (and guy too). Prayer changes things, and this book will help transform us as we engage in conversation with the source of all power, Jesus!"

Julia A'Bell, lead pastor, Revitalise Church, Australia

"Debbie invites you to journey with her in having daily conversations with God. In *She Prays*, you will discover a confidence to open your heart to God in conversation, and in doing so you will draw closer to him. He will reveal his character and grace to you in ways you could have never imagined. Enjoy the journey and watch your faith grow right before your eyes!"

Rev. Doug Clay, general superintendent for the Assemblies of God, USA

"If you've ever thought, *I want to pray, but I don't know where or how to start*, you've found a mentor! Through accessible Scriptures, personal stories, and doable steps, Debbie will guide you into the development of a hope-filled daily devotional practice. As a friend, I know that prayer isn't just a theory for Debbie. Believing prayer is at the very foundation of her love, life, and leadership."

Dr. Alicia Britt Chole, author of *40 Days of Decrease*

"You can't write a book on prayer if you don't pray. Debbie Lindell is one of the most powerful and prayerful women I know. I watched from afar a few years ago as she walked through brokenness and still held her head high and encouraged others. As I've gotten to know her and her husband, John, better, I've been blown away by their steadfast faith in God and their consistent commitment to the call of prayer. In this thirty-one-day journey, Debbie beautifully illustrates the purpose, potential, and power unlocked in prayer. *She Prays* extends an invitation to every woman, regardless of age, background, or pedigree, to become the person God has ultimately called her to be—one of powerful, effective,

"Personal. Poignant. Accessible. *She Prays* will help you savor the privilege and power of prayer with a renewed awe at the tender care and absolute sovereignty of our heavenly Father, who listens to, delights in, cares for, and answers his children. With humor and warmth, Debbie Lindell infectiously communicates his invitation to communion made possible for us in Christ. Grab your girls and dive into this resource!"

Shelley Giglio, Passion City Church

"If you have ever struggled to know how to pray or what to pray for, this book will be a gift and a guide. Debbie takes our hands and walks us into the presence of our Father."

Sheila Walsh, author of *It's Okay Not to Be Okay*

"Prayer is a divine and profound invitation to partner with, engage with, and lean into the heart and intent of heaven. My gorgeous friend Debbie, over her many years of following Jesus and pastoring a thriving church, has gathered and now composed a beautiful journey sure to bring truth and revelation to every reader. She helps you to pray with assurance that your heavenly Father loves you, listens to you, and desires to converse with you."

Bobbie Houston, co-global senior pastor, Hillsong Church

"I absolutely love Debbie's new book, *She Prays*! Even though this is designed to be a thirty-one-day devotional, I could hardly put it down. Finally someone writes a book that not only stirs up the desire in us to pray but also increases our faith that the prayers will actually be answered. Whether you are male or female, young or old, this book will surely inspire you to take your prayer life to the next level. Debbie's book clearly reveals prayer to be an exciting journey and adventure. Because she is my close friend, I know that this is the way she lives her life, and we can all join her."

Nancy Alcorn, founder and president of Mercy Multiplied

"Debbie is a woman of prayer. She lives this message of constant conversation with Jesus as a lifestyle and example. In *She Prays*, Debbie removes the shame and disappointment that we often attach to our possible lack of prayer, and intimate prayer. Even though this book wasn't written for me, it blessed me. I can't wait for my wife and daughters to immerse themselves in this powerhouse devotional."

Jeremy Foster, lead pastor, Hope City

"Even the most seasoned believer can struggle with prayer. But in her book *She Prays*, Debbie Lindell reminds you of the great joy and privilege of communing daily with your creator. She invites you to bask in your heavenly Father's love for you and teaches you how to intercede with confidence in his promises. If your desire is to know God better and to pray with more power, you'll definitely benefit from *She Prays*."

Kristen Feola, author of *The Ultimate Guide to the Daniel Fast*

"*She Prays* is a powerful and deeply personal devotional that welcomes each reader into an intimate journey of prayer in their relationship with God. I truly love and appreciate the way Debbie Lindell opens up her heart and life experiences and through them teaches us how to grow in our own communication with God. After reading each chapter I was left longing to hear the voice of the Holy Spirit more clearly and experience his presence more closely in my own life."

Helen Burns, pastor, TV host, author, and international speaker

"Debbie Lindell is someone I look up to and admire greatly. I'm so excited my good friend wrote this devotional. She is an amazing, powerful woman of prayer and knowledge. The way she explains God's Word is fun, practical, and encouraging. She has a love for women and is so full of love and life. This book is going to be an incredible tool that every woman needs to have. I know it will inspire and encourage all who read it."

DeLynn Rizzo, director of ARC Women

"Prayer isn't just a tool; it's a weapon to wage war. In the simplest of ways, Pastor Debbie Lindell guides us through the understanding, practice, and application of prayer. This resource will help beginning prayer warriors and sharpen seasoned saints through simple reminders and easy ways to communicate with God. I love Pastor Debbie and know her words—like her heart—will jump off the pages of *She Prays!*"

Bianca Juarez Olthoff, teacher, preacher, and bestselling author of *Play with Fire* and *How to Have Your Life Not Suck*

"As a dear friend to me and a mentor to thousands, Debbie has a passion to lead women of all ages into a deeper and more intimate relationship with God. *She Prays* will do just that for you, as each devotional builds your faith and takes your prayer life to a whole new level. This book has a timeless message and is one I will treasure and share with others for years to come."

Taylor Madu, speaker and founder of Social Girls

"Debbie Lindell has been a friend and colleague for some time, and I am honored to endorse her new book. You'll be encouraged, surprised, and blessed by her writings. She is an individual who is honorable, a lover of God, and someone who believes in and stands for truth. I cannot wait to see where this project will lead and what doors the Lord will open moving forward—the sky's the limit!"

Havilah Cunnington, author, speaker, minister, and founder of Truth To Table